KILLIAN DE LUCA

DE LUCA SERIES

BOOK FOUR

JACLIN MARIE

PLAYLIST

ALL THE STARS	**KENDRICK LAMAR**
GET YOU	**DANIEL CAESAR**
HABITS OF MY HEART	**JAYMES YOUNG**
FIRE N GOLD	**BEA MILLER**
CAN WE KISS FOREVER?	**KINA**
LOVE HURTS	**PLAYBOI CARTI**
TALKING TO THE MOON	**BRUNO MARS**
SAVE YOUR TEARS	**THE WEEKND**
MOON & STARS	**$NOT**
DADDY ISSUES	**THE NEIGHBORHOOD**
FALL IN LOVE	**$NOT**
LATCH	**DISCLOSURE**

BLURB

REIGN

Killian De Luca is a lot of things.
He is a liar, aggressive, and will destroy everything good
and beautiful in your life.
But what did I do? I ended up helping him and falling in
love with him instead of trying to hate him.
And now that I'm sitting here with stars in my eyes
looking at him, I have no clue how this all will end.

KILLIAN

I tried to warn her.
I told her to not make me fall in love with her.
But it's too goddamn easy.
When she stares up at me with stars in her eyes and daisies
in her hair, it's so easy to hopelessly fall in love with her.
My end is near, I can feel it.
But she has no clue.

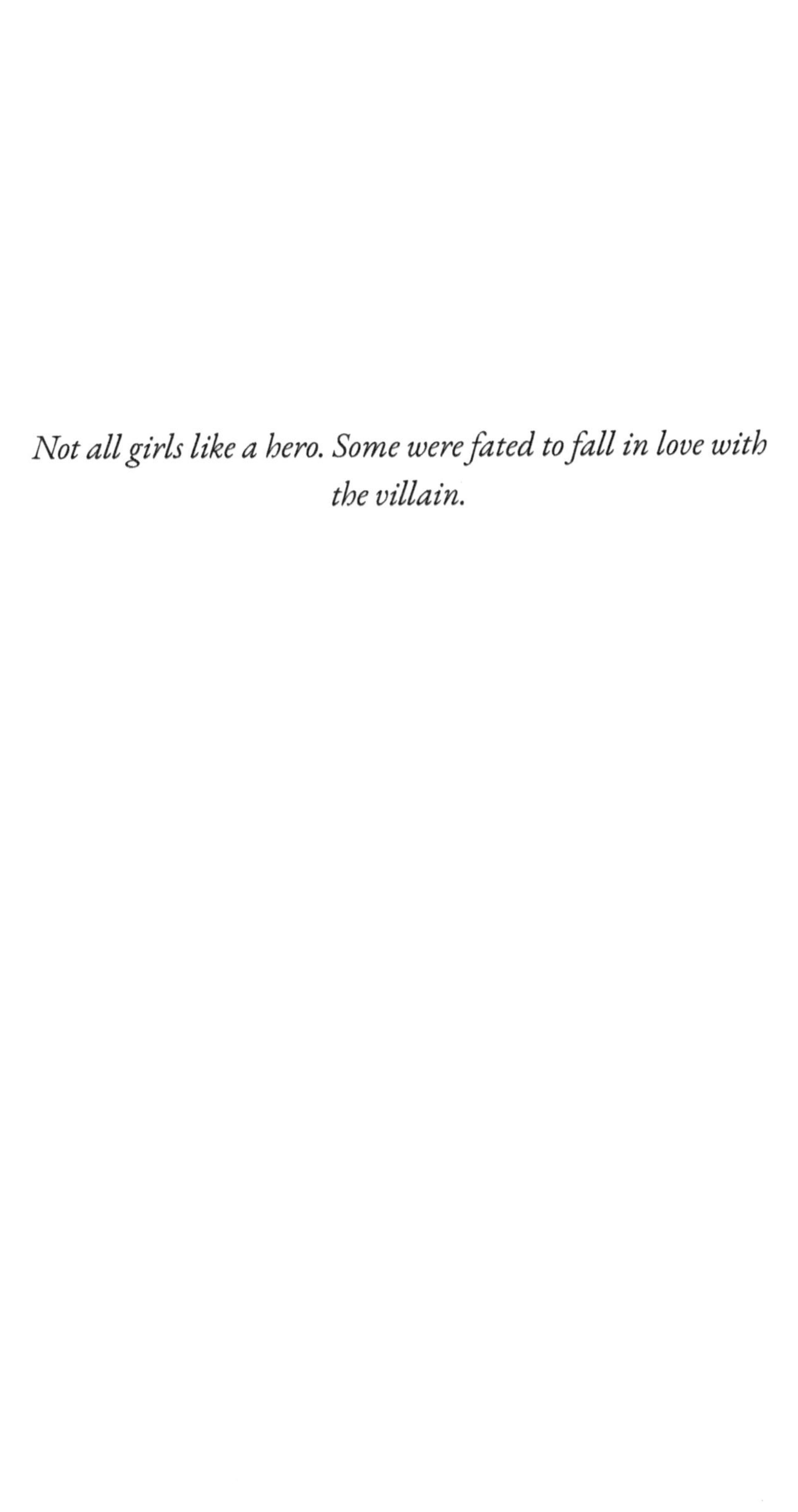

Not all girls like a hero. Some were fated to fall in love with the villain.

When you see something you want, you don't stop at anything until you have it in the palm of your hand. I wanted to be able to hold fire in the palm of my hand and not get burned. When I finally held the flame in my hands, I did anything to protect it, anything to keep it without getting burned. But in the end all I did was get destroyed. Even though I'm alive and well, I feel as if I'm about to die everyday. All thanks to the devil, Ace De Luca.

\- KDL

PROLOGUE
KILLIAN

AGE FOURTEEN

MY DAD SAID IN ORDER FOR PEOPLE TO BE AFRAID of you, you always have to appear bigger. Only way to do that is to become stronger, have more money, become more powerful.

But the most important thing that Ace De Luca ever taught me was you have to not care.

If you don't care, then there is no point for anyone to try and piss you off. One of the main things you have to have to not care is no feelings or strings.

My dad fucked up there because he has my mom, who he would die for.

He said that mom helped him stay alive in a way, which I don't understand and never will because love is something I never understood in general. Watching my dad be a man who has no remorse for those who are not blood made me vow to never have any strings, and if I fuck up like him, to keep those strings close so no one will be able to cut them.

As my family and I walk towards the ball room, cameras flash our way which makes it blinding for us to see where the fuck we're going. People are telling us to look in all kinds of directions, but we don't pay any attention.

My mom is smiling at my dad while Thalia just has that resting bitch face that she always has. I'm observing because that's the best thing I can do.

"Welcoming, Ace De Luca and Aria De Luca," the announcer says in the mic. As we walk closer towards the ballroom, I see small groups of people from various crime organizations.

There is the Yakuza; Japanese organization, Clanuri Interlope; Romanian organization, Chicago Outfit, which is the American organization led by my uncle, La eMe, the Mexican organization, and many more that are just too much to list.

I know a lot about the business side of what my dad does because he taught me young, and I'm still learning. I need to learn if I want to be on top someday.

At a young age, I already know exactly what I want.

I've always been a needy kid but living in this kind of world, the dark and ugly, how else are you supposed to be?

"I'm going to go find Jane," Thalia says before walking away without another word.

"Thalia!" my dad yells, his jaw clenching while my mom calms him or at least tries to ease him by resting her hand on his chest and whispering in his ear. "She always does this and if she doesn't want to get fucking killed, she needs to stop and listen."

"She's a teenager, Ace. They don't care and won't listen. You'll just end up arguing with her like you always do in front of everyone," my mom explains, which sort of eases my dad even though I know he wants to say something back to her. "Let's go sit down. I'll text Layna that Thalia is looking for Jane."

My mom and dad walk towards our assigned table while I follow behind them.

This suit I'm wearing is itchy and I'm close to ripping the thing off. My dad always makes me wear a suit, whenever I am in meetings with him, observing, or at events like this. He tells me it's because I need to get used to it and when I told him, "When I rule the world, I won't need to wear suits." He replied with, "Well if you want people to respect you or be afraid, then you must listen and do as I say."

Arguing with my dad is like arguing with the wall. In

his mind, his word is law. That goes for everyone except my mom.

She is the only one who can do whatever she wants without getting my dad's wrath.

I sometimes think that he might love her more than anything else in the world whether that be him or even Thalia and I. I try not to think of it because it hurts.

"Ladies and gentlemen, please take your seats," a man says, getting everyone in the room's attention. "Tonight, we are here . . . "

His words drift off as I scan the room, seeing who's here and who needs to be looked out for.

When my eyes catch bright blue ones, I feel like I'm at a beach with deep, vivid blue water. The sun shines down on the water, creating a glow and sparkly blue color.

And when she smiles it feels like everything seems like it's actually okay. Like the world isn't falling apart around her.

Why is a girl like that at an event full of people with guns in their pockets and blood on their hands?

She seems like the type to ignore everything around her as she dances around murderers and on pools of blood with a smile on her face.

I keep staring at her, confused but also enchanted. She looks at me with a smile that makes my chest ache.

They say the eyes are the window to a person's soul.

They tell you whether that person is kind and has a good heart or if there is darkness and fire in them.

This girl who is staring at me with a small smile on her face, looks like the most innocent person I have ever laid my eyes on.

I'm almost jealous of her.

"I hope everyone enjoys their night. We'll be announcing awards after the briefing," he says before walking off the stage.

"I'll be back, *amore*," my dad says, making me look at him as he stands up after kissing my mom on the forehead.

"Can I go outside on the balcony?" I ask my dad.

"Why?" my dad asks, furrowing his eyebrows down at me.

He does that a lot.

Questions me.

It annoys me to the point of no return.

"I want fresh air."

"Let him go, Ace, he'll be fine," my mom says, looking at me with a smile on her face.

I love my mom. Every time she smiles at me like that, I always feel safe and like nothing could happen to me. I know I said my dad would do anything to make sure she stays happy and smiling but me, I wouldn't die for her, I would probably burn the entire world to the ground for her. I've always been closer with her rather than my dad even though she says I'm a lot like him.

"Fine but check in in twenty minutes. I'll be back by then."

I nod my head before getting out of my chair and walking towards the doors that lead to the balcony outside.

Every time we go to these stupid events and galas, I always end up waiting outside for my family to be done fucking around. My mom always wants me to stay with her but it's always so boring talking to my uncles and aunts. They ask the most ridiculous questions like what I have been learning in school, any girlfriend yet, and other bullshit.

I would hang out with Thalia but all she does is gossip with Jane or argue with Alexander.

Once I am at the edge of the balcony, I rest my hands on the railing and look up at the sky.

The stars in Bulgaria seem to shine brighter than they do in Italy.

This is the first time I've been to Bulgaria because my family never had a reason to come here until now. The Bulgarians joined the families not too long ago. Maybe three years ago? But this year they hosted their first gala because they got the pleasure of hitting the top five in the families.

My family, Italians, are the first in the rankings while the other side of my family, the Americans, are third in the rankings. The Bratva has been demolished because of the issue that happened with them and my dad years ago before Thalia was born, but there is always a possibility of them coming back in the future.

"Hi." I hear a soft voice making me turn my head. It's the girl with the big blue eyes and warm smile from earlier. I look at the dress she is wearing and admire the white fabric that makes her skin glow. I look at her face and she has her hair down and messy. It looks like she didn't even brush it. "I'm Reign." She thrusts her hand towards me.

I look down at her hand and look back up at her. "Killian."

Despite me not shaking her hand, Reign still smiles and walks closer to me. "So why are you out here by yourself Killian?"

"Because I don't want to be in there," I say, pointing to the doors that lead inside the building.

"Why?"

I shrug and look back at the sky. "Because I don't like people."

"You don't talk very much, do you?" I look back at Reign and her head is tilted a little and her smile is gone.

She now just looks confused as she narrows her eyes at me and doesn't smile.

"I don't like talking to people," I say bluntly.

"Why not?" She furrows her eyebrows, and her nose scrunches a little bit.

Damn she asks a lot of questions.

"Because it's a waste of time when they don't listen."

"I can listen," she offers, smiling softly. She puts her hands behind her back and walks closer to me. Why is she walking closer to me? "But if you don't like to talk then I can do most of the talking. My family hates that I talk too much, and I wish there were more people I could talk to because I feel like they don't ever listen to me either," Reign rambles before looking at the sky above us. "I sometimes go outside my house and sit on the grass to stare at the stars. I'll talk for hours to myself while looking at them. Kind of weird right?" Reign snickers while still keeping her eyes up at the sky while smiling.

I look at the stars and they shine brightly down at us.

"As long as nobody catches you talking to yourself then it's not weird," I say before looking back at her.

Reign looks at me and her smile brightens almost making me want to smile.

She looks like a good girl.

And good girls always want a bad boy, even if they don't admit it.

"Killian, I think that you and I could be really good-" before Reign can finish, I hear someone yell her name.

I turn my head and see the Bulgarian *stronzo* from the stage walk outside with a vein prominent on his forehead. He must be mad but at what?

"Reign! What are you doing out here?!" the Bulgarian *stronzo* says before turning his eyes away from Reign's to meet mine. His face forms a look of disgust, and it makes me want to kick his shin to show him something really disgusting I can do. "Why are you talking to him?!" he hisses at Reign.

I clench my fist as I see Reign try to look away from the man, who I assume is her dad.

"We were just talking, papa," Reign mumbles.

"Not with him," her dad hisses.

"Hey, what's going on out here?" I look to my left and see my dad walking outside of the building to where Reign, the Bulgarian *stronzo*, and I are standing. "You, okay?" my dad asks me once he stands by my side. I nod my head and my dad looks in front of me and he tenses immediately. "Malcolm," my dad states and he look down at Reign who is staring at my dad.

"Ace. Is this boy yours?" Malcolm asks while glaring at me.

"Yes. What's the matter?" my dad asks with a stoic expression on his face as he speaks calmly with Malcom.

"He shouldn't be anywhere near my daughter," Malcolm says while pulling Reign closer to him.

I can't help but look at Reign. Her hyper, easygoing personality vanishes, and now she shies away while still looking at me. I can't help but worry if she is okay or not.

"This is the one time a year that all families are civil, and you are really going to go after two teenagers who are hanging out? Really Malcolm? Not very mature if you ask me." My dad narrows his eyes at Malcolm.

"If he comes near my daughter one more time, I will make sure to cut his head off. Don't underestimate me, Ace. You may be the devil everyone says but I am not afraid of you," Malcolm states with confidence and I can't help but snicker. Anyone who isn't afraid of my dad is stupid because he is the one person who will you make cower from just a simple glare from him. This Bulgarian *stronzo* obviously has a death wish. "Got something to say, son?" Malcolm glares at me.

I'm about to open my mouth to say something, but Reign's soft, calm voice speaks up.

"Let's just go, papa. Mama and Baba are probably waiting for us," Reign says while trying to pull her dad away from my dad and me.

But before Malcolm does leave my dad speaks up. "Careful, Malcolm. Not a lot of people walk away with two feet and a pair of eyes after threatening me or my family," my dad warns, and Malcolm looks back at him.

"You have no clue what I can do, De Luca. You be careful," Malcolm says before walking away while holding Reign's hand.

The last thing I see of Reign is her bright blue eyes piercing into mine.

All I know is that I want to see her again and hear what she has to say about everything.

ONE
REIGN

AGE SIXTEEN

"MRS. ROB CAN SUCK MY DICK, REIGN. I SWEAR she has some sort of weird obsession with me with how much shit she says," Angela complains as I try to concentrate on the words in the book I'm reading.

Angela is always complaining about her teachers because they are always up her ass, rightfully so because she never listens in class. She thinks everyone is the problem but her, but I can't say anything because she's my best friend and would probably think I'm betraying her.

So instead, I just pretend to listen and give a simple "Oh" or "Oh my god" so she thinks I'm listening to her.

"Have you finished the homework?" Angela asks.

"Yea. I finished it in class while she was going over it. It's super easy."

"Can you send it to me then? I won't have time to do it tonight. Me and Claude are going to FaceTime."

I want to roll my eyes but instead I just say, "Sure. I've got to go. Mama is calling me down for dinner."

She thanks me and tells me bye before I hang up the phone.

The only reason I'm friends with her is so that I don't get tossed into the wrong crowd at school. Everyone at school is super mean and cruel and now that Jamie is gone, I don't have anyone to protect me. So, I started hanging out with Angela who happens to be the type of person I would normally stay away from.

I still talk to Jamie but not that much since he is busy with Triple A, All Assassins Academy. Which is a private school that trains killers and creates monsters.

He is going there to learn the basics because he wants to be a hacker, which he technically already is because he's a genius. He told me he wants to learn more combat skills which is why he went.

I put my book down and close my laptop before putting both on my side table. I reach over and unhook my phone from the charger at the same time I feel it vibrate with a text.

I assume that it's Angela asking for the answers but when I look at the screen, I see an unknown number.

Reign?

I furrow my eyebrows before unlocking my phone and reading the phone number. It's a Bulgarian phone number so it could probably be someone from my school.

Yes? Who's this?

They respond almost immediately as if they had been waiting for my text.

Call me your Star.

How'd you get my number?

Don't worry about it. Instead, how about you tell me what you're doing right now.

I don't even know you.

You will. Now indulge me.

What if you're some murderer or trying to gather information from me to kill me?

You're a mafia princess with a lot of power. You shouldn't worry about someone behind a screen.

How does this guy know I'm related to the mafia? How does this guy know who I am in general?

I should be showing this to Papa or Jamie so they can deal with it, but I can't help but keep typing. I feel adrenaline run through my veins.

You aren't supposed to know that.

I know a lot about you Reign Pierce. I know you have these bright blue eyes that make people stop in their tracks and just stare into your eyes for hours. I know that you love talking to the stars because no one at home listens to you. I know that you only hangout with that certain crowd because you're too scared to be alone or bullied at school because your high school is known for that type of shit. I know your favorite color is white and you love daisies because your granddad would always give you them as a child. I also know that at night, when no one is looking, you like to touch yourself to those erotic books you read. Tell me I'm wrong.

Blush creeps up my neck and flushes across my cheeks.

Oh my god.

What a weirdo.

Is he a stalker or something?

My phone dings with another message.

Now you're wondering if I'm outside your window or have a camera in your room, but I don't. I just know you.

Who are you?

Can't reveal myself quite yet, Reign.

Tell me a clue.

I'll do you one better. We'll keep talking until I think you might have a clue as to who I am or until we meet again.

We've met before?

Yes.

Should I be scared?

Definitely.

Tell me a clue.

Does this mean you're in?

Yes.

As I wait for his text to roll in, my toes curl in anticipation.

I should be showing this to Papa so he can handle it, but this feels like a fun forbidden secret, like the ones from my books.

It's fun and exciting.
Can't be that bad.

We met under the stars.

Two

Killian

AGE TWENTY ONE

ON PEOPLE'S TWENTY-FIRST BIRTHDAY THEY ARE either going out to clubs, drinking their little hearts out, having celebratory sex, or some other shit that just slowly wastes your life away.

But for me, this is it.

The day I have been waiting for since I was sixteen years old when my dad told me I was going to end up taking the role soon.

Even though it won't be mine for long, he says that I should still have the honor of taking the role.

Thalia, my older sister, was supposed to be taking the role but after her husband died, she decided to turn the role down. Her husband ended up just being in a coma and he magically came back to life.

She is living on an island in the Mediterranean.

I look at my dad who is sitting at his desk while reading the sacred paper that I have to sign, basically selling my life away to this family. Once I take this role I can never back down from it and if I ever do that means death.

"But you know the deal, Killian," my dad states, making me focus on him. "There is one last thing you need to do before you're officially named capo," he says before looking at me instead of the papers.

There are multiple steps to become a capo in general. Different families have different rules and traditions.

Some require an arranged marriage with a powerful leader or showing how to run the business side of things by conducting trades or relationships with different groups.

I know how to kill, torture, conduct trades, form relationships and alliances; I know it all.

The deal I made with my dad is that I have to produce an heir right after I finish the last task.

Which just so happens to be killing another leader.

And that will be done hopefully in the next few months.

"I'm not worried," I state, making my dad's face form into a scowl.

He doesn't like how I'm not taking this as seriously as him.

The reason I'm not worried is because I don't care enough to be worried. I know what I have to do. I have been waiting for this day since I was told I was going to take this position. I know how to kill a man that is impossible to kill. I have studied ways to kill my dad as practice. The hard part is the aftermath, not the actual killing.

Ripping out his tongue and shoving it down his throat making him choke on his own breath isn't hard. Everything you have to deal with after, the meetings, threats, and all of the other bullshit the families throw at you.

"I don't think you understand how tedious it is to kill a leader. You have to be aware of all of your surroundings because as soon as you get into that country you are targeted, and someone will want your head. There are men guarding him at all times and when you finally kill him, you have to get your ass out of that country as soon as possible," my dad scolds me, making me want to roll my eyes.

"Again, I'm not worried."

My dad sighs and leans into his chair. "You remind me a lot of myself, Killian." He rubs the back of his head.

For a guy in his fifties, he's a good-looking guy. He still looks young for his age and girls at my old school would throw themselves at him, not knowing he is the age of their dads.

My mom would always laugh, knowing that my dad wouldn't love anyone other than my mom, even after she dies my dad will still be faithful to her.

My dad would kill for her, and I would do the same.

The love I have for her is unexplainable. She is my safe space and every time she's around I feel strong enough to do anything. She loves me and it feels nice but at the same time it hurts. Out of everyone in this fucked-up world, I relate to her the most.

Recently she was diagnosed with breast cancer.

It's bad.

No one likes to think about it or talk about it because if we do, it will feel more real. She is always in bed because of her chemo treatment. She is weak and tired all the time. When her hair started falling, I held back tears because it was becoming too real.

I won't have my mom in my life soon. It hurts to think about.

She puts up such a strong front in front of my sister and I, but I know when those doors close behind my dad she cries in his arms and tells her how scared she is and how she doesn't want to die yet. My dad loves her, and you can tell by the way he looks at her and holds her as if she is his world.

The love he has for us is nothing compared to the way

he loves my mom. I don't think he could love anyone or anything as much as he loves my mom.

I can't even begin to think about love because for me it's pointless.

I can't trust myself to love anyone because when the time finally comes, I would have to let go.

I tilt my head to the side as if mocking my dad. "Isn't that a good thing?"

My dad chuckles. "For your mom and I, no. But for the family, it's a great thing. You're guarded. Keep guarding yourself Killian. You never know who you're going to run into during the job."

His lectures make me needy for a fucking cigarette. He needs to hurry up with this meeting.

"I'm not worried. Are we done?" I raise an eyebrow and look down at him.

Irritation fills my dad's eyes, and he bites the inside of his cheek before grabbing a paper.

"What's your legacy, Killian?"

"To carry on the family business. To carry on the Italian Mafia our family has built over the years."

"And what have I taught you Killian?"

"To protect myself and only myself."

"And what will you do, Killian?" My dad leans his arms on his desk and keeps his eyes on mine.

"Kill Malcom Pierce. The leader of the Bulgarian Mafia."

THREE
REIGN

AGE NINETEEN

MY FIST CONNECTS WITH PAPA'S PADDED gloves.

"Harder," Papa grunts, making me punch the padded glove harder. "Harder, Reign," he repeats, making me do it again. After ten minutes of repeatedly punching my Papa's gloves, we stop and have a small break to drink some water. "So, are you nervous?" my Papa asks.

"Me? Nervous? Never," I say with a teasing smile.

My Papa gives me that scolding look that he knows I hate. "I'm serious, Reign. I can't lose you during this mission," my Papa says sternly.

My parents are always so worried about me, especially Mama.

"And I'm serious too. I'll be fine, Papa. Don't worry," I assure him while still smiling because he loves it when I smile.

"Reign, it's not that I'm worried. I'm just anxious about you going on your first mission. Alone, might I add?" my Papa says as he looks down at me with worry.

My Papa, Malcolm Pierce, the leader of the Bulgarian mafia, is one of the softest leaders I have ever met. But that's probably because he's my Papa and he is supposed to be all soft around his only daughter. He is all about loyalty and pride. He has a very hard time trusting people outside of family, if he trusts you or even lets you get near his family then you are considered lucky.

He rarely lets me out of the house. The only person he lets me hang out with is Jamie who is my best friend. We have grown up together and have known one another since we were babies. My Papa and Jamie's Papa have known each other for a while. They are very close business partners and they've become best friends over the years.

"Papa, seriously, don't worry about me. I'll be fine. It's not the first time I've been on a mission," I say while placing my water on the weight bench.

"But the thing is that you have never been alone on a mission, Reign. I don't want anything to happen to you."

"And nothing will," I assure him again.

"Reign, not to be a dick but you don't even know how to take someone down." Papa narrows his eyes on me before taking a huge gulp of his water. "I just want you to come back home in one piece."

I have a mission coming up in a few days and for this mission, I have to kill this person who my dad found out was a mole in our mafia. He is going to be at one of our warehouses. My papa wants me to gather information out of him first before I kill him.

Luckily this warehouse is in our country because I don't think Papa would be able to handle me being out of the country.

"I understand, Papa. But I'm nineteen. You have to learn to let me go." I place my hands on my hips and raise an eyebrow at him.

Papa smiles at me but it almost looks sad. "Reign, you're my daughter. I don't think I will ever be able to let you go. You will always be my little girl."

I smile at Papa and kiss him on the cheek. "I love you, Papa. But once I turn twenty-one you have to be able to let me go," I said while narrowing my eyes at him.

"I will. But your Mama will be a hard one," Papa chuckles while getting his stuff on the bench.

"True. She cried at the thought of me living by myself." I smile while reminiscing about Mama crying.

I told her I wanted to move out and she started crying and then yelled at me for being so "ridiculous."

Papa and I get our stuff and walk out of the home

gym. "So, you understand your mission and what you have to do?" Papa asks, while raising his eyebrows at me.

"Yes." I roll my eyes at him.

"Tell me. What do you need to do?" Papa stops walking and stands in front of me.

"I have to kill Anton Invano who will be working in the warehouse on Friday this week," I stated, with a teasing smile.

"Okay, and how will you do it?" Papa puts his hand on his hip and stares down at me with a questioning look that is supposed to look intimidating but it's really not.

At least not to me.

"I will be in your office and call him up to, and I quote, talk to him."

"Okay, and when he is in the office, then what?"

"You really want a play-by-play?" I laugh.

"Yes, Reign!"

I laugh. "Once he is in the office, I will hold a conversation with him and then ask some questions about the other mafia. I will get information out of him and then kill him."

"And you will stay safe while doing so. Correct?" Papa raises his eyebrows at me, and I nod my head. "Good. 'Because I can't lose you Reign."

"You won't!" I yelled playfully. "I swear Papa, I'll be careful," I assure him, and he pulls me in for a hug.

"You better be. I can't have you dying on me Reign. I

need you to stay alive." Papa narrows his eyes at me, and I chuckle.

"I will! Don't worry."

Papa kisses the top of my head. "Good, now let's get some dinner. I'm hungry and you know how I am with your mama's cooking."

Papa and I walk inside the house and go to the dinner table. I wanted to shower but Mama is super strict on having a family dinner at a certain time.

It's just me, Mama, Papa, and Baba who live in this house. We have such a big house for only four people living here. We used to have Dyado, but he died when I was a kid.

"How was the workout?" Mama asks as Papa, and I walk inside the kitchen.

"Good. Papa taught me how to punch harder when fighting," I say as I sit down next to Mama at the table.

"As long as you're having fun," Baba says with a warm smile on her face.

Baba and I are super close and I'm lucky to have her in my life. She is always there for me whenever I need her, same with Mama but sometimes I need Baba to talk to. Mama can't take me seriously since I'm her only child.

"I am. But I think I may need a new trainer. Papa's getting kind of old," I joke, and Papa rolls his eyes at me before sitting next to Mama.

He kisses her forehead and whispers something in her

ear making her blush like a teenager. I can't help but smile at them. They look so happy and in love and I just hope to experience that someday.

"Stop lying. I'm the best damn trainer you'll ever have." Papa looks away from Mama and jokingly glares at me.

Four

Reign

Papa didn't let me leave the house without a list of specific instructions he wanted me to follow or at least remember to make sure I don't die, not that I'm going to.

I'm not worried. I'm excited to see how this mission goes. I know I should definitely take this seriously but I'm just happy that Papa finally let me do this by myself.

To be honest I don't want to do this whole assassin and mission stuff forever. I actually want to become a nurse. I love helping people and the idea of helping them. But I also love the work my dad does because there is secretly a dark and depraved version of myself that only my Star knows about.

I look down at my messages with him, rereading the ones from this morning.

You nervous for today?

No, I'm excited. I think it will be fun.

Killing someone gives you a different type of adrenaline rush. I think whenever I kill someone that's when I feel the highest form of adrenaline.

I've never killed someone before.

Don't die.

Never. Who would you have to stalk and talk to if I did?

That was the last conversation we had.

He didn't reply or send a reaction to my message which is normal.

He knows I'll text him when I get home and if I don't, he always texts me.

A knock sounds on the door making me put my phone in my pocket. "Come in," I say before Anton walks in my Papa's office.

I told him to come to my Papa's office so that we can *chat* on my Papa's behalf but I'm actually just going to kill him.

"You wanted to see me, Ms. Pierce?" Anton asks as he closes the door behind him.

"Yes. Please, sit," I say as he sits in the chair in front of me. "Couple questions regarding your mission to

Spain the other week. You said that some of the drug shipments sent to their warehouse were missing, correct?"

"Yes, ma'am."

"Do you happen to know which crate boxes they were? All of the boxes have a number and all of them go by order, but you didn't give us an order number."

"I spoke to your dad about the shipments the other day."

Liar.

"What were the numbers?" I ask again before looking down at his leg that's bouncing up and down.

"Numbers 1552 and 3728," Anton states.

"What was the mission Papa assigned to you again?" I ask, acting confused.

"Just to be a mole but he also sent me for those shipments which I didn't find."

"So just to be clear, you were able to make it out of Spain without getting what my Papa asked for? You have been in this family for years and you know how my dad is, yes?" I ask, raising my eyebrow.

Anton gulps and nods his head. "Yes, Ms. Pierce."

"Then why didn't you do more? You could have gone to the main office in that warehouse to figure out what happened with those shipments. You seem nonchalant about this mission." Anton opens his mouth, but I don't let him get a word out. "Don't apologize because I don't need that. My Papa doesn't care for that. He cares about answers."

"Well, I-"

"You're taking too long to answer." I stand up and rest my hands on the desk. Adrenaline is pumping through my veins, and I love how the rush feels. I feel so powerful and it's almost a euphoric feeling. "Why did you not get those shipments? Why did my dad later on find out you were snooping through his office? And then not to long after, while he was searching through the papers on his desk, those papers regarding those shipments just disappeared?"

Anton's face pales.

I take a deep inhale and suddenly start coughing.

Why does it suddenly smell like smoke? I disregard it, probably someone smoking a strong cigarette downstairs.

"Miss, are you alright?" Anton asks before coughing a little as well.

I take my gun out and aim it at Anton. "Who are you working for?" I ask and Anton widens his eyes and holds his hands up.

"Woah, woah, woah. You don't need to do this, miss. I swear I'm not-"

"Don't make me ask again. If you do, I'll shoot you and send my Papa to take care of your family," I say, lying about his family.

His family is innocent and doesn't deserve to be caught up in the aftermath, but he doesn't know that.

"Please don't. I-I swear I don't-" A shot rings through the air as Anton's body slumps to the side with a bullet through his head.

I start coughing more as I realize smoke is entering the room.

What the hell is going on?

I put my gun in my waistband and head towards the door. I wince once my hand touches the knob, my burning as if I touched fire. What the hell?

I use the end of my shirt to open the door and when I do, I see smoke and red flames everywhere.

I look over the railing and down at the box shipments seeing them all set on fire. I cover my mouth with the top of my shirt and squint my eyes because of how much the smoke is burning my eyes.

Fire is crawling up the stairs so there's no way to get out.

I look down the railing and see a spot where I can jump and get out.

I can make it.

The second floor isn't that high of a jump.

I get on top of the railing and ignore the burning pain on my palms as I hold myself up.

Don't think, just jump.

I close my eyes and jump down as I land on my feet, strings of pain shoot to my ankle. I cough even more as fire and smoke surround me.

I look around the warehouse for an exit that's not covered with fire. While looking around my eyes start to feel heavy.

My energy from all the adrenaline starts to wear off.

I hold onto a crate nearby that hasn't been hit with fire yet. I cough and slowly get on my knees.

It's fine. I'll just take a minute to catch my breath, and everything will be fine.

I won't prove Papa wrong.

I can't.

I lean my head against the crate and just rest my eyes.

Only for a few minutes.

I need to think of what to do.

What would Papa do or Jamie?

What would Star tell me to do?

I open my eyes and look up, seeing a dark figure in front of me. They walk closer to me making a man's figure become clearer. He has a tall, muscular build and his eyes pierce through me.

"Help," I whisper, almost desperately.

The man tilts his head and I notice his green eyes glinting at me.

My eyes slowly close and then blackness surrounds me.

FIVE
KILLIAN

I REST AGAINST MY BUGATTI AS I WATCH THE warehouse go up in flames.

The orange and red mixing together makes the blood in my body warm. I love the way fire looks, so pretty you want to hold it in your hands, but you also don't want to get burned.

Everyone has their weapon or specialty in the organized crime scene. My mom's is knives, my dad's is fire and various torture methods, and Thalia's is stiletto heels and knives. She likes stabbing her sharp heels into anyone who poses a threat.

I got my love for fire from my dad.

It's ironic how it's bad for me like how most things are.

I control my breathing and ignore the erratic beating of my heart as I walk towards the building on fire.

I cover my mouth with my jacket and walk in. I look around for her as I try to ignore the burning sensation surrounding my heart.

My dad said that Reign Pierce, the Bulgarian Princess, was having a meeting here and I'm supposed to be saving her from a mission that I manipulated.

Nothing a little fire can't destroy.

My dad had a mole working for Malcom and he told us everything we needed to know about what was happening.

I move closer to the crates and see a body leaning against one, struggling to hold her head up.

Reign Pierce.

The girl I met under the stars.

Reign trembles on the floor before looking up at me. Blue eyes stare up at me and she whispers the word, "Help."

I tilt my head while looking down at her, all helpless and in need of saving from a prince.

Too bad she got the villain.

Her eyes close and I'm pretty sure she fainted.

I lean down and pick her up, bridal style. I go back out the way I came while controlling my breathing and ignoring the burn.

I walk all the way towards my car parked on the side of

the road and rest her on the grass. I lean against my car and stare down at her, admiring her features but I wish she could open her eyes to let me see those blues again.

Reign looks more mature than she did when I was fourteen at the gala when I first saw her. Her hair is long and dark. Her cheeks are round making her have that young face but not so round to the point where she doesn't have a nice jawline. Her lips, plumped and pink, make me wish I could see what they look like when she's on her knees begging for my dick.

Reign's breathing steadies out and she starts to slowly wake up. Her eyes flutter open and she squints before looking around slowly and sitting up.

"Where am I?" she coughs out, her voice a little raspy.

"Safe. Out of the fire," I say, still not taking my eyes off of her.

She looks up at me and furrows her eyebrows. "What? No, I could have gotten out on my own," she says and stands up too quickly to where she limps and almost falls.

I catch her by the arms, her face close to mine. Her lip's part but she still looks pissed that I saved her.

"From what I saw a few minutes ago, it didn't seem like it."

She gets out of my arms and steadies herself on her own. "Who do you think you are?"

"I think I just saved your life." Reign glares at me with

those beautiful blues. "Be grateful because I could have just left you to die in there."

"I had everything under control."

"Not from where I'm standing," I say, making Reign look behind me and at my car. Black paint with a custom blue paint on the sides, mirror caps, and the grill. "If I didn't save you, you would have been dead. You should be thanking me." I lean off my car and unlock it.

"Like I'll be thanking you anytime soon."

I furrow my eyebrows at her. "You have a comeback for every little thing someone says?"

"Not my fault my Mama raised me to stand up for myself."

I roll my eyes and turn to my car. "Get in."

"I don't know who you are. I won't get in a car with someone I don't know." I turn to look at her.

"Reign Pierce, right?" I ask.

Reign furrows her eyebrows and nods. "Yes. How do you know that? Who are you?"

"Killian." I open the door. "Now get in and I'll explain more on the way."

Reign hesitantly gets in the car. I close the door after her and get in the driver's seat. I start up the car making the engine roar to life.

I pull onto the road and drive towards her estate.

"Killian. Killian De Luca?"

I look at Reign and see recognition finally taking over her face as she studies me.

"Yes." I look back on the road.

"Why are you here?"

"I need your dad's help."

"For what?"

"To kill my dad."

Reign doesn't say anything which makes me look at her.

She looks innocent sitting there wide eyed, her eyes matching the interior of the car, while wondering why I would want to kill my dad when in reality I'm out to get hers.

Six

Killian

The car ride was surprisingly quiet. Reign wasn't talking, instead she was just staring out the window which I'm glad for because I had no interest in talking at the moment.

I just want this mission over and done with. I'm not going to lie, it's nice I have something or rather someone to occupy my time with and Reign seems like the perfect distraction to not think about the reality of everything going on.

"How do you know my address?" Reign asks as we enter her gated neighborhood.

Her house is the last one on the hill, surrounded by big gates and a bunch of security.

I shrug. "It wasn't hard to find." I eventually pull up

to her gated house. "Tell the guards to open the gate," I demand as a guard walks up to my car.

"Does my Papa know you're coming?" she asks.

"No, now do it." I roll down the window and Reign turns toward the guard.

The guard looks surprised seeing Reign in my car. "Hello, Ms. Pierce. Who's this gentleman?" The guards ask, looking at me with a skeptical eye.

"He's just a friend, Finley," she says politely.

The guard looks away from Reign and rests his eyes on me, studying me.

I am two seconds away from running this *stronzo* over with my $5 million car and then crashing through the gates.

"Are you going to listen to her or are you going to keep eye fucking me?" The guard straightens his stance and walks back to the small booth. The gates open as I say, "Your men here suck." I pull into her estate.

"They have trust issues. Papa always says to be careful who you're around because you never know what role they could play in your life."

"And what role do you think I play?" I ask her, turning my eyes away from the driveway to look at her.

Reign studies my face intensely. Those blue eyes of hers make that thing in my chest beat a little too fast for my liking. It's like she can easily read me without even doing anything.

Reign Pierce is just another girl who is innocent and knows nothing about what's happening in the real world around her.

She is mindless and has no clue.

"Right now, you strike me as someone who will cause trouble in my life. Maybe the kind of trouble I need."

"The trouble you need, huh?" I ask, a smile threatening to spread on my lips.

Reign blushes and looks out the window.

When I pull up to the front of her house, Malcom and two women are waiting on the porch.

Reign gets out of the car when I put it in park. I get out and close the door as Reign goes up to her dad and hugs him.

He holds her in his arms, making sure she's alright while the two women surround them.

Her mom, Lia Pierce, brings her into her arms and hugs her tightly. "Oh, baby you're okay!"

"No more missions, Reign," Malcom speaks, fucking finally.

He doesn't seem to notice me as I lean against my car and watch the small family make sure Reign's okay.

"What?" Reign exclaims and gets out of her mom's hold to turn towards her dad. "That's not fair? Why?"

"I almost lost you. I heard about the fire and I'm not letting you go out on another mission. Something like this could easily happen again and I can't risk losing you."

"I was doing fine! Even before Killian-"

Malcom's face morphs from a concerned dad to a fucking angry mob boss in seconds before he turns his head and looks at me. "Killian?"

"You. You saved my granddaughter?" Kyra Nikolova, Reign's grandmom, says while pointing at me.

"You saved her?" Malcom asks, walking closer to me. I nod my head which makes him furrow his eyebrows. "Why?"

I rest my hands in my pockets and lean off the car. "My dad disowned me. I was going to your warehouse to speak to you regarding him but then I found your daughter with your warehouse up in flames. I've come to ask if-"

"No," Malcom says instantly. "You really think I'm going to let an Italian join my family? You think I would help an Italian?"

"I don't associate with them anymore," I lie through my teeth smoothly. "You're really not going to consider it because of my dad and who I am to him? You don't even know exactly what I want yet."

"Malcom, he has a point. You owe him Reign's life," Lia says, resting her hands on his arm.

"She's not wrong. You're all about loyalty and giving people chances," Kyra agrees.

Malcom crosses his arms, looks me up and down,

studying me. My eyes go to Reign, and I notice her staring at her dad, hope filling her eyes.

Malcom glares at me and bites the inside of his cheeks before saying, "Fine. We'll see who you really are," he says before turning around and walking back inside the house.

My eyes go back to Reign who has a smile on her face.

Why does she always feel the need to smile?

Seven

Reign

We follow my papa as he stomps inside like a child.

Okay maybe not like a child but he sure looks like one when he's huffing and pouting. I notice Baba looking at Killian with interest as he stands near the doorway, not knowing what to do.

"He looks damaged," Baba says, whispering so only Mama and me can hear. "He's just so serious and seems closed off."

"He's a madman, Ma. Of course, he is closed off. Ace probably taught him young," Mama comments as she looks at Killian, who is looking around the house with a bored expression on his face.

Papa went to his office, probably to drink as much brandy as he can to forget about Killian's existence.

"Who's Ace?" I ask Mama.

"He is the Don of the Italian Mafia. His daughter was supposed to take the role, but I heard that she didn't want it anymore after her husband almost died. Killian, I assume was supposed to take the position but as he said, he's disowned."

"I wonder what happened. Ace would never disown his only son," Baba says with a skeptical tone.

"Ace is always hot and cold," Mama says. "But I heard he was worse before Aria came into the picture."

"She is such a sweet woman. I met her at one of the galas and she was talking to me about her daughter and how she was trained. Very different from Ace," Baba says.

"Does her daughter still participate in the business at all?"

"I am pretty sure she does." I see Baba look back at Killian. "Reign, I think you should show Killian to the guest house."

I raise my eyebrows at Baba "What? Why me?"

To be honest I'm kind of scared of Killian. He gives me a feeling that I've never recognized before. I have no clue how to talk to a man like him, which is odd because I usually love talking to people, no matter who they are.

"Well, I know that it may be hard for him here. Seeing as your dad doesn't like him so I think you should show Killian around and make him feel comfortable. Your dad said he wants Killian in the guest house so you should take him to it."

"I agree. It must be hard coming to a different family and asking for their help," Mama agrees.

My eyes go to Killian, and I pause as his green eyes collide with my blue ones. He isn't smiling or giving me a specific look. He is just openly staring at me.

I give him a small smile but nothing on his face changes much.

"I guess I can."

"Maybe he can even show you some new techniques for fighting or missions. I heard he was sent to a private academy where they taught him how to be one of the best assassins. Plus, he was trained by Ace and Aria. I think if Killian showed you some stuff you might become better than your dad thinks," Baba says, making me look down at her.

She has a smirk on her face, and I can't help but smile at her.

She loves scheming.

"Okay." I walk towards Killian who is still in the foyer. "Hey."

Killian still has an expressionless face as I stand in front of him. Now standing face to face with him I notice how tall he is and openly admire his features silently. He has striking green eyes that look down at possibly anyone to intimidate them. It's probably not hard for him to look down at someone with his height. I'm about 5'8" while Killian has to be standing roughly over 6'1" for sure. He's wearing a suit, but I can tell underneath the fabric he is full of muscle.

"Did you come here for a reason?" Killian asks, making me meet his eyes.

"I thought I would show you where you'll be staying. The house is starting to kind of settle down since it's getting dark. We usually have family dinner, but you know since you're here and everything-"

"Where's the room?" Killian cuts me off, still holding eye contact.

I blush, realizing I was talking more than I should've. "Right, sorry. Follow me." I turn around and walk towards the backyard. I show him the massive pool over-looking the city and the garden where I love to spend time, just to look at the flowers. I spend most of my time in the garden or at the beach when it's midnight so I can talk to Dyado. We walk up to the front step of the guest house, which is massive. Papa likes his privacy so whenever guests are over, he throws them here. "Here it is." The house is white and has two floors. One kitchen, living room, bedroom with a bathroom and a walk-in closet. Killian walks inside the house and inspects everything. As we walk through the house, I watch him. "Thank you." Killian turns his head to look at me. "For helping me." I clarify.

Killian leans his body against the back of the couch. "What kind of assassin are you anyway? You almost got yourself killed."

He could have just said 'you're welcome' like a normal person.

"I'm just starting out. It was one mess up. Won't happen again."

"You wouldn't last a day on your own without your family or your dad's men," Killian comments. "I'm surprised you didn't die before I saved you."

My hands clench by my side and I feel myself growing annoyed with what he's saying.

I mean I'm still learning, and my Papa never taught me young because he only saw me as his little princess, still does. He doesn't want me in this kind of business, but I just want to see what it's like.

"And I suppose you can do a better job at teaching and training me than my dad?" I raise an eyebrow at him.

Killian snickers. "Yea."

I take a step closer to him which Killian notices by the way he observes me.

"Then how about tomorrow morning, before breakfast, you do a training session with me?"

"I doubt you could keep up."

"You'd be surprised."

Killian licks the inside of his cheek and leans off the couch to stand about a few inches away from me. "Your dad and I are very different when it comes to training. I will break you, Reign. I don't train pretty," Killian says in a low voice, almost threatening.

"I can handle it."

"Doubt it."

"Then tomorrow."

Killian nips his bottom lip as he looks down at me and I swear I see something dark flash in his eyes before he nods. "Fine. Tomorrow at 5:30 am. Don't be late."

EIGHT

KILLIAN

MALCOM IS DOING PULL-UPS ON THE METAL BAR in their home gym.

I woke up around 4:00 in the morning just to see what time Malcom usually does his workout. From one of the past moles that worked in the house they told me that Malcom would start his workout in the early mornings.

During his workouts, he's by himself, not around family or focused on what could possibly be a threat to him.

Malcom releases the metal bar and plants his feet on the ground. He grabs his towel from the weight bench and wipes the sweat off his forehead.

I rest my hand on my gun that's tucked into my waistband as he grabs his water bottle and takes a sip.

As I'm about to pull it out I hear footsteps walking

nearby. I remove my hand and look behind me only to see Reign with clothes in her hands and a small smile on her face.

Why does her smile make my heart clench?

And why is she smiling this early in the morning?

"Morning," she says and hands me the clothes. "Baba found a change of clothes for you. She thought you'd be more comfortable with that instead of your suit. She has more clothes just until we can get you a wardrobe set up here. But-"

"Thanks," I cut her off.

Her grandma has been giving me weird looks ever since I arrived. It's not the kind of looks that make me think she doesn't trust me. It's more like a sympathetic look and I hate it.

I hate when people do that.

I hate when people feel sorry for me and give me sympathy because it's only a reminder.

"Well, I know you probably didn't want to train or work out in the clothes you were wearing so I thought these would be good."

I honestly thought she was going to sleep in this morning. That's why I chose to do this early. I was hoping to study his routine, maybe get a kill in and just be done.

Reign is wearing athletic shorts that compliment her long pale legs and a black shirt that shows off the silhouette of her breasts and then her snatched waist.

And let's not forget about that smile she wears with every single goddamn outfit.

"They're fine," I say, walking past her and walking towards the house.

"You still don't talk very much do you," Reign comments.

"So, you do remember me from that night." I confirm.

"It's hard to forget someone like you," she says, which makes my heart clench again.

I don't say anything to her as I get inside the house and slam the door shut.

I strip my white dress shirt off and dress pants. Last night I slept in my briefs and assumed I'd be stuck in these clothes for a while since Malcolm isn't very fond of me, so I didn't think he'd give me clothes.

The clothes Reign gave me were black shorts and a white sleeveless compression shirt. I only change into the black shorts since I don't like working out with shirts on since it's uncomfortable.

I have my white tennis shoes from yesterday so those should work.

I get out of the house and see Reign squatting down and looking at a flower bush.

I caught a glimpse of them yesterday as well as the garden they have. I close the door behind me making

Reign turn around to face me. The smile wipes off her face when her eyes dart to my bare chest.

I ignore the feeling of butterflies in my stomach as she admires my chest and the tattoos that crawl up my arms.

"Ready?" I ask, walking towards her.

She meets my eyes and I notice her face flushes red. "Yea, what do we do first?"

I walk towards their home gym as she follows me. "What's your favorite combat method?"

"Well, I'm familiar with hand-to-hand combat. Papa taught me a lot of combat moves," she says. "What's yours?"

"It's not a combat move, but it's my favorite choice of weapon."

"What is it?"

"Fire."

"Really? Why?"

"Because it can do a lot of damage while still looking breathtaking."

"You probably learned how to walk through fire since you got me out of the fire yesterday so easily." She jokingly says.

If only she knew how hard and damaging it actually was for me.

Once we get to the gym, I walk over to the punching bag. "Show me what your dad taught you." Reign walks to where I'm standing in front of the bag. She wraps her hands but doesn't put gloves on. For such a small girl with small hands, she should be wearing gloves when punching a punching bag. I don't stop her as she walks towards the bag and starts punching hard. Another mistake which I furrow my eyebrows at. My dad always said to control your punches and to not go fast at first because you never know who you're fighting. You could be wasting all your energy punching hard at first instead of evening every punch out. Is her dad purposely trying to get her killed in the field? "Stop," I say and walk towards her.

"Why? What's wrong?" Reign asks, her breathing getting heavy.

"Are you tired?" I cross my arms over my chest which makes Reign's eyes dart to my arms before meeting my eyes.

"No. Why?" she says, trying to control her breathing.

"'Cause you breathing like a dog who just ran down the street on a hot day tells me otherwise." I narrow my eyes on her. "Stand straight, slop slouching first." Reign straightens up quickly. "I'm pretty sure your dad is setting you up to fail."

"Why do you say that?" She looks up at me through her eyelashes.

I get closer to her. "Because how you punched the bag was one of the best ways to get you tired and killed when fighting someone. You became sloppy after a minute. You shouldn't be punching the bag that hard for the first few minutes. Because when you become tired and sloppy like that," I put two fingers against her temple like I'm aiming a gun "boom, you're dead."

"They aren't that sloppy," she argues.

"Your breathing shouldn't be so heavy. You should be able to hear what's around you. Close your eyes and drop your hands." Reign gives me a look before closing her eyes and dropping her hands from her waist and letting them hang by her side. I go to stand behind her and place my lips near her ear. "I want you to focus on the things around you. What do you smell? What do you feel? What do you think about when fighting? What do you hear?" I whisper, my lip grazing her ear as she shivers against me.

"I smell your cologne and sweat. I feel cold air hitting my body and your lips near my ear."

"What do you think about when fighting?'

"I think about the stuff Papa has taught me and how I want to make him proud."

Mistake number one.

Her dad has shit lessons.

"And what do you feel? What are you focused on right now to make your breathing controlled?'

"You."

Stupid girl.

She has no clue I'm going to burn her to the ground.

NINE
KILLIAN

I have been training Reign for about an hour and a half.

She's not completely terrible.

If she was my daughter, I would never put her out in the field, but I guess Malcom doesn't care as much about his daughter as I thought.

She is good at some stuff; I'll give her that. She is aware of what's coming at her and quick on her feet.

She definitely needs to build up her stamina, so I made her do a mile sprint without taking a break.

Thalia and I would always do sprints to build up our stamina and endurance, so I'm used to sprinting three miles. The assassin academy our dad sent us to was very strict. We had strict schedules there, diets, lessons, anything you can think of.

"How do you know so much about training?" Reign asks before taking a sip of her water.

We are pretty much done with the "training session" that Reign labeled it even though we were just working out.

We have to head inside for family breakfast. Reign said that her mom is strict when it comes to family meals.

"My mom and dad are some of the most strategic and powerful people in the world. They weren't like that without proper training. My sister and I were taught by them and also went to an academy." I grab my shirt from the bench since I doubt Malcom won't shoot my head if he sees me breathing near his daughter while being shirtless.

Reign would look at my chest and get distracted every so often while working out and it did make me feel good since she couldn't keep her eyes off me.

I know how innocent Reign actually is.

I know she's never had a boyfriend, but I also know that one guy, who's no longer alive, fingered her with the same fingers that I ended up cutting off.

"Your sister, Thalia. Is she Donna?" Reign asks, making me look down at her.

"I don't know, and I don't care," I lie.

"Well, I think Mama is done with breakfast so we should go in the house."

"I'm allowed to?" I ask while following her out of the gym.

"Oh yea, Papa should have settled down from yesterday so you're good. Plus, Mama said to tell you to come inside."

Meals at my house would consist of our old Chef named Lana, who died a few years ago from a heart attack, cooking for us every night. Ever since she passed, we've never had another chef. My mom and dad would cook and sometimes I would help. Reason why my dad would never hire a new chef is because no one could cook like Lana and my dad is also a control freak who wants to make sure everything is perfect.

We walk inside the house, and I see Lia placing plates on the table while Kyra is sitting at the table sipping tea and Malcom just glaring at me.

"Good morning, guys." Kyra beams at us. Reign hugs her grandma and kisses her cheek. "How was your guy's workout?" she asks, looking between Reign and I.

"Good, Killian taught me a lot of new stuff in the gym," Reign says, sitting down next to her grandma.

Kyra smiles at Reign and looks at me. "Sounds lovely. What about you Killian? Sit down, please."

I take my seat next to Reign which happens to be facing Malcolm. "Fine."

Kyra assumes I'm not going to say more so she looks at Malcolm. "How are things with business, Malcom?'

Malcom glares at me before saying, "I don't think it would be wise for me to discuss this when we have an Italian at the table."

"'Cause that would be a fucking tragedy, wouldn't it?" I mumble and see Reign look at me through my peripheral vision.

"Watch it. I'm letting you stay in my house for free without any of my men breathing down your neck with a knife to your back. Be grateful, brat," Malcom sneers at me.

"Papa, can we please just have a nice breakfast?" Reign asks as her mom sits next to her dad and places a hand on her husband's arm.

"I agree. How about we talk about something else other than politics and business?" Lia suggests before turning her attention to me. "Killian, how do you like the guest house?"

"It's comfortable," I say, before taking a bite of the eggs on my plate.

"I'll have one of the maids bring some clothes. I have them getting some things for you so it should all be there before the end of the day."

"Thank you," I say quietly, which makes Malcolm mock me like a child.

Lia slaps his thigh which makes Kyra and Reign laugh. "What did you guys work on today in the gym?" Kyra asks, sneaking a look at me while I'm silently eating.

"Killian taught me how to control my breathing better and he also made me sprint a mile. Not jog but sprint! I was dying!" Reign exclaims.

"Sounds like he worked you out," Kyra says with a small smile.

Malcom's face turns red, and a vein looks like it's going to pop from his forehead.

"Hello Pierces!" a deep voice yells from the hallway.

A boy with platinum blonde hair walks in the dining room.

Who does this guy think he is walking around with that hair?

Alexander would dye his hair to make it lighter because he thinks he's like some fucking hotshot when in reality he just looks like a fucking college frat boy who drinks to fill his liver.

"Jamie!" Malcom smiles for the first time since I walked in the room.

I've known about Jamie for a while. He is one of Reign's best friends but that's only because Malcolm and his dad are best friends. I also happen to know that Malcom wants Reign to marry this prick, but Reign would never do that because she only sees him as a friend, a brother even.

Doesn't mean I don't like or despise him any less.

Jamie is a college frat boy wannabe that happens to know how to hack like fucking Kevin Mitnick. He knows his shit for being so young. He's enrolled at All Assassins Academy going on his last year before he graduates and starts working with the family.

"Malcom, pleasure as always." Jamie smiles at Malcom before coming around to Reign and resting his hands on her chair. I eye his hands near her back and refrain from breaking all his fingers off so he never fucking hacks again. "Feel like getting in some trouble today?"

"What kind of trouble?" Reign smiles at Jamie.

"The best kind. How do you feel about paintball?" Jamie asks with a teasing smile.

Reign's smile widens. "I think it sounds like fun." She turns her head to look at me. "Killian, what do you think?" I look at Jamie who stares at me with a skeptical look. I shrug before taking a last bite of my breakfast. "That's not a good enough answer." Reign looks back at Jamie. "Can Killian come?"

Jamie leans away from Reign's chair and raises an eyebrow at me. "Who are you anyway?"

"Killian De Luca. He is gracing us with his annoying presence for the next few weeks until I figure out how to get rid of him," Malcom says, back to glaring at me.

"You're a pleasure to spend time with, Malcolm. I'll make sure to get you a dad's Day gift since you're basically taking over."

Jamie gives Malcom a look and Malcom just clenches

his fists around his utensils, still acting like a fucking toddler.

I swear Landon, my nephew, acts better than him.

"Killian's new to Bulgaria and I want to show him around," Reign says with that fucking smile on her face.

"I guess it's fine. I'll just have to tell the rest of the group."

"I'm sure they'll be okay with it," Reign says, giving me an assuring smile.

Doubt it.

TEN

KILLIAN

I DIDN'T WANT TO DO ANYTHING TODAY.

I was planning on staying in the house all day and catching up on work or texting my Star.

My Star being Reign, but she doesn't know that.

Lia gave me some casual clothes that Malcom doesn't wear anymore. Malcom glared at me when I walked out of the house and then I heard him and Lia arguing about me before leaving.

I couldn't help but snicker at him because he and my dad are so petty and act like goddamn children not getting their way.

I brought my gun with me and slipped it in my waistband.

I have more guns and shit in my car, just in case.

Reign rode with me in my car even though Jamie told

her to go with him. Reign said she was going to go with me since she wants to make sure I actually make it there. Jamie was trying to race me to the paintball place, but his SVJ could barely even keep up with my Chiron.

During the car ride Reign kept talking about everything and anything there was to talk about. When we passed by a park, she started storytelling about the memories, and she also talked about Malcolm and how he can be a bit much.

But don't worry, she said that he will like me soon.

I almost laughed at that which she noticed.

Reign is his sun, he would never let anyone, or anything touch her unless he says so.

Good thing I'm not good with following directions.

When we get to the place, we go inside to meet with the rest of the group. Reign introduces me to everyone, but I forget their names after five seconds.

"Have you ever been paintballing Killian?" Jamie asks as he puts on his gear.

"No."

"It's like shooting a gun. You should have no problem with that, right?" Jamie says a playful smirk on his lips.

"Are you insinuating something?" I raise an eyebrow at him.

Jamie puts his hands up. "Just trying to make friendly conversation, man."

If he keeps trying to talk to me, Reign will no longer

have a best friend to talk to. He's been getting on my nerves since Reign told her Star about him.

"Well, we should get into groups," Reign suggests, thank God. "Jamie will be leader and then so will Andrei."

Jamie ends up picking first and of fucking course he chooses Reign. She smiles and walks towards him.

"I'll take the new guy," Andrei says, pointing to me.

I don't walk next to him; I stay leaning against the wall until all of them pick all their team members.

We go into the paintball room where it's pitch black. Everyone gets into their hiding positions, and I decide to go into the back of the room where you can barely see anything.

The timer ends and some members from each group go out of their hiding spot and start shooting.

I notice one of the girls, who was trying to flirt with me, come out of hiding.

I aim my gun for her leg, and she yelps and trips over her feet.

A small smile forms on my face as I see her on the floor in pain.

"I think shooting your teammates is against the rules." I turn my head and see Reign aiming a gun at me.

"She was annoying."

"Don't disagree with that," Reign says. "And you're supposed to be having fun."

"I like having fun by myself," I say and lean my head

against the wall, closing my eyes. I feel a jolt of pain on my calf making me hiss from the pain. I look at Reign and see she has a small guilty smile on her face. "Stop, I'm not playing these games with you."

"You're no fun." She rolls her eyes playfully.

"I'm not here to entertain people."

"Too bad," she says before she shoots me again on my other leg.

"Stop that." She shoots me again on the arm, making me more annoyed and wanting to shoot her. "Reign," I warn her, in a low voice.

"Killian," she mimics. "I'm going to keep shooting you if you don't play."

Stupid fucking girl.

She wants to play?

"Keep shooting me and I won't be gentle with what I do to you, Reign," I threaten.

But that does nothing to stop her. She aims the gun and shoots me in the arm again. I don't waste any time before bringing up my gun and shooting her on her thigh.

"Ow!" she winces and looks down at the paint on her thigh.

She glares at me and is about to shoot me again, but I beat her to it and hit her on her waist.

She gets a shot in, and we are just slowly walking closer to each other, just fucking shooting each other.

Once I'm close enough to her, I take her gun and toss it to the side.

She backs up until she hits a wall. "I told you I don't play," I say, my face leaning down so we're about an inch away from each other. "Shoot me again and I'll make sure to make the next shot hurt. Don't. Test. Me." Reign looks up at me with those innocent blues and I swear I could probably go on my knees with how she's looking at me. She's looking at me like I'm about to burn her world to the ground. She doesn't say anything, so before I do something I regret, like squeezing her throat in my hand, I turn around and am about to walk away. But after I get a few steps away I feel a shot on my back. I throw the gun to the floor and next thing I know my hand is on her throat while my other is on the wall near her head. She drops the gun and places her hand on my chest, probably feeling my heart beating against my chest rapidly. "Did you not understand what I just told you?"

"You're too stubborn to admit you're having fun. Just be normal for once and have fun. I bet you've never experienced fun."

I laugh lightly and shake my head. "You have no clue who I am or what I can do, Reign. Stop acting like it."

Reign gulps against my hand on her throat and I swear blood rushes down to my dick.

"What if I want to? What if I want to know more about what you're constantly thinking about or why you're always quiet? What's underneath the hard exterior?"

I lick my bottom lip lightly and I see Reign's eyes flash to my lips before meeting my eyes.

Stupid fucking girl.

"Then you're in for a hell of a ride, Reign Pierce."

ELEVEN
REIGN

KILLIAN AND I HAVEN'T SPOKEN TO ONE another since we left the paintball arena. The moment between us in the arena ended as quickly as it started.

His hand left my throat when the bell rang, and he disappeared in the shadows while I met with the rest of the group.

We all left the arena and when we got outside to the parking lot, I saw Killian waiting next to his car, texting on his phone.

I said bye to Jamie before heading over to Killian which brings us to right now, in the car where we still haven't said a word to one another.

I don't take back what I said about getting to know Killian. I want to know the kind of person he is because of how different he is from me. I don't want to just learn about him, but I also want to learn from him and how he is so strong and stoic.

So, I asked my Star for advice.

He always knows what to say without judgment.

> How do I get to know someone who doesn't want to talk?

Why?

> Because he interests me. I'm curious about him.

You know curiosity killed the cat, right?

> Good thing a cat has nine lives.

All I can tell you is to be careful. You don't want to get burned, Reign.

I texted him right after the moment between Killian and I because I was desperate to know.

I don't know what makes Killian so different compared to all the other guys I've met. Jamie told me to be careful with him and I know he's worried since he doesn't trust Killian but for some reason, I see him in a different light.

"Can you go to this address?" I ask Killian, showing him my phone.

We get to a light which makes Killian stop and look at my phone.

His eyes move to me, giving me a questioning look. "Why? Trying to kill me?"

"No, I just don't want to go home yet," I say, which makes Killian nod his head. He takes my phone to follow the directions.

The drive is quick as Killian takes the canyons, driving probably over 160 kmh, even around the corners. While driving he rolls one of the windows down making my hair flow around.

A smile forms on my face as he drives fast.

I always love drives that Robert, my bodyguard, would take with me when going to the beach. It's just a time where I don't have to think about my dad or what anyone really thinks of me.

I can give myself some time to relax and not think so much.

Eventually, we get to the parking spot in front of the beach. Killian parks the car and doesn't say anything as he turns the engine off.

"Where are we?" he asks.

"Follow me and find out." I give him a teasing smile before getting out of the car.

Over the hill of green grass is the beach. I sometimes go in the water when it's hot but tonight the stars are prominent like they are every night.

Because this beach is so far from the city you can see the stars shine brighter.

"What is this place?" Killian asks as I sit down in my usual spot.

"I always come here whenever I feel like I need to be away from home or just need to talk about everything that's on my mind."

Surprisingly Killian sits down next to me. "I remember you telling me when we were kids, you would go outside to talk to the stars since no one at home would listen to you."

I furrow my eyebrows at him, another smile threatening to spill on my lips at the fact that he remembers. "You remembered?"

"I remember a lot of things about you, Reign," Killian says, looking up at the sky. "How'd you find this place?"

"Robert was driving me through the canyons one night and we took a wrong turn which made us end up here," I explain, while playing with the grass. "When we got here, I ended up sitting here for hours just talking about everything and anything."

"Why do you talk to the stars?"

"They listen without judgment." I look at Killian and see he's staring at me.

The moonlight is shining down on us. Killian almost doesn't look real with how prominent his jaw is and the way his eyes shine under the moon.

One look from him will probably make any girl's heart shatter.

"That's a good reason."

"Dyado said that 'The people with the best heart and greatest intentions are watching over us from the sky.' Maybe that's another reason I like talking to them so much. Because I know he's up there and listening to me. I sometimes think he is giving me advice that I need."

"How'd he die?"

"Heart attack."

It's quiet for a few moments before Killian says, "I'm sorry."

"You don't need to be." I shake my head at him softly. "Everyone dies eventually. He had a long and healthy life. He once told me that Stars are dead too. They burned out thousands of years ago, but their light still hits us. Kind of like ghosts. So Dyado is still here even though he died. He's watching over me."

Killian's eye twitches, the only reason I notice is because I'm just paying attention to him and every breath he takes basically.

I wonder what he is thinking about so hard that makes him keep everything in and not talk or express his feelings.

I just want to know what someone like him, dark and mysterious, is constantly thinking about.

"If you come here to rant to the stars then why bring me here?" he asks.

"Because like I said at paintballing, I want to get to know you."

"One question. You only get one question, but I get to ask you one first."

I feel myself smile widely, excited that he's indulging me. "Okay, that's fair."

Killian turns his body towards me and leans on his hands. He looks down at my lips, for a second, I think I'm hallucinating or something before he meets my eyes again.

"What's your favorite animal?"

"A lion."

"Why?"

"Because they are powerful and strong. They are beautiful but also dangerous."

Killian nods his head. "Beautiful things hurt."

"What's yours?"

"Is that your question?" Killian raises an eyebrow at me.

I blush. "No."

"Ask," Killian whispers softly.

"What are you afraid of Killian?"

Killian's jaw clenches and his eyes darken. "My heart." I furrow my eyebrows. Why would he be afraid of his heart? Like loving someone? I want to ask more but Killian stands up. "Come on."

My mood dampens because the small moment we had together just vanished like it didn't even happen.

Like I dreamt of us talking under the stars.

Twelve

KILLIAN AND I GET BACK TO THE HOUSE JUST IN time for dinner.

The drive home was quiet. I would stare at Killian every so often and I would catch him staring at me, but we didn't say anything to each other. I didn't want to push his limits since I feel like that question about his fear was close to his limit.

Why would Killian be afraid of his heart?

I don't understand but I plan on finding out.

"Reign, how was your day?" Baba asks before taking a bite of her steak.

"It was good. Paintballing was fun. Jamie and my team won. For lunch we ate at this cute little diner near the paintball place."

"And how about you Killian? How was your day?"

Baba asks Killian who is already finished eating almost everything off his plate.

Whenever Killian stays quiet or in his own world, I always think that he might pull out a gun and start shooting the place down.

But that's just my crazy overthinking.

"It was fine. How was yours?" he asks, which surprises me because he never really asks any of them questions since he came here.

Baba smiles at him. "It was great. Lia and I made some candles and then did some gardening outside," Baba says while Killian keeps eye contact with her, listening attentively but not smiling.

Killian looks every bit powerful and confident. So devious. So, in control. Much like the devil.

Everyone says Ace is the devil, but I don't think they've met his son.

Killian doesn't act out of control unless he needs to, even then he still keeps a calm composure.

And I feel like that makes him more dangerous.

"How about you honey?" Mama asks Papa.

"It was fine. I had some issues with another family, but it's handled now," he says, sneaking a look at Killian.

"Well, that's good that it got resolved. Would be horrible if something happened," Mama replies, not really paying much attention to Papa and his business while she eats.

She doesn't care much about the business Papa does, she just wants to make sure everyone's alive and healthy.

Papa side eyes Killian again. "No, we wouldn't."

The sound of the metal utensils makes a loud clatter. My eyes go to Killian who's resting his hands on the table and glaring at papa.

"If you want to talk shit about me, say it to my face instead of being fucking shady. No one likes a coward."

Papa smirks. "Who says I'm talking about you?"

"I'm not a kid anymore, Malcom. You sure as hell aren't one either so I'm not going to explain it to you. Stop looking at me like I'm about to do something wrong. If I wanted to do something, I would have lit your ass on fire the moment I dropped Reign off yesterday."

It's dead silent in the room as everyone at the table stares at Papa and Killian, wondering who is going to shoot who first.

I look down at Killian's hands and see them gripping his thighs.

Baba clears her throat, making the glaring competition between Papa and Killian end.

Baba gives me a teasing smirk and winks at me before focusing her attention on Killian. "So, moving away from that conversation. In a few days I was supposed to be volunteering at a nearby beach to pick up trash. My back has been killing me today from gardening so I wanted to ask you and Reign if you guys could be kind and do that for me."

"What?" Killian, Papa, and me ask while looking at Baba with wide eyes.

"Yes, my back is hurting and aching. You guys know I'm getting old so I can't do much about it. I was going to ask Reign, but you know how she is. She can't be outside all alone with the sun beating down on her, my poor baby," Baba says, perfecting the role of a concerned grandmom but I know how mischievous she can be.

"Baba-"

"You wouldn't say no to your dying Baba, would you?" Baba cuts me off and raises her eyebrows at me.

I feel Killian's eyes burn a hole on the side of my face. "Yea, of course Baba. Only if Killian is okay with it?" I say, looking at Killian.

He looks at Baba before looking back at me, probably thinking of whether to say yes or no.

Eventually he nods his head. "Fine. Just this once."

The rest of dinner goes by quickly without any arguments.

Eventually everyone heads to their rooms for the night. I watch as Killian walks out the patio backyard door.

When I go to my room, I can't help but look out the window. Killian is still standing outside the house with his hands in his pockets, looking up at the stars.

For some reason I can see progress with him.

Even if we just spent one day together.

There's hope to make him talk more and just be a happier person and not so stoic.

Killian looks away from the stars and goes inside the guest house.

I walk away from the window and lay on my bed.

I close my eyes and place my hands on my heart, feeling how hard and fast it's beating.

"What am I going to do?" I ask myself.

My phone vibrates in my pocket. I sit up and take my phone out and see a message.

> How'd it go with that guy?

> Not horrible. He indulged me. I think I'm going to make progress with him.

> Why do you want to get to know him?

I think about that for a moment.

Killian is just some guy from another Mafia family.

He's not special to me or anything.

I guess I just like helping people.

And Killian looks like he just needs a friend or someone to talk to.

He's been taught to not trust anyone or be open, but I want to prove him wrong.

Killian is just a boy whose heart hasn't been loved enough.

> I think he needs a friend or just someone to talk to. He's different from everyone else I know.

Wow, replacing me already?

> Never :) I just think he doesn't have a lot of people he can trust or rely on which can be lonely.

Did you end up finding out anything?

> Yea. Just one thing. He's afraid of his heart which doesn't make much sense to me.

Maybe he's scared of getting hurt.

> Everyone gets hurt. It's inevitable. You can't control what the universe has in store for you.

Usually, the people who try their best not to get hurt are the ones that get hurt the most.

Thirteen

Killian

Why do I feel glad that Malcom hasn't been home since last night?

During dinner he told all of us that he had to take care of an emergency. He kissed his wife and Reign before glaring at me and leaving in a rush.

I don't have to worry about him today or killing him.

But the only reason I'm here is because I have to kill him, it's part of my duty.

It's been almost a full week since I've been here, and I've maybe only attempted to kill him once.

So why can't I fucking get it over with?

Maybe it's because whenever I see Reign, I think about ways to see that annoying smile on her face.

Thinking about these kinds of things makes me feel guilty.

We haven't hung out much since her grandma told us about picking up trash at the beach. The only time I "hangout" with her is when we're training or when she's talking to me about fucking flowers in the garden.

We text almost every night because she always needs to vent to her Star about her day. She rarely talks about me, the only time she does is when her Star wants to hear updates about the boy she's trying to fix.

It's amusing to me how she is texting Star about me, telling me all the details and what she thinks of me.

She wants to fix my broken heart that is damaged beyond repair. She has no clue how broken it is and what it takes to fix it.

Working out together is a nightmare because she comes in with tight clothes that show off her perfect waist, perfect legs, and perfect tits. It makes me want to wrap my hand around her throat again, shove her to the nearest wall, and show her what those clothes make me want to do to her.

But in reality, I'm trying to focus on training her, so she doesn't get killed in the field.

I'm not a fuck boy or a player.

Yes, I think about sex like every regular guy but not to the point where I need it every day or week.

It's been a while since I've been in bed with a girl because I'm too busy focusing on work, but I swear to

God, every session with her makes me act like a teenage boy with hormonal issues.

My phone rings on the side table next to the bed. I grab it and feel my body tense when I see my dad's name.

He hasn't called since I landed in Bulgaria.

I sigh while answering the phone. "Dad."

"You sound tired. What are you doing?" He says, not bothering to say hi.

"I'm in bed."

"It's almost noon over there, Killian. What are you still doing in bed?" I hear my mom ask from the other side of the phone.

She should be the one in bed and not worrying about me.

"I'm tired."

"Not good enough," my mom says, making me roll my eyes.

"What's taking so long Killian?" my dad asks, not even caring about my health unlike my mom.

No, don't expect Ace De Luca to do that.

He is all business.

"Malcolm hasn't been home," I lie.

If I told him the truth, of how I am constantly trying to find ways to see that stupid smile on her face, he'd probably yell at me and tell me to stop being pussy whipped.

"Not good enough. You can get him alone even when he isn't in the house, stop acting stupid."

He knows I'm not stupid.

If he thought I was he wouldn't have sent me to kill Malcom.

"I'm not stupid. I'm not going to attack when I'm not even ready. Do you think if I would attack him at his office, where there is surveillance and security everywhere, that someone wouldn't catch me? Get real." I run my hand down my face, getting frustrated with this piece of shit I call a dad.

"Watch it. Just because you're about to become capo, doesn't mean you get to disrespect me," my dad lectures.

It's quiet on the line and I'm about to hang up before my mom cuts in. "How are things with the girl?"

"Fine. She doesn't suspect anything."

"She's smart. I ran through her records and found that she was one of the top five in her classes. Be careful around her."

I'm not worried.

Reign isn't stupid. But her head is in the clouds most of the time.

She doesn't worry about anything because in her world, there is nothing to worry about. No one will let the princess fall.

Reign is very different from me because in high school all I would do is smoke and sleep my way through. I knew I had another life ahead of me, so I wasn't worried about my career.

I never wanted a career like regular people had. I knew I was meant for more than college, trade school, or a regular boring job.

Ever since my first kill, I knew that's what I was meant for.

It's just the rush and then adrenaline of a kill that makes me feel so powerful, like I can do anything and no one can stop me.

It almost makes me forget about the endings and what my life will look like soon.

"I know she is," I agree with my dad.

"How are you holding up after the fire incident?" my mom asks.

My heart clenches at the reminder.

My caring mom, always reminding me of my health.

"I'm fine."

"Is your-"

"I'm fine, mom. If I wasn't I wouldn't be here," I snap without meaning to.

"Hey. Fix your tone when you're speaking to your mom like that," my dad yells from the other side of the phone.

"Baby, I'm just worried. I want to make sure you're taking care of yourself," my mom says softly.

And what about worrying about your own health issues? You're fucking dying, and I can't save you.

Instead, I'm sent to another country to kill a guy your husband hates.

"I know, I'm sorry. But we already discussed this, and I don't want to talk about it," I explain, calmly this time. "How are you? Are you resting?"

"I'm okay, baby. You don't need to worry about me," my mom reassures me.

I don't believe her though.

I know the end is near.

She's growing weaker every day and there isn't a damn thing I can do about it.

"I've got to go," I say before hanging up and tossing my phone onto the end of the bed.

I get they care and worry.

But it would be easier if they didn't sometimes.

My phone buzzes on the bed. I groan and grab my phone.

How can I make a person want to
open up?

Oh Reign, you have no clue how bad I'm about to fuck you up.

FOURTEEN

KILLIAN

I SLEPT IN BY MISTAKE THIS MORNING. I WAS supposed to wake up early to catch Malcolm in the gym.

He came back from work late last night, I heard him come in and decided I was going to catch him in the gym this morning but I fucking slept in.

For some reason I'm not worried and I don't feel anxiety crawling up my neck worrying about it.

Instead, whenever I am about to go to sleep and get a text from my Star, I always end up feeling guilty.

I never feel guilty because what's the point?

But I would never be able to look Reign in the eyes and see those tear stained cheeks as she cries over what I did to her dad.

Or who knows, maybe she's the forgiving type and she'd forgive me.

She seems like the forgiving type.

My dad's right.

I can't be pussy whipped and ruin my only shot at what I've been destined for since I was a kid.

It's my mission and the last thing on my "checklist" to become capo.

But the guilt I would feel when looking at Reign pisses me off.

She'd get over it.

I look at myself in the mirror.

"What the fuck?" I say to myself.

I can't marry her.

I just want to fuck her until everything expires, and I'll be good.

Those blue eyes are just the blue eyes I want to see until I die. I don't want to marry or have children with her.

It's not that serious.

I'm overthinking this whole thing.

I'm just thinking too much.

I've known her for a week, and I'm obsessed.

Well, I've known her longer than that but just being around her makes everything seem so quiet and like everything makes sense.

It shouldn't go like that.

She's just a fucking girl.

But being with her makes me feel calm and like my heart isn't constantly racing.

A knock on my front door makes the overthinking pause. I look back at the mirror one more time before leaving the bathroom. I already know who it is before I even open the door.

Reign is wearing a bright smile along with a white bathing suit top and blue shorts when I open the door.

Is she insane?

It's cold as fuck in this country and she's wearing that to the beach as if she's going in the water?

I know it's summer here but it's still cold.

I'm used to the hot and sunny weather in Italy.

Her eyes dart to my bare chest and the smile wipes off her face. I can't help but smirk at her and lean against the doorway, crossing my arms over my chest.

I love how she stares at me openly, with no shame. It makes me feel good and my dick hard.

"Isn't it too cold to be wearing a bathing suit?"

Reign looks away from my chest and blushes. I mean I look at Reign all the time, the difference is that she just doesn't catch me.

"The weather isn't bad today for the beach and I'm not going in the water. I just didn't want a weird tan," Reign explains before she looks over my attire, her eyes staying on my dick for a few seconds too long before meeting my eyes. "Are you wearing that to the beach?"

"You want me to?" I raise an eyebrow at her.

Reign blushes again while trying to hide her smile. "If you want."

I lick my bottom lip, my eyes darting to hers. I shake my head lightly and lean off the wall. "Give me a second," I say before walking inside the house. I get changed into a pair of gym shorts and go back downstairs to Reign who is looking at the flowers. I saw the flowers that Lia and Kyra planted yesterday in front of the house. They are white roses and opium poppies. Reign is about to touch the rose bush as I close the front door. "I would suggest not touching the rose if you don't want to get pricked." I say, walking towards her.

Reign turns around. "Do I sense tenderness? Didn't think you could feel that kind of emotion towards another human," Reign teases and a smile threatens to spill on my face.

"Don't get ahead of yourself, Reign. Just wanted to make sure I won't be picking up trash by myself." I walk past her. "Come on, I don't want to stay at the beach all day."

Reign and I get inside my car and the drive to the beach is about twenty minutes.

When we get to the beach Reign, and I split up and start picking up whatever trash we see.

Never in a million years would I think I'd be at the beach on a weekday, picking up trash for an old lady.

But my mom would always tell me to respect my elders, no matter what. My mom is huge on respect as well as my dad. You never know what role people will play in your life so you should show everyone respect. My dad is only respectful to people who show respect to him.

The only person he doesn't respect or give a shit about is my uncle Alex, my mom's brother. They have been bickering like children, going back and forth for over twenty years and they still can't manage to get along.

My sister and I find it funny while my mom finds it immature and stupid.

Family dinners with those two are always the best.

Reign and I have been picking up trash for more than an hour now and we are getting closer to the water since there is just some leftover trash in that area.

I'm getting bored and my back is aching from all the bending down. Pretty sure there is going to be a burn on my back too.

I get we're helping the planet but who the fuck would actually want to do this during their free time?

I walk up to Reign, and she looks up at me with a questioning look in her gaze. She has sweat on her forehead and chest from the heat beating down on her skin.

Guess it's not as cold as I thought it would be.

"When can we leave?"

Reign stands up and shrugs. "Whenever we want."

"Great because I want to go back."

I start to turn around, but Reign doesn't move. Instead, she drops the trash bag and walks towards the water.

"The water isn't too cold," she says, dipping her feet in.

Reign shivers her before looking at me. "Are you trying to get me to go in the water?"

A small teasing smile appears on her face. "Would you go if I asked?"

"No." Reign rolls her eyes and all of a sudden, I have the urge to grab her by the throat and threaten her to do that again so she can see what the outcome will be. I feel cold water splash on my chest and run down my stomach. "Reign," I warn as I see a smile spread on her face, a mischievous smile.

"Just put your feet in. It's not that bad."

I cross my arms over my chest. "Come on, stop fucking around and get out."

Reign's eyes dart to my chest so I take the time to stare at her. Her body is glistening with sweat which makes her look absolutely radiant. Her skin glows with the sun beaming down on her, complimenting her skin perfectly.

Water splashes on my face making me focus my attention back on Reign who is holding in a laugh.

Next thing I know I'm in her face, my hand around her throat as I pull her close to me. "I said, stop," I demand in a low threatening voice.

Reign nips her bottom lip before water splashes on my leg.

Fuck this.

I grab Reign and throw her over shoulder as I walk towards the water. "Killian! I'm sorry. I'm sorry! Please, Killian-" Reign yelps and screams while scratching my back.

"Should have thought about that before splashing me, Reign."

And for the what feels like the first time in a long time, my lips tilt in a small, barely there smile as I throw her in the water.

FIFTEEN

REIGN

I FORCED KILLIAN TO HELP ME PLANT DAISIES IN the garden.

Out of all the flowers Baba and Mama have planted, there are no daisies and daisies happen to be one of my favorite flowers.

So, because Killian and I haven't hung out since the beach, which was a few days ago, I decided to have him help me.

Yes, we have meals together and train together every day, but we barely talk during those times.

During training, Killian is always barking out orders at me while I try my best not to faint from how hard he pushes me.

He never lets me take a break.

I asked him one morning why he always pushes me so

hard, and he told me, "Because your dad doesn't. You haven't reached your full potential because he isn't pushing you."

And Killian isn't wrong, but God I wish he was.

But during workouts we train and then he works out while I'm doing whatever conditioning he makes me do. Sometimes when we are punching the bag, he is behind me, and I feel his body heat against me and then his deep breathing in my ear.

Sometimes he puts his hands on my waist to position me and I know he knows that he has an effect on me. He isn't stupid. He sees the blush in my cheeks and then the goosebumps rising on my skin.

He will also tease me and dip his fingers below my waistband and rub the skin there but that's it.

Nothing more.

And don't get me started on him staring at me during dinners.

I always feel eyes on me and sometimes Killian smirks whenever I blush at him.

Papa notices the looks because he always clears his throat extra loudly and starts picking a fight with Killian on purpose to get Killian's attention off of me.

But the stolen glances and the lingering touches, need to calm down because my heart is too sensitive for Killian's reckoning force. Killian and I are so different I could never see myself liking him but when he touches me and looks at me, it makes me feel all hot and like there are butterflies in my stomach.

I've never had a boyfriend; I've told Star that. He told me it's good I've never had a boyfriend because boys can do some pretty good damage to girls with innocent hearts like me.

Star told me, don't trust a guy if they don't break down their walls for you.

I told him about the things Killian would do and Star would just say be careful.

Guys like Killian would break a girl like me.

"Are you ready?" I turn around and see Killian, blocking the sun from my view. He is shirtless, of course.

I asked him once why he is always shirtless and Killian told me, whenever he was home, he would never wear a shirt because he wanted to be comfortable in his own home.

And now that he's living here, he wants to feel the same way.

Which I don't mind because his body isn't the worst thing to see first thing in the morning.

"Yea. I've just been maintaining the rest of the flowers," I say, moving to the side so he can sit. Killian sits down next to me and leans on his hands as he observes me. "So basically, all we have to do is water all of them and then start planting these ones that Baba got from the market. It's not that hard. I've been gardening since I was a kid, so Baba taught me everything she knows-"

"What do you want me to do?" Killian asks, interrupting me.

I smile, realizing I was oversharing. "Just water them. It's not hard and you can't mess up on that."

"You saying I can't take care of a flower?" Killian raises an eyebrow at me.

"No. I'm just saying you'd probably ruin them with your hands. You don't seem like the gentlest person to be taking care of flowers."

All of a sudden, Killian's lips are close to my ear, and he whispers soft and sensually, "I can show you exactly how gentle I can be, Reign."

I turn my head to make eye contact with him and I feel the brush of his skin on my cheek. "I doubt you could be gentle."

"What makes you think that?" Killian tilts his head to the side.

I look down at his lips before looking at his hands.

His hands have small scars and cuts on them with a few tattoos on his fingers. He is wearing two rings on one hand. One of them looks like an heirloom and the other is just a chrome hearts band.

His tattoos consist of stars on his wrist leading up to his ring finger while the pointer finger has a sword tattoo on it. Another one on the center of his hand says, "Devils

Don't Sleep" and the last one on that hand has a small smiling face with x's as eyes.

"Your hands. They don't exactly scream 'gentle'." I meet his eyes and realize we are closer. My heart is beating so fast to the point where I think Killian can hear it. Killian licks his bottom lip, and he looks like he's about to move away but I say, "Show me."

Killian's jaw hardens and I see his hands form in a fist.

"Why would I do something stupid like that? I could break you."

"Then prove it," I urge him.

I see doubts in Killian's eyes but for a second, I swear I see something darker flash in them, like he wants to give in to the urge as if he is a drug addict and I'm the drug he shouldn't take.

Killian's breath hits my lips making them part and I swear I feel the brush of his lips before the sound of a phone going ringing makes him back away from me.

He cusses in Italian and pulls out his phone.

He picks up the phone, gets up and walks away while talking in Italian.

I didn't run but with how fast my heart is beating, it feels like I just did.

Sixteen

Reign

It's been two days since I last spoke to Killian.

He doesn't do the training sessions with me anymore in the morning. The only time I would see him is at meals.

Baba and Mama have asked him what he's been doing and why he's rarely in of the house.

He would make up some excuse about not feeling well before continuing on with the dinner not talking.

My dad the other day asked me what's going on with Killian and why he hasn't been in the gym training me. I tell him I don't know but I have a feeling it's because of our almost kiss or whatever that was in the garden.

I don't usually go to Killian's house to get him for dinner but I'm over the silent treatment with him.

I just want everything to be back to normal.

I tried talking to Star about it, but Star told me I should leave him alone. Star doesn't get it though because he isn't the type of person to worry about anyone.

When I get to the guest house I knock on the door and wait for Killian to pop out. When he does, he's only wearing basketball shorts and nothing else. His hair looks like it's been ran through by his fingers.

Killian trails his eyes down my body like I'm his mark. His eyes pause on my bare legs before meeting my eyes again.

"What?" he asks, opening the door wider.

"Dinner is starting soon but I wanted to talk to you."

"Yea I know it is." He walks inside the house, his bare back facing me. His muscle clench with every step he takes as I follow him inside and close the door behind me. The place is actually quite clean. Killian cleans up after himself so well and you can tell. There aren't clothes everywhere and when I catch a look in the kitchen, it doesn't look messy at all. "What do you want to talk about?" Killian asks as he walks towards the room.

I follow after him. "Things have been weird between us lately." Killian turns to look at me and he grabs a white shirt from the bed and throws it on.

"What makes you say that?" Killian crosses his arms over his chest and raises an eyebrow at me.

I nervously grip the bottom of my skirt. "Well after what happened in the garden-"

"What happened in the garden?" Killian asks, acting like he's actually confused.

I laugh lightly because he has to be kidding. "We had-"

"Nothing." Killian walks towards me. "We had nothing, Reign. Nothing happened that day. You'd be crazy to think something would."

I furrow my eyebrows. "You're the one who was making eyes at me."

Killian narrows his eyes, and they darken just like they did in the garden. "What eyes?"

He knows exactly what he's doing. "That. Your pupils get bigger which makes you look like you want me or something."

Killian's lips lift in a small smirk and take a step closer. "I don't want you, Reign."

"Then stop looking at me like that."

Killian leans down and his eyes go to my lips before meeting my eyes. "Could say the same for you. Staring at me constantly and blushing when I don't wear a shirt." Killian's smirk widens. "I mean admit it, you love the attention I give you. You love seeing me walk around everywhere shirtless. Don't be a hypocrite," he says before passing by me, knocking his shoulder into mine.

He leaves his room and goes out the front door after putting his shoes on.

I try to calm down and force myself to walk out of his house.

We're not finished.

Killian can't just project all this on me when I didn't even do or initiate anything.

When I walk into the main house everyone is sitting in their seats and Killian is sipping on water, smirking when his eyes catch mine.

I sit down with everyone else at the table as the workers start bringing in dinner.

"Today I had the chef make some pasta. I wasn't in the cooking mood today," Mama explains.

"What'd you do today, Mama?" I ask.

Mama starts explaining how she worked in the garden with Baba, she did some reading and went to the store with Papa.

Papa and Mama try to go out regularly because they like pretending they have a somewhat normal life.

So, a day with just them two and rarely any bodyguards up close to them, they enjoy it and spend it quietly together.

While she explains more about her day along with Papa cutting in, my eyes go to Killian automatically.

I don't know why I can't keep my eyes off him.

Killian is like the black devil. Not the red, no.

The red devil is the one that everyone is afraid of because he makes his presence known, kind of like Killian's dad.

But Killian, the black devil, he is the devil you never see coming. Quieter and deadlier.

It's the ones that everyone will scream for.

Killian's eyes meet mine.

Us staring at one another feels like a lifetime and Killian's lips lift in a small smirk. I don't smile at him even though I want to.

He doesn't deserve my smile after what he said to me about being a hypocrite.

He is the one who started this.

Yes, I urged him but that's because if you start something you should at least finish it.

I feel a hand, warm and rough, slide onto my bare thigh. I look away from Killian and see his hand on my thigh. I blush immediately when he grips my thigh tightly before rubbing his hand up and down.

I've had one guy in my life touch me like this, but I don't remember feeling so hot and sensitive. That guy wasn't a boyfriend, he was just a little talking stage, but nothing ever came out of it except for him fingering me, which honestly was a small let down.

A few months later that guy disappeared and there was trace of him found everywhere.

Jamie tried to find out what happened with him but nothing major came up.

No guy has touched me since, at least not until Killian.

"Reign," Papa says, making me look away from my lap and try to focus on Papa.

"Yes, Papa?"

"I asked how your day was," Papa repeats but I can't stop thinking about Killian's warm hand on my thigh with his rings sending jolts down my body.

"It was good." I force a smile on my face. "I worked out in the gym, did some reading and even talked to Jamie for a little bit."

I take a deep breath in and press my thighs together when I feel Killian slide his hand up and towards my inner thigh.

"And you Killian?" Papa asks, glaring at him.

Papa still doesn't like Killian, but he is learning to control his anger and dislike around him.

Killian runs his thumb up and down in my inner thighs which sends chills to the spot between my legs. I try to press my legs together more, but Killian doesn't let me, keeping them spread a little.

"Boring. I didn't do anything," he says nonchalantly.

"Have you talked to your dad at all?"

"No. I told you already, he kicked me out. Ace De Luca won't call, he wants to see me running back," Killian says with a smooth tongue while I'm over here blushing and going crazy over a small touch.

"And you're not going back why? I'm just curious why all of a sudden you and Ace had a falling out."

Killian looks up at Papa and says in a low, almost threatening voice, "That's for me and my dad only to know. All you need to know is one of these days, I'll be asking for your help."

Papa rubs his chin and gives Killian a skeptical look. "And what do I get out of it?"

"You finally will get to kill the man you hate the most."

SEVENTEEN

KILLIAN

I KNEW WHEN REIGN AND I FIRST MET THAT I was going to be the villain in her story.

That's currently the role I'm taking over now.

I'm the villain in Reign Pierce's happy, happy story.

But it's too perfect to not pass up.

I've known that from the moment Reign bothered me that day of the gala, we were written in the stars.

Us meeting under them and confessing things we've never told anyone; it was meant to be.

The day Reign and I were in the garden, it was my dad who called my that day. He reminded me of my mission, like he does almost every day and asked why I'm taking so long. I eventually got him off my back but then I started to think about Reign.

I can't become attached to someone like her knowing what the outcome will be for both of us.

We can't happen.

But then she looked up at me with those big blue eyes and I snapped.

Her eyes. God her fucking eyes. They kill me.

I was over what my dad said, and I suddenly just didn't give a single shit anymore.

I tried hard to stay away from her and close myself off, but she makes me want her like she's some fucking drug.

My walls are slowly crumbling. You wouldn't notice it, but I notice it. In the way Reign smiles, my heart cracks a little or when she laughs or gives me that mischievous, teasing look, my heart feels like it just wants to fall.

I don't know how I'm doing it so well, holding it up.

During dinner last night she kept trying to get my hand off her thigh, but I wouldn't let her.

I like seeing her squirm at the table in front of her family. It made me want to take her to her room to see how far I could push her to ruin that perfect good girl image she puts up in front of everyone.

I can push that good girl side out of the way and see what I really want to see. Reign completely at my mercy, screaming and crying for me.

I missed breakfast today, which I'm sure Lia wasn't happy about, but I couldn't give two shits.

I wanted to sleep in and relax. I was supposed to meet

with Reign for training but I'm just holding off a little longer until I decide how I'm going to play this whole thing with her.

Right now, I'm in the main house because there was no more coffee in the guest house, so I needed to drop by to get some.

When I do, I see the coffee maker all filled up.

Thank the fucking lord.

I start making the coffee until I hear footsteps enter the kitchen.

"We missed you at breakfast," Kyra says, walking past me to get something from the fridge.

"It's not good to lie."

"Good thing I'm not lying because one of us at least missed you," Kyra says, making me look at her.

She has a stupid smile on her face, and she is wiggling her brows at me.

Reign Pierce is going to perfectly ruin my ending.

"Then she's stupid," I mutter.

"You don't mean that Killian."

This lady is fucking crazy. I'm surprised she isn't in a nursing home yet.

"You have no clue what I mean, Kyra," I say while pouring my creamer.

"I know someone just like you." I raise an eyebrow at Kyra. "My husband and almost every other made man is just like you. I see the way you sneak looks at my granddaughter. Malcom and Lia see it too. That's why Malcolm is scared of you living in our home."

"He doesn't have to worry. I'm not touching her."

Yet.

"That's a lie. You know it and everyone else knows it. It's almost like your guys' story was already written for you."

"Why do you think that?"

"Because Reign has changed since you showed up. I know my granddaughter and she's never acted like this with a boy."

"Changed how?"

Kyra leans against the counter. "Her cheeks are more red than usual, especially when she is deep in thought about something. She is always smiling or trying to hide behind her long hair whenever you're around. The looks you give each other from across the table show. And if nothing happened yet, then something will," Kyra explains which makes me crack my knuckle with my finger. "I think you're afraid of her because perhaps you feel something for her. You don't want to feel something for anyone because it's easier for you." Kyra isn't wrong but I'm not going to tell her that. I'm afraid that Reign will make me miss something when I already had a perfectly placed plan for everything. Reign wasn't involved in my plan; she wasn't even thought about. But all of a sudden, she pops into my head when I think of the end.

"You can disagree all you want but I know the look on your face right now. You're scared and Reign is happy. That's usually how it works for boys and girls when they start liking or even loving each other. It's a hurtful realization."

I take a sip of my coffee.

"She'll be disappointed."

"No, she won't. I know you won't try to hurt her because I can already tell how much you care about her."

Crazy fucking lady thinks she knows me.

She has no fucking clue.

"You're crazy to think I'm going to fall or even allow myself to fall in love with her," I say, trying to convince myself more than her.

Kyra pats my shoulder. "But you see Killian, I'm positive that it's just beginning. And once it starts, there is no way you'll be able to stop it." She smiles at me before walking past me.

Eighteen

Reign

I'M TIRED OF THE SAME TRAINING.

I'm tired of Killian avoiding me like the plague.

I'm just sick of him looking at me from across the room, smirking but not actually saying anything to me.

It's almost like he's daring me to make a move after the stunt he pulled during dinner a few days ago.

I tried to keep in a gasp so many times, especially when he would slide his hand a little too high and rub his thumb on the inside of my thigh. I couldn't stop squirming in my seat, and it felt unbearable to sit next to him.

After dinner was done, I jumped out of my chair and ran upstairs to my room. This time I've been the one avoiding him because every time I think about him, I think about that moment during dinner and then how we were almost about to kiss in the garden.

I hope he thinks this much about me, and I drive him out of his mind, it's only fair.

During meals he gives me looks and sometimes would try to slip his hand on my thigh, but I don't let him. We haven't spoken much because we are both playing the game of who will cave first.

And it won't be me.

But I do need his help with something.

I knock on the front door of the guest house. It's not long before Killian opens the door, wearing nothing but black sweatpants.

His hair is a little wet and water droplets fall from the ends onto his skin making him look godly.

"Done staring?"

I meet Killian's eyes and force a smile on my face. "I'm not here to stare at you. You should really learn to put a shirt on."

"You staring at me makes my dick nice and hard. Why would I want to do that?" Killian raises an eyebrow at me while my face turns tomato red, and the smile wipes off my face.

Good thing everyone in the house is sleeping. So, we don't have to worry about anyone possibly waking up.

I clear my throat and try to calm down my rapidly beating heart. "You can't say things like that."

"What do you need, Reign?" Killian crosses his arms over his chest.

"Can I come in?" I ask, looking past the front door in the house.

He opens the door wider to let me in. I walk in slowly as I feel Killian's eyes watching my every move. I feel the gun in my waistband burn against my skin.

Killian closes the door behind us and heads to the couch. On the TV, there's a football match between Romania and Germany.

"I didn't know you liked football."

"I was a striker in high school." Killian sits on the couch. "So, what do you want?" Killian looks at the clock on his phone. "It's one in the morning and you decide to come knocking on my door for...?"

I grab the gun out of my waistband and rest it on the table.

Killian's eyes follow the gun and then look up to meet my eyes.

"I want you to teach me how to use a gun."

Killian licks the inside of his cheek, staring at the gun. He rubs his chin and looks up at me. "Why?"

"What do you mean?"

"Why do you need to know how to shoot a gun? Don't you already know how to shoot one?"

I lick my bottom lips before saying. "I only know how to shoot a Glock. Not a pistol." I shrug.

"You aren't afraid of guns?"

"No, I've grown up around guns." Killian reaches towards the table and grabs the gun. He inspects it and then checks the cylinder. Killian then turns the gun upside down and dumps all of the bullets on the coffee table. "What are you doing?"

"You should be scared of a gun, especially if you don't trust the person behind it." He grabs one bullet from the table and puts it back inside the cylinder. He clicks it in place and turns off the safety. "Come here." I look at him then the gun. I don't know a thing about Killian, I have no clue what kind of person he is with a gun but for some reason that doesn't stop me from walking towards him.

I stand in front of him and wait for the next demand he says but instead he grabs me by my thighs and sits me on top of his lap. My hands automatically drop to his chest to steady myself. Killian's hands rest on my hips, making me feel chills rush down my body.

My body feels so warm against his. He almost feels like a blanket protecting me from anything and everything.

How could an enemy feel this good?

"What are you doing?" I ask, adjusting myself on his lap. When the spot between my thighs meets his erection, I squirm and take a deep breath in.

I can feel his bulge pressing against me even though I try to ignore it.

Killian's hands flex on my hips, running his thumb up

and down as if it calms him. "A game my dad told me to never play. Russian Roulette." My heart rate speeds up, and I try to stay calm.

I know how Russian Roulette works and I know how the game ends.

Someone dies.

Nineteen

Reign

"Why would you want to play that? You're not even Russian."

"Because it's perfect to teach you how to shoot a gun. It will give you the basics." Killian hands me the gun. "Put your finger on the trigger and shoot." I give him a look, but he ignores it. "You want to learn, don't you?" I nod my head and lick my lips. "Aim the gun towards me." I do as he says, hesitantly. I press it against the middle of the chest. "Now pull the trigger. I already turned the safety off," Killian says and then he slides his hands up to my chest, resting it where my heart is located.

Killian can for sure feel my rapid heartbeat as it beats underneath his hand.

This should scare me.

My mind should be screaming at me to run and get the fuck out of his house.

But no, instead I lick my lips before pulling the trigger. It clicks but nothing comes out.

All the pressure weighs off my heart from the fact that a bullet didn't pierce through his chest. I blow out air and a tear falls from my eyes. I look up at Killian and focus on where his hand is.

He snaps out of it and grabs the gun. "I feel like because we're playing this game, I should at least know a little more about you."

Killian nods his head. "One question each shot." Killian aims the gun for my heart. "What's there to smile about?"

The gun against my chest makes my heart race again. Being on both ends of the gun is an experience some would never want to have. Me on the other hand, it's an experience I'll never forget. The way being on different ends of the gun and how they make you feel is scary. Being behind the gun makes you feel powerful and like you can do anything. But being on the end of it makes you feel like you're at that person's mercy.

"The fact that you're alive," I answer. "You could be dead or have cancer or something way worse but you're here, in the moment, breathing, feeling, listening."

It's quiet, the feeling of anxiety creeping up my neck

wondering if I'm going to die or not. A click rings in the air, and nothing comes out.

I take a deep breath and laugh a little. "I feel like one round is actually enough."

I go to move off his lap, but he keeps his hand on my hips firmly, not letting me move. He adjusts his lap and moves his hips against mine. I gasp feeling his erection rubbing against the spot between my legs.

"You're the one who wanted to play with big boy toys, Reign, now you're going to learn." He places the gun in my hand.

I place the gun against his head, and he leans back against the couch and his body relaxes. He seems so chill, as if we aren't playing a suicide game. "Why are you afraid of your heart?"

Killian's hands clench around my waist and his jaw clenches. "You can ask any question you want, Reign, except for that one," he says in a low, deadly tone.

"Why-"

"Ask another one," he demands.

"Are you afraid of dying?"

"No, I've accepted it," he says now waiting for me to pull the trigger but the more we play the more chances of risking one of our lives. There are five empty slots and one bullet, but I don't know which slot Killian put the bullet in. "Pull the trigger, Reign." I don't move which makes Killian wrap his hand around mine holding the gun. I worry as Killian pulls the trigger with me, my stomach feeling like it's going to drop.

The gun clicks as our fingers press the trigger. "Killian, I don't-"

Killian drops the gun in my lap and his hands wrap around my throat to pull me closer.

His lips touch mine and he officially loses the game.

He kisses me as if he's been starving and waiting for it. His hand on my neck flexes and he nips my bottom lip causing me to moan. My hands rest on his chest and I feel his heart beat, fast and hard.

He is a beast feasting me as if he's been waiting for this since that day in the garden.

The forbidden aspect of this kiss and how I shouldn't be kissing my dad's enemy's son makes the veins in my body pulse.

I feel like I'm going to pass out with how eager Killian is kissing me, like if he stops, he might just die.

Like kissing me is the only way to keep his heart running. I try to match his intensity, but he doesn't let me. He bites, groans, tugs, and erotically forces his tongue between my lips.

"Killian-"

"We aren't done." He presses the gun against the spot between my legs and I feel goosebumps spread across my skin everywhere. "What do you think about when you're all alone in your shower, running your hands down you're body?" Killian asks against my lips. I can't answer because the fact that he has a gun rubbing against my pussy makes me dizzy and when his lips tug and kiss mine I just want to close my eyes and fall into his orbit. "I know you're a virgin, Reign, but not for long," he whispers. "I'm going to claim you and make you mine so many times to the point where you won't question who you belong to." He rubs the gun back and forth fast, pressing it hard against my clit.

"Killian, please-" I beg, feeling myself coming closer to the edge but Killian cuts me off.

"Tell me Reign. What do you think about?"

Why did I wear thin shorts here?

I can feel the hard ridges of the gun against me, playing with me.

"I used to think about a shadow. Usually, it would be my Star and his dirty words because he would sometimes flirt over text," I explain, remembering the times Star and I would playfully flirt, and he'd say dirty words to make me wet. "But lately it's been you. You in the shower with me, playing with my nipples."

Killian kisses down my neck and he licks my nipple through the thin tank top. I flush all over and moan. "These nipples?"

"Yes," I moan, rocking against the deadly weapon on his lap. "I would imagine you playing with my pussy or you thrusting inside me roughly."

"You like it rough baby? I could break you," Killian says while lightly biting on my nipples.

I arch into him and feel myself getting closer while rocking against the gun.

Oh my god, this is a fucking gun.

What is wrong with me?

"Killian-"

"I could break you." He tugs me closer, his lips now a centimeter away from mine.

"Then break me," I whisper, running my hands down his bare chest.

His abs tense under my touch. He leans back down and bites onto my nipple hard. I moan and thrust against the gun but suddenly it's gone, and he points it at the wall.

"Break for me," he says before shooting the gun.

He tugs my nipple making me scream as a shot rings through the air.

Twenty

Killian

Last night with Reign seemed too good to be real. Everything about her is perfect and God when the time comes, it's going to be hard to just simply leave her.

I want to take her with me, stick her by my side and stitch us together.

Her coming apart on top of me has definitely been added to the list of the top three things I loved watching. And I know for a fact that I want to see that all over again but this time on my dick.

After she came on top of me and flinched from the sound of the gun, she scrambled off my lap and mumbled something before leaving through the front door.

During breakfast this morning she wouldn't make eye contact with me.

Just to fuck with her a little bit I placed my hand on

her thigh, and she kept trying to take it off. It's funny seeing her squirm under my touch. I like how much I affect her.

After breakfast Malcom asked to talk to me and I have a feeling it's because of the gun shot last night.

After I shot the gun, the guards came to the guest house and asked what the shot was about, but I told them it wasn't from inside the house. I do have my gun and the gun that Reign left in the house. Both of them are hidden in a secret compartment because I have no clue if Malcom is having his men search the guest house when I'm not around.

I knock on Malcolm's door, and he says, "Come in."

I push open the door, my eyes going to Malcom who is sitting at his desk.

Right now, would literally be the perfect time to kill him.

He's all alone, no guards or anyone watching him.

It would be quick and easy.

"Are you going to sit?" Malcom raises an eyebrow at me.

I clear my throat and sit in front of him. "You wanted to talk?"

"Yes. Two things I want to talk about." Malcom says. "First, the shot that rang last night."

"Yes, you've had your men search the guest house and they didn't find anything. Can't blame me on that one."

Malcolm's jaw clenches. "I know, brat. I was thinking that maybe it was one of the neighbors. I know a house down the street, not to far, full of college boys who renovated part of their house into a shoot range." Malcom explains but I already knew that. I make sure to know where Im staying at because you never know. "I'm hiring extra security around the perimeter and inside the gates to make sure our safety isn't compromised."

Yea but what he doesn't know is that the gun shot that rang was the same gun I used to make his little princess come.

He doesn't need to know the details though.

"Understood. What else? I know you don't care that much about me to give me heads up so it must be something else."

"Yes," Malcolm brings out a folder. "It's about Reign." Anxiety ripples throughout my body but I stay calm. "She's been asking me for another mission to go on. I don't want her to go on one after the fire incident at the warehouse," Malcom explains. "I want to make sure Reign is able to complete this mission with no fuck ups. The warehouse was completely out of hand and I don't want something to happen like that again."

"Okay, why are you telling me this?" I raise an eyebrow at him.

He has no fucking clue that I'm the one who screwed

over Reign's mission to kill Anton. She was doing pretty good until she almost died on the floor.

"I want you to go to Paris with her and watch over her during this mission. Her birthday party is coming up and for her gift she wanted this mission."

And you just can't say no to your little princess.

I know her birthday is soon, like in less than two weeks.

"She wanted a mission in Paris?" I narrow my eyes at him and rub my chin.

"Killian, I don't like you-"

"Fuck, there goes my plan to be best friends," I say sarcastically.

Malcom glares at me. "Listen, brat, you and Reign have spent a lot of time together. I may not like you, but I know you've done a great job training her. She speaks highly of you which makes me trust you to go with her on this mission." He explains. "I know you'll protect her if anything goes wrong. If you're anything like your dad, I trust that you will show no mercy to those on the mission. That's why I would feel more comfortable with you there since you know your shit."

"I appreciate it, but I don't feel like babysitting."

Malcom rolls his eyes. "You aren't babysitting. You're just watching over her and helping her out with the mission. That's all."

I lick the inside of my cheek and think.

Reign and I, alone in France for a few days.

What trouble could we both cause?

I look at Malcolm and he's watching me intensely, probably trying to figure out what I'm thinking.

I know exactly what kind of trouble Reign and I could get into, but I also know I wouldn't want to watch over her during a mission. I don't like the fact that I have to worry about someone or hold responsibility over someone.

That's why I don't really want kids.

But at the same time, Paris with Reign, alone for a few days, sounds like just the kind of trouble I need.

"Fine."

TWENTY-ONE
REIGN

After the whole gun thing that happened with Killian, I've been avoiding him.

I guess now it's my turn to avoid Killian at all costs.

I have barely said any words to him since that night and now me and him are stuck in a plane together, less than twenty minutes away from France.

For my birthday I asked Papa if I can go on another mission, and he said I could as long as I bring all my guards plus Killian.

When I said no to Killian coming, Papa seemed shocked that I said no. I'm always trying to include Killian in things and Papa sees I'm getting along with him, so he was curious as to why I said no to Killian coming.

But Papa doesn't know that he made me orgasm from a gun sliding back and forth against me. He doesn't know that Killian, the guy he currently hates the most, bit and tugged on my nipples to make me orgasm.

That's all I can think of when I look at Killian. No one has ever handled me so roughly and intensely.

It makes me wonder what else he can do. The dark and curious side of me is yearning to know and learn more from him.

Right now, he is sitting on the right side of the plane, looking at something on his phone while I'm on the left side holding a book in my hand, pretending to read.

I keep looking up at him and have been stuck on the same page for about an hour. It's a smutty page from this book called Lies Of My Monster, it's a mafia romance by one of my favorite authors. Ironic how I'm reading about the mafia and actually living in one.

One of the smut scenes is happening and every time I read a few lines I immediately start thinking of Killian and everything he did to me that night.

He doesn't notice I'm staring and if he does, then he doesn't say anything.

Killian hasn't been distant or anything, he's been normal, maybe a little more flirty and talkative to me than usual but we don't hang out much anymore ever since that night which was Monday and today is Friday.

Since then, Killian has been discreetly grabbing my hand and rubbing his thumb on my fingers or palm. He sometimes trails his fingers up my arm, sending shivers down my spine, when we're at the dinner table. Let's not even get started on the thigh grabbing. Every breakfast and dinner Killian always has his hand on my thigh, despite me trying to move it because I can't risk Papa killing him for it.

But when I run up to my room, I smile because I love the forbidden aspect of this.

It's the fact that no one knows what we're doing because it's wrong.

We shouldn't be doing this, flirting, the small touches and linger of the fingers, it's wrong but it feel so right.

The fact that no one can know what we're doing behind closed doors because it's not right for either of us.

He could get killed and Papa could hate me.

It's not right but being with Killian, I can't keep the smile contained.

Every touch, every linger of his fingers makes me want more.

But I'm way too scared to actually ask for it.

He hasn't said much since Papa said he was going on the mission with me.

Killian asked me what clothes I brought, to start conversation, to which I replied a few dresses and cute skirts. He said those weren't good enough for a mission and that I need better clothes because it's not fashion week. He made me put some other clothes that are more fit for a mission before he finished packing.

During the whole flight we haven't said much.

"Ms. Pierce and Mr. De Luca, we're about to land so if you want to put on your seatbelts for landing that would be great," the attendant says before going back to the dickpit.

I listen to her and put my seatbelt on while Killian, who thinks he is a badass or something, just continues going on his phone.

The plane lands smoothly without any issues. Killian and I get off and get inside a black Escalade that was already waiting for us. The drive to the hotel is quiet.

Killian is still on his phone, barely looking at me which makes me want to grab the phone and literally throw it out the window.

"So." I clear my throat.

Killian looks at me. "So?"

"So have you ever been to Paris?"

Killian types on his phone. "Yea, a few times." He puts the phone in his pocket when he's done and then gives me his full attention. "What about you?"

"I've been a bunch. I love Paris. The food is one of my favorite things about Paris."

"Who have you gone with?"

"Just family." I wonder if he's ever came here with someone special. Usually, Paris is for couples who are in love and possibly about to get married. Paris is a place full of love. It's quiet for a few more minutes before I get over the silence and awkwardness. "So, we should probably talk about-"

"About what?" Killian furrows his eyebrows, looking genuinely confused about what we should be talking about.

"About the whole gun, Russian Roulette thing." He stays silent, still looking genuinely confused as if it never happened. "Where you made me do that thing on the gun."

Killian licks his bottom lip slowly and nods his head. "And? What about it?"

So, he does remember.

"I feel like we should probably set boundaries maybe? I mean it got out of hand-"

"Reign." Killian cuts me off and I feel myself blush and narrow my eyes on him. "What happened that night, will keep happening. You wanna know why?" Killian says quietly, leaning closer to me.

"Why?" I say in a low tone, still staring up at him.

"Because from the moment you looked up at the stars with those big blue eyes of yours, I knew I was going to make you mine one way or another Reign." Killian reaches his hand towards my lips and his thumb grazes my bottom lip. "What happened Monday night will keep happening because I want you. And I always get what I want, Reign." His touch feels like fire on my lip, but I don't lean away from him.

I like the feel of his touch.

Killian is aggressive and dark, and it makes me want to know more.

It makes me want more.

"Ms. Pierce and Mr. De Luca, we're here," the driver says, ruining the small moment between Killian and I.

Killian leans away and his touch disappears. He gets out of the car and a valet opens my door.

Killian and I walk inside, side by side, towards the front desk. The woman behind the desk smiles widely before saying, "Hi, welcome to Ritz Paris, are you guys checking in today?" the woman says with a strong accent.

"We made a reservation. It's under Malcom Pierce," Killian says.

The woman types a few keys on her computer before looking up at us. "You guys booked the Windsor Suite?" Killian nods his head. "Perfect. Here is your key card to the private elevator." She slides a card to Killian. "James will escort you to the room."

Wait there's only one room?

TWENTY-TWO
KILLIAN

"YOU NEED TO STOP FUCKING AROUND AND GET this job done," my dad demands angrily over the phone.

It's been more than three weeks since I arrived in Bulgaria.

In those three or so weeks, I haven't even attempted to kill Malcom.

Not when he was alone in the gym or in the office.

Not when he asked me to help out his daughter with this ridiculous mission.

And guess what?

I don't give a shit.

Especially when my dad is yelling at me from the other end of the phone.

I stepped out of the room so that Reign couldn't hear my conversation with my dad.

Right now, she's unpacking her stuff in the room while I'm on the balcony.

Malcom told me to take care of the rooms and then threw me his AMEX.

I took care of it alright.

$14,000 a night in a suite room with a view of the Eiffel Tower almost as beautiful as Reign. If I'm going on a trip with my enemy's daughter, I'm damn sure going to make it a good vacation.

Of course, he doesn't know that those charges are for a suite room instead of a luxurious double.

momfucker keeps calling me brat.

"I am. I'm not in Bulgaria right now."

"What?"

"I said, I'm not in Bulgaria, right now," I deadpan.

"Why not? Where are you?"

I look at the Eiffel Tower. "Paris. It's a beautiful day out here. Not many tourists either."

"What are the fuck are you doing in Paris? You should be in Bulgaria killing that asshole," my dad screams through the phone making me roll my eyes.

He's always had serious anger issues. That's where Thalia gets her anger issues from but her husband, Alexander, knows how to handle her. He always has, which makes me know for a fact that he is the perfect match for her.

"I'm gaining their trust. Calm down," I say calmly

even though I feel my heart fucking clench. "They want me to make sure the girl is safe on her trip."

"Malcom's such a fucking pussy when it comes to that daughter." Pretty sure my dad is rolling his eyes. "Killian, you need to stop fucking around. This needs to get done. You only have so much time-"

"I know," I cut him off harshly, more than I wanted to. That control and calmness slipping slowly. "You don't have to remind me, I'm not stupid."

"Then why isn't it done?"

"I don't question you, I expect you to do the same."

"Last time I checked, I'm the one in charge. So, when I say jump, you ask how high. When I want an answer, I get it. So, stop acting like a child and get the job done." The sound of a door opening makes me turn my head. I see Reign walking out of the bedroom wearing a skirt and a white halter top. "Killian-"

I hang up and shove the phone in my back pocket.

Her long legs make me feel hypnotized and the halter top she's wearing shows off her smooth shoulders and makes me want to rip the thing off so I can see what's underneath.

"Why are you wearing that?"

"We're in Paris. I was going to walk around the street and look at the shops."

I furrow my eyebrows at her. "We're here for a

mission, not to shop. Get dressed into something more comfortable to train in."

Her eyes sparkle and a small smile lifts on her face. "We're training again?"

"Why wouldn't we?"

"Well, you stopped the training."

"And you stopped showing up," I backfire.

She crosses her arms over her chest making her breasts look fuller. "You never mentioned it to me. How am I supposed to know what you're thinking when you never tell me?"

My lips lift in my smirk, and I shake my head lightly.

The way she gets so angry over not knowing anything about me is funny. She knows everything about her Star, but she has no clue that she is looking right at him.

When I first started texting Reign, I knew that she was an innocent timid thing, but I also knew she had a little bit of darkness because why the hell would anyone confess their secrets and darkest thoughts to someone they don't even know?

Don't worry Reign, I'm going to tap into the darkness for you.

Twenty-Three

The mission that papa told Killian and I about seems pretty simple.

We have to go into one of the French's warehouses to steal one of the drugs that they wouldn't sell papa.

Papa wants to duplicate the drug and sell it for a cheaper price than the French are selling it for.

He told me the story to give me some context. He said when he tried to buy this drug from them, they charged a lot so now he needs to go through different measures to get this drug and sell it.

Papa said this mission should be easy and quick, but in case anything happens I have Killian.

He's making me wait outside while he scans the area to make sure we're all clear.

We trained last night even though I was way too tired to do that.

Last night was weird. Killian left right after and then I woke up to him waiting for me in the living room. He didn't sleep in the same bed or possibly the same room as me last night.

He says all these things about being his, yet he couldn't bear the thought of sleeping next to me.

I don't even know why we got this suite since there are two people and clearly two people will sleep in two separate beds.

Killian walks out from the corner of the building. He's wearing a black long sleeve compression shirt under the bullet proof vest. The vest is filled with all kinds of different knives and bullets for his gun. He's wearing black trousers and black shoes.

He looks like a fallen god, especially with the small strand of his hair falling from his face. I can't help but want to push the strand back like he does with me sometimes when a strand of my hair falls.

I hate how he looks so effortlessly good while I look like I've been put through the ringer.

I'm wearing a long sleeve dark gray shirt with black skinny jeans and a huge vest, a vest bigger than Killian's that's for sure. When we were in the car, I asked if the big vest was necessary and he said, "For me no but for you yes.

Your safety is top priority, so I don't want to risk anything."

I tried not to feel butterflies in my stomach as I looked out the window and felt his eyes on me.

I ignored the way my heart sped up and forced away the smile I wanted to show him.

He's the enemy technically, but God he doesn't feel like one.

"Are we ready to go?" I ask, walking towards Killian as he fixes his earpiece.

"Almost." When I'm close enough he grabs me by the neck, butterflies bursting in my stomach and fire spreading across my skin. I stare up at him while he plays with the earpiece and clicks a few buttons on the side. "Can you hear me?" I nod my head, still staring up at him. He lets me go but doesn't take a step back. "Okay, I need you to listen to every single fucking word I say, you understand?" I nod my head. "No, Reign. I need your words. I need you to tell me. Because if you fucking die in there..."

He trails off, licking his lips and shaking his head lightly like he's actually afraid.

"I'll be okay. We'll be okay." I give him a reassuring smile.

He doesn't smile back but that's okay.

Killian leads the way towards the entrance of the warehouse. I follow behind him quietly as we go inside. It's pretty empty in here, surprisingly. Probably because all of them are having lunch or something since it's the middle of the day.

"Do you-"

"Shh." Killian cuts me off.

I follow him through the warehouse. He keeps his gun aimed at eye level and turns in all kinds of directions while I'm following him, my stance the same as his.

A figure catches my attention to the left, I turn swiftly and see a man walking towards one of the crates.

I don't think, I just shoot.

Killian turns his head and then looks at the man's slumped body on the floor. His jaw clenches when he looks back at me before continuing his walk.

We silently shoot anyone we see, him more so than me since he sees them before me. Killian covers for me as I look for the crate and read the box numbers.

"I found it," I say softly, making Killian turn his head to look at me.

I take the small powder filled baggy and hold it to his face. He looks at the bag then back at me.

"Guess you're not horrible with missions like I thought."

I smile at him, and I swear I see a little sparkle in his eyes and a twitch of his lips.

But the moment ends as quickly as it started when a shot rings through the air. Killian grabs me by the waist and hides us behind a crate.

They scream something in French and Killian curses.

I look at him and see him loading his gun. "What do we do?"

"Follow behind me. Don't move or compromise your position behind me or you will get shot. You understand?" I take a deep breath and nod my head, trying to calm my breathing down. "Fucking Reign, I need you to tell me you understand." Killian grabs me by the chin to make me look at him. "Just calm down and follow my lead. You got this."

"Okay."

"Okay." Killian stands up. "Stay close."

Killian gets out of the hiding spot and shots start firing at us. I aim my gun and shoot over Killian's shoulder while Killian covers me. He shoots whoever he sees in sight with no mercy.

It's like he's wearing a mask. His concentration is locked on getting us out of here, wound free. He's making sure to cover every inch of space, looking everywhere to find any possible targets. He'll protect me. He won't let me die.

He wouldn't.

His dad may hate my dad, but he won't let me die.

A guy runs up to us and before Killian can do anything, I push him out of the way and stab the guy with my knife.

"Reign!" Killian yells but I can't pay attention to him.

Too much happens at once. The bag of the white powder falls from my hand. "Reign, take fucking cover now!" Killian yells as he shoots people, covering for me. "Reign, get the fuck out of here, that's an order." I shoot my gun while keeping my eyes on the drug. "Fucking Reign!" Killian says at the same time I get the drug bag. He grabs my wrist and covers me with his body while he shoots in all kinds of directions. "Get the fuck out of here. I'll cover for you, just run through the front."

"But-"

"Don't fuck with me right now, Reign, just do it," Killian says.

And I run.

I aim my gun high, covering my face and shooting anyone who's a threat, which is basically everyone.

When I finally get outside, I don't stop running until I'm near a car that's parked in the woods nearby.

The doors unlock and I get in and look out the window while calming down my breathing.

"Miss are you alright?" the driver asks but I can't answer him.

Not as I see the warehouse go up in flames and Killian walking out like he's Satan arising from Hell.

Twenty-Four

Reign

It's been quiet since Killian got inside the car and said, "Drive."

He didn't say a word or even looked at me. His face is covered in ashes and I see some bullet holes in his vest. His shirt is dirty and his hair is a mess.

I can't help but want to fix him and make him look like the Killian that I'm used to, the one with the playful smirk and smile.

But his finger anxiously taps his thigh as he keeps his eyes on the window.

When the warehouse blew up in flames, I knew Killian somehow was the cause of it.

Seeing the warehouse in flames gave me Deja Vu from the time our warehouse in Bulgaria blew up in flames.

But Killian isn't the type of person to do that. Not intentionally.

"Kill-"

"I don't want to fucking hear it, Reign." Killian says roughly, still not looking away from the window.

I know I fucked up.

I know I should have listened and just did as he said but then what was the point of going through all this if we didn't have the bag?

This trip to France would have been pointless and papa would have been disappointed.

The rest of the drive to the hotel is spent in silence as we both look out the windows. I took off my vest because it was getting stuffy in the car but Killian still has his on, looking super roughed up.

When we get to the hotel, the driver parks the car. Killian gets out while the driver comes around to open the door for me.

I keep my eyes on Killian as I follow him slowly to the elevator. People in the lobby are looking at us like we're insane but obviously Killian doesn't care.

All eyes are on Killian and he doesn't even care or shows that it affects him. Watching him walk past a crowd of people who are staring at him while he has a straight face and a powerful walk makes me intimidated.

I was always a little intimidated by Killian just because

he has a lot of power, not because of his status or last name but because of the way he carries himself.

We get in the elevator and stand side by side.

After a few seconds of silence, I feel chills and goose-bumps crawling up my chest because of the fact that I have to say something to him.

"So we-"

"I thought I said I didn't want to fucking hear it?" Killian looks down at me. His jaw clenched and his eyebrows furrowed down making him look so royally pissed off. "Obviously you have some serious listening issues or else you would have heard me and followed directions during that mission, but you didn't."

I stay quiet for the rest of the elevator ride because I don't want to make Killian even more pissed off then I already have.

I almost feel like a child getting scolded even though Killian and I are close to the same age.

The elevator bell rings and we get out and enter the hotel room.

Killian starts taking off his gear while walking towards the room.

I keep my eyes on him, waiting for his move. I know he probably wants to yell and lecture me like a child.

But I also know that he is out of sorts and unpredictable right now.

He probably wants to take a shower and not talk until he's ready.

That's fine.

We can talk things out when he's done.

Everything will be fine.

Killian soon opens the bedroom door and walks out in brand new clothes and hair a little damp. He's wearing a white dress shirt with the first few buttons unbuttoned and then black trousers.

"Where are you going?" I asked, standing up from the couch.

"I need a fucking drink and probably a smoke after that shit show today." Killian says while fixing his cuffs.

"Killian, I'm sorry-"

"Reign, when I tell you to do something, you fucking do it. You don't make excuses or get the fucking bag off the floor, you do as I ask." Killian says while slowly walking closer to me until both of our toes are touching one another.

"I didn't think-"

"That's right. You didn't fucking think because if you did then you would have known that you could have died! You think I want to see your body lifeless on the floor?" Killian yells, getting slowly in my face but I don't move away from him. He's right. I shouldn't have compromised myself and I should have listened to him. "You could have fucked died, Reign. Then what? What would I say to your dad? Your mom? Kyra?"

"I just knew we needed the bag Killian. Coming to France would have been pointless if I didn't pick it up." I try to reason but Killian doesn't care.

His jaw is still clenched tightly and his face is getting closer to mine as he gets more frustrated.

"That doesn't matter, if you're fucking dead. Don't you get what I'm trying to tell you?"

"I'm sorry. I didn't mean for you to get mad or to cause an issue. I just wanted to help."

"Next time, do as I say. Understood?"

I roll my eyes and Killian's jaw hardens and the look he gives me turns into something more furious but also dark.

"You aren't the boss of me. You didn't have to come on this mission and-"

Killian grabs me by the throat and pulls me towards him.

My heart starts racing and I swear the spot between my legs pulses as I remember that night with his gun.

"Say that again." He demands.

I open my mouth, but before I can get a word out I feel Killian's rough and demanding lips on mine.

I gasp into the kiss and just melt in his arms as he holds me against him while kissing me roughly. I press my hands on his chest and he laps lips with mine before thrusting his tongue in roughly.

Everything about him is so demanding and rough. He just takes and takes without any remorse, only thinking about himself.

Killian's other hand trails onto my waist and pushes my body closer to his.

His body heat against me, making me feel all hot. I want to be closer to him.

Inside him.

I want to be able to be so inside him to the point where I can hold his heart in my hands.

It's like his kisses awaken my soul and when he pulls away I feel so deprived and empty.

Who knew I would crave someone like Killian.

"Don't ever doubt me and who's in charge between the two of us. I'll fucking ruin you Reign and you won't even be able to do a thing about it."

Killian then turns around without another word and leaves with the elevator.

Twenty-Five

Killian

It's close to 2:00am when I enter the suite. The lights are all shut off, but the curtains are open making the room have some natural lighting from the moon.

I definitely feel more relaxed than I did when I left the room. My body feels relaxed from the two glasses of the bar's most expensive scotch.

My dad called me, but I didn't answer. I think my mom sensed something was wrong because she texted me.

> Hi baby. I know your dad tried calling but you didn't answer. I want to make sure you're okay and taking care of yourself. I love you. You better call your Mama soon. I miss you.

I just hearted the message because I didn't feel like responding but she had to know how I was doing.

I walk through the suite and go towards where the bedroom is. I open the door slowly and look towards the bed.

I don't see Reign's face, but the blankets are covering her figure as her chest rises and falls. I can hear her small snores.

Ever since we landed in France, I haven't slept in the bed with her.

It's a temptation to say the least. Being near Reign when we're in public and I can't even touch her is enough for me to want to grab her and take her to the nearest corner to devour her.

Or whenever we are at the table back in Bulgaria and she gives me those innocent glances or blushes, it makes me want to throw her on the table, wrap her legs around my fucking head and make her see stars.

Obviously not in front of her family though.

Fuck it, tonight I'm over me pulling away.

In the warehouse today, I honestly thought I was going to lose her. I was fucking terrified, and I swear I felt my heart, my useless fucking heart, beat so rapidly and hard against my chest I thought I was going to die before saving her.

I've never cared enough about dying or if anyone else died for that matter, but that changed today.

I was prepared for my mom's death and someday mine as well.

But for some reason, seeing Reign cover while people started taking shots at her, I felt my heart almost catch on fire and burn.

So yes, I did lecture the living fuck out of her and yes, I would 100% do it again to make sure that shit doesn't happen in the future.

I had to leave the room before I took her neck in my hands and strangled the living fuck out of her for not listening to me.

I walk inside the room and towards the bed. I sit down next to her legs and move the covers down so I can see her face.

Her soft, pink lips are parted, and her long eyelashes caress her under eyes while she sleeps calmly.

She has one hand under her head and the other resting on her chest. I reach over and move a strand of her hair away from her face, softly caressing her soft cheek with my thumb.

My eyes go down to her chest and I move her hand and lay it on the bed. I reach towards where her heart is and lay my palm on her chest, feeling her steady and calm heart beating against her chest.

I close my eyes and just feel her heart.

For some reason, feeling her heart makes me feel calm, like the world is suddenly silent and that I have nothing to worry about. It feels like it's just us two in the world.

Just two steady beating hearts with nothing to worry about.

"Killian?" Reign's voice makes me open my eyes. I look down at her as she reaches up and holds my jaw in her soft, fragile hands. I lean into her touch and move my hand away from where her heart is. "What are you doing?" she whispers.

I lick the inside of my cheek. "Today you fucking scared me, Reign. I've never been scared of anything in my life before but today I was so fucking scared," I admit.

"Killian, I'm fine-"

I shake my head. "No, you don't get it. My heart was fucking pounding, Reign. I was afraid of losing you."

Reign sits up and scoots closer to me. She rests her other hand on my jaw. "Why? You're Killian De Luca. You're not afraid of anything. Half the time I think you want me to die," Reign tries to joke but she's got it all wrong.

Yes, I've known that my obsession with her since that night under the stars meant something, but I never thought I could be afraid of losing someone or dying before someone else in my life.

At least not until I truly got to know Reign in person, instead of over a stupid phone where she thinks she is talking to her Star.

Tonight, she messaged him. Saying she fucked up and didn't know how to fix it.

I didn't respond because I didn't know what to say.

I probably would have said to not be fucking stupid.

"Everyone is afraid of something. You just have to find it," I admit.

Reign looks down at my lips swiftly before meeting my eyes. I want to pull her closer and kiss her again.

Probably even do more than kiss her.

It's been more than three weeks and this girl can have me on my knees without asking.

"Why me? You kiss me, flirt with me, protect me? Am I just someone who you are passing time with?"

I furrow my eyebrows at her and move her hands off my face to hold them in my hands. "I don't know why. I'm not really used to feeling like this with someone. I love and care about my mom, but it's never felt like this."

"What does it feel like?" Reign whispers and I feel myself getting deadly close to her.

It feels like my heart is going to catch fire any second now.

It would be fucking ironic.

Instead of answering her I grab her jaw and pull her towards me. I groan, taking her mouth. A strong, hot current that always feels like fire sparking between us sweeps through my body. I immediately deepen the kiss, needing more.

Reign leans back against the bed, and I follow with her, kicking off my shoes and getting on top of her, my leg between hers, pressing against her hot pussy. She's wearing the same fucking thin ass shorts she did when she was coming all over the gun in the guest house.

My tongue dips into her mouth and she caresses her tongue against mine as she moans.

I place one of my hands on the bed while the other trails to her stomach, dipping below the waistband of her shorts, pausing slowly to see if she pulls away from me but like a good girl she doesn't.

My dick hardens behind my trousers and I just need more room.

I can feel how soft her skin is against my body. My heart starts racing and I'm trying so hard to control myself with this girl.

"You're so fucking beautiful." I bite her lip making her arch her back. My hand dips below her panty line and Reign still doesn't do anything to stop me. "Tempting," I whisper, my fingers inching closer and closer to her hot, wet pussy. "And you don't even know it. The fact that you're all innocent about it makes me want to ruin and fuck you all up. No one will be able to have you other than me."

When I press my finger against her clit, Reign moans against my lips. I trail my kisses down her neck, wanting to hear her moans instead of muffling them.

I play with her clit and slowly tease her tight and drenched hole with my middle finger.

When my lips finds Reign's nipples she whimpers and pushes her chest towards my head. She arches her body, almost taking my hole middle finger inside her. She hisses but she doesn't look like she's in pain.

"Killian, please," she begs, sweat forming on her forehead already.

I nip on her nipple and sink my middle finger inside her slowly. She swallows it up and moans, gasping at the fullness.

"You're so tight, baby. No one's touched this cunt, yea?" I rub her clit in circles while using my middle finger to thrust in and out of her. Reign shakes her head as I bite her nipple hard before licking it. "Say it. No one touched this cunt."

"No, you're the only one," she moans, gripping the sheets in her hand before holding onto my shoulder. She squeezes her thighs together and thrusts against my fingers.

"You get so soaked for me, I can slip right in. I could make you see fucking stars."

"Killian, I'm close, please," Reign begs, her nails digging into my shoulders.

"I know, baby," I say, feeling her walls clench onto my finger. I thrust my finger in and out of her faster. "Right there, come for me. Come on baby. Let me know what this pussy feels like when your come for me."

Reign moans loudly, dragging her nails down my back as I bite and suck her nipple while she comes on my fingers.

I play with her clit until she's all spent, and my fingers are drenched. Reign's eyes fall and her breathing slowly evens out. She takes deep breaths to calm down, her chest rises and falls with both her nipples poking through the wet patches from me sucking on them.

I take my fingers out and kiss her forehead.

"Where are you going?" Reign asks as she feels me get up.

"Don't worry, I'll be back." I say before going to the bathroom and grabbing a towel.

I wet it with warm water before returning back to the room. I take Reign's shorts and underwear off before resting the towel against her pussy. She moans and squeezes her thighs against my hand between her legs.

I clean her up before throwing the towel on the floor.

I get up and start taking my shirt off.

"You're not leaving, are you?" Reign asks, her eyes open and now looking at me.

I don't answer her as I get in bed beside her. "Go back to sleep." I wrap my arm around her waist and pull her closer to me before closing my eyes.

I rest my hand against her heart, falling asleep with her steady heart while comparing it to my broken one.

Twenty-Six

Waking up this morning felt different.

Sleeping with Reign, made me feel calm like I would live another day without any worry.

I slept my hand hand on her chest where her heart is located. Hearing the steady beats of her heart made it so easy to sleep.

I woke up this morning with a small hard on, especially since Reign kept scooting closer to me and rubbing up against me.

I whispered in her ear that if she kept doing that shit then I might as well just take my briefs off and thrust inside her.

She stopped immediately and tried to move away from me, but I didn't let her.

This morning felt like the calm before the storm. I kissed her and then went to take a shower.

This whole day we spent it eating food and watching movies inside the hotel.

It was a relaxing day. I wish I had more days like that, with her especially.

Now I'm waiting downstairs for her, outside the car because I'm taking her to see the stars.

She doesn't know that though.

When Reign finally walks out of the hotel, with a bright smile on her face, she's wearing a white dress that stops at her mid-thighs.

The dress is too high for my liking, but I don't say anything because she looks beautiful, nonetheless.

"Where are we going?" she asks and I grab her waist in my hands and smirk down at her, admiring the way her skin glows with the white dress.

"You'll see," I say before opening the car door for her. She gives me a teasing smile and gets in. I follow after her and close the door.

The car drives off and my eyes go back to Reign.

She blushes while I admire her. "What?" she asks.

I shake my head and lick my bottom lip. "Nothing."

"Then why are you looking at me like that?"

I raise an eyebrow at her. "You really want to know?" Reign shrugs. I smirk and lean down so my lips are next to her ear. My hand slips onto her thigh and goes underneath her dress. "All I'm thinking about right now is taking you back to the hotel and ripping that dress off and then making you beg and scream for me to make you see stars."

I lean away and look down at her which is turning red. I refrain from laughing at her and instead look our the window while placing my hand on her thigh.

"That's inappropriate."

I look down at her and ask confused. "How so?"

"You can't say things like that," she says, scolding me but I know she loved it. The way she clenched her thighs together says otherwise.

"Why?" I tilt my head slightly.

"Because it's crude."

I smirk and chuckle lightly. "Reign, that was nothing. I bet you a million bucks I could make you come with my words alone."

Reign's eyes heat up.

As her Star, she always tells me how she'd like to experience rough and degrading sex. She likes being praised of course because she's a good girl at heart, but her curiosity gets the best of her sometimes.

"I don't think so. Words can't be that powerful."

"Don't challenge me, Reign, I'll prove you wrong right here, right now, in front of the driver." I give her thigh a tight squeeze again.

Reign looks at the driver before turning to look at the window, staying silent for the rest of the ride.

I chuckle lightly and just admire her for the rest of the ride.

Who knew I would have made Reign speechless.

When Reign finally looks at me, it's when the driver parks the car in front of the dock.

I thought that because it's going to be our last night in France, I would take Reign out, especially since the mission yesterday took a lot out of her and was stressful.

We both need a night out, so a dinner on the Seine River underneath the stars sounded perfect.

"What are we doing here?" Reign asks, I open the door and offer my hand to her.

"Follow me and you'll see."

Reign grabs my hand, and we get out of the car. "I'll be here waiting, Mr. De Luca," the driver says, and I nod my head at him before walking towards the small yacht that's parked in front of the dock.

Reign says nothing, completely and utterly in awe as she looks at the boat. I help her onto the boat since she's wearing heels. Even though they aren't tall or anything, I still wanted to have a way to put my hands on her, just to feel her.

"Welcome Mr. De Luca and Ms. Pierce. I'm Alan and will be your captain tonight. Dinner will be served in a bit but until then you can have a look around and take a seat on the deck," Alan says in a strong French accent so you can barely understand him.

Reign smiles before looking up at me. "Why'd you do this?"

Alan leaves and I hold Reign's hand in mine while walking towards the deck of the yacht.

I lift my shoulders.

I don't fucking know why.

Maybe because I felt bad for yelling at her and this seemed like the perfect way to mellow down and just relax with one another.

Just a night under the stars.

"Because I wanted to," I answer.

It's not the one she wants but it keeps her from asking even more questions that I don't know the answer to.

Once we get on the deck, Reign's smile widens as she looks at what the crew set up. There is a blue blanket laid out with a bunch of white and blue pillows. The setup they did is amazing and exactly what I asked for. A small table is in the middle for dinner but that won't be until later.

"Killian, this is so beautiful." Reign smiles up at me before walking towards the blanket. I refrain from smiling down at her because her fucking smile, I swear it does something to that thing inside my chest. We sit on the blanket next to one another and the sun finally sets making the sky dark so you can see the stars. All perfect timing. A waiter comes to give us two glasses of wine plus the bottle. Reign can't stop smiling and I can't stop staring at her in awe, almost wanting to smile myself. "Tell me why you really did this."

I look at Reign and see her eyes almost begging me.

All big and innocent.

I want to confiscate that innocence and just put it in a jar so I can keep it forever, only for me to see and have to myself.

"Like I said, because I wanted to. It's a perfect way to end a trip to France, yes?" I raise an eyebrow at her.

She blushes and looks up at the stars. "You know what would make this night even better?"

"What?" I ask, I can't stop the small smile on my face because I have a feeling, I already know what she wants.

Another secret.

Another truth.

Another thing about me that makes her closer and closer to getting to know me.

"I want to know one thing that no one knows about you." Reign looks at me.

I lick the inside of my cheek and lean closer to her so my face and hers are centimeters apart. "No one knows how much I want to stay alive in this world because of you."

Reign tilts her head slightly without realizing it. "What do you mean? How can I make you want to stay alive? You barely even know me."

"I know a lot about you," I say confidently. "I know

you love the color white. Your favorite flower is any white flower because you like white. I know you like lions. You love talking to the stars because no one listens to you rant at home. You like helping people and that's mainly why you're doing all this mission stuff to help your dad. You want to become a nurse after all this because you like helping people. Pretty sure your life goal is to make an impact on someone's life. Your favorite song is any song by Cigarettes After Sex. You love helping your grandma with tasks so she can rest. You mostly talk to the stars because your grandpa is up there listening to you, and you were always closer with him. And that's not even all of it Reign. I know a lot more too." I lean even closer, until my lips are grazing hers. "I know about your deepest and darkest fantasies that you want to indulge in but are too scared because you have this whole innocent good girl facade up, but I know, Reign. I know everything."

Reign looks shocked with everything I said. She backs away a little, but I follow. "How do you know all that?"

"I have my ways," I say before kissing her.

It's become my new favorite thing to do.

I never realized that I have favorite things to do until now. Before Reign, I thought life was meaningless and I couldn't care about the outcome of things.

But then Reign happened and suddenly everything matters.

I kiss Reign like I own her, because I do.

My hand holds her throat as I control the kiss. My tongue slips inside as I play with her tongue. She keeps one hand on my chest, grasping my dress shirt, pulling me closer subconsciously.

"Fuck, what am I going to do with you, Reign?" I ask, not breaking the kiss. "Don't make me fall in love with you."

The night is filled with endless talking from Reign, me interrupting her by kissing her and making her blush.

I think spending nights like this with Reign is also a new favorite pastime of mine.

TWENTY-SEVEN
REIGN

I ADMIRE THE LONG WHITE DRESS THAT STOPS AT my ankles. There is a small bow on the heart-line of the dress that just makes the dress even more beautiful. Small details matter when it comes to dresses.

Mama's necklace is around my neck. It's a silver chain with a small star pendant that has a blue diamond in the middle. Dyado gave it to her and after he died, she wanted me to have it, so I feel like I'm closer to him.

It's been a day since we landed back in Bulgaria and preparations for my birthday party started before, we arrived. Events like birthday parties are a big thing but after France with Killian and dinner under the stars with him, I felt like that was enough and we didn't need to do anything else.

Dinner under the stars with Killian was perfect and I don't need anything more.

We had a nice steak dinner and crepes for dessert. After laying together, looking up at the stars, and kissing because Killian couldn't keep his hands off me, we left the yacht and went back to the hotel.

We didn't have sex or anything which I'm thankful for because I don't want to rush things with Killian but at the same time, I'm always expecting something to happen, maybe because I do want something to happen.

I can'r seem to make my mind up with him.

He hasn't kissed me much since being back in Bulgaria just because now we are under close surveillance with Papa and his guards watching Killian's every move. But during dinner last night he would give me sneaky looks and trail his fingers along my thigh to make me blush and squirm.

Killian knows the effect he has on me, and that fact is so dangerous because he could make me kneel to him if he wanted to.

My mom just left the room after doing my makeup and helping me get ready. My hair is in loose curls and the makeup is light.

Looking in the mirror I can't help but smile at myself, happy with how I look and how beautiful I feel.

The smile on my face feels different too. Sure, I've always smiled because I never had anything to be sad about but for some reason this smile doesn't feel forced, it feels natural.

It doesn't make sense to me.

A knock on my door makes me look away from the mirror. "Come in." The door opens and Killian walks in. He's wearing a white dress shirt, black trousers, and white Loro Piana shoes.

Killian's hair isn't styled, it never usually is because he's always running his hands through the strands. Killian's messy hair fits him well because although he is all about control, his hair is the only thing that isn't in place or perfect like the rest of him.

Other than the tattoos, but I'm pretty sure those are because he wants people to be scared of him because somehow tattoos make men more intimidating.

I meet Killian's eyes and he's looking at me with a heated stare, not saying anything. He looks so dangerous and cruel with his dark hair and aura; it matches him perfectly.

"You look nice," he compliments, which makes me blush a little.

"Thank you, so do you." Killian closes the door. He doesn't say anything as he walks closer to me. My room isn't that spectacular, and I think this is the first time Killian has been in my room. I just have a bookshelf next to my white desk. There is a huge vase filled with white tulips on my desk and then you have my bed in the center of the room with white and blue bedding. "Is it busy outside?" I ask, trying to calm down my racing heart.

"There are a good amount of people." I let out a breath I didn't know I was holding and look at myself in the mirror. Killian comes behind me and he looks down at me with those eyes again, those damn eyes. "You shouldn't worry though because you look beautiful."

I turn around to face Killian. His size compared to mine should make me feel unsafe but if anything, it makes me feel safer than I have with any other guy.

Killian isn't a small guy; he has a good amount of muscle on him plus his height.

"Thank you, I'm glad you approve," I joke.

"I would approve even if you were dressed in sweatpants and a baggy t-shirt." Killian narrows his eyes to my lips before meeting my eyes again. "White looks good on you."

"Black looks good on you," I say, keeping the intense eye contact. It's like Killian is undressing me with his eyes and it sends chills down my spine and makes my nipples pucker a little bit. Killian takes a step closer. "What are you doing?"

Killian doesn't answer, instead he grabs my waist to pull me closer and he covers my lips with his.

My hands go to his chest, not to push him away but to hold on to him to keep me from falling.

I can feel my heartbeat in my ears if that's even possible.

The kiss starts off as one simple kiss and then it turns into two.

Then three.

Four.

Five.

The world around us disappears and it's only Killian and I.

Killian and Reign.

I like it.

I want to keep all the kisses Killian has given me in a jar just in case he ever decides to leave, I'll still have his kisses.

Killian's tongue runs over my lips, and I moan. His other hand trails to the side of my neck and he tangles his fingers through my hair, pushing my face closer to his.

Our hips rub against each other making Killian groan.

Yes.

He backs me into the bed, and I end up falling with Killian on top of me. His lips move down from my mouth, and they start making their way to my neck.

He kisses, licks, sucks, and bites.

I'm pretty positive I might get a hickey from how he's sucking on my sweet spot. I clench my thighs together and moan softly.

"Fuck Reign, you're making this so much harder for me," he moans, moving back to my lips.

"Harder how?" I say in between kisses. "You're the one who's going to make me look like a mess in front of my family."

"I approve of you looking like a mess, especially since I'm the one who causes it."

Oh god.

Twenty-Eight

Killian

Fuck.

It was too tempting to not kiss her.

And then what happened after that, well that was because I couldn't control my urges and how bad I wanted to see her come undone by a simple flick of my finger on her clit.

She's too perfect to not obsess over or praise.

She deserves to be put on a pedestal and fawned over.

I mean seeing her in that dress with her dark hair and those goddamn innocent eyes made me want to ruin her and fuck her all up so that no one could have her other than me.

And I'm going to.

Do I care?

Apparently not.

I don't care about the problems that getting involved with her will bring me.

Maybe I just need to fuck her out of my system, is what my mind is thinking. This crush, this obsession that I've had since I was kid has been building and maybe I just need to act on it.

No, I need to kill Malcom.

Kill Malcom.

Kill Malcom.

Kill fucking Malcom.

Such an easy job that I should have done weeks ago like my dad said but no, Reign is his daughter and of course she has to make things difficult for me.

So untouchable and so forbidden it makes me want her more.

You want what you can't have.

After kissing her and making her come on my fingers, she fixed herself up while I watched her and smirked because seeing her all messed the fuck up just by my fingers is amusing to me.

It made me start thinking how she'll look after getting destroyed by my dick. The dark and depraved thoughts make my dick ache, but I continue sipping on the brandy they're serving.

There are a lot of people downstairs for Reign's birth-day, most of the family and some friends that are close to the family. I recognize some of the men here just because of the countless galas I've attended.

That fucker Jamie is here, walking around in a dark navy suit, talking to different people with a golden smile on his face.

And then Kyra, who keeps eyeing me ever since I got downstairs.

She doesn't know shit.

Everyone stops talking and I look at the top of the stairs where everyone else is looking.

Reign looks like she did before, except she's probably glowing from the sweat and her cheeks are still a little red.

But hair and makeup are in place, and you wouldn't know what happened to her unless you were in the room.

Reign walks down with a small smile. Her eyes go to me, and I smirk which makes the blush on her face return.

I almost want to take a picture and put it as my lock screen.

The party is being held in one of the many rooms that Malcolm has. You could consider it a ballroom but it's not as big as ones you see in the movies.

I watch as Jamie wraps his arms around Reign, making sure it stays friendly.

They talk for a little before Reign gets pulled into another conversation with someone else. I keep my eyes on her as she makes her rounds. My eyes also catch Kyra as she watches me watch her granddaughter but like I mentioned, I don't give a fuck.

Kyra won't do shit.

My eyes go to Malcolm as he watches his daughter with a smile on his face. Lia is holding his arm while also smiling, both of them proud of their daughter.

Malcom asked me how the mission went, and I told him the truth. She's doing great but she needs more work. She's too oblivious but she has determination. She just needs more training is all.

I could have killed Malcom then and there or even now to make it all dramatic, but I'm prolonging it.

I'm prolonging it because of the time I want to spend with Reign.

I needed to find a way to make sure I can have Reign no matter what in the end.

You won't.

Maybe I should tell Reign everything.

I need to tell her about her Star, me killing her dad, the accidental fire at the warehouse, how this story will end.

But I also have my dad to worry about. That momfucker won't stop blowing up my phone like a whiny little bitch.

When Reign walks up to me, my mind goes blank, and I feel the beating of my heart slow down after the constant overthinking. "Does Killian De Luca want to give me the first dance of the night?" she asks with a teasing smirk on her face. I grab her hand and let her pull me towards the middle of the room. "All The Stars" by Kendrick Lamar and SZA plays softly through the speakers. Reign puts her arms around my shoulders, and I place my hands on her waist. "You weren't kidding about the number of people here."

Another thing I like about Reign is that she isn't afraid of getting what she wants when the public looks at her. She is confident in front of everyone with everything she does and asks.

But when it's with people she's close to, she shows her true self and I love how she's able to do that with me.

It makes me know that she is safe enough to be vulnerable with me.

"They're here for a reason."

"It's just a birthday." Reign rolls her eyes playfully. "Can I ask you another question?"

"Why?" I furrow my eyebrows at her.

"Because I can't keep kissing someone that I don't know anything about."

But you just happen to know some of my secrets that no one knows or would dare ask of me.

"Only if I get one question in return."

Reign nods her head. "Deal."

"What's one thing you want to do before you die?"

Reign big blue eyes burn a hole in my soul if that's even possible.

Those big blue eyes keep fucking me over.

"I want to be able to impact someone's life in a drastic way or I want to be able to know what it feels like to be in love. Like the true love you read about in books or see in Disney movies."

And that's why I'm scared of her. Because of stupid shit she says like that, that is impossible for me to give her. "Why don't you want to be loved?"

I lick my lips and almost lie but what's the point?

At the rate I'm going, I'm truly fucked.

But I think I always knew that and didn't care.

A new thing I want to experience before I die is being loved by Reign Pierce.

"Because it will be easier in the end."

Reign tilts her head slightly and furrows her eyebrows. "End? What end?"

"You only get one question."

"But I want to ask more. Like what your favorite color is, what you like to do in your free time, why you're so quiet all the time, what's one thing you want to do before you die, your favorite animal, and-"

"Okay," I cut her off, making her rambling stop and a shocked expression appear on her face.

"Okay?" she repeats, another fucking smile wanting to make it's way to her face.

"Meet me at the hill tonight if you want to know."

A smile finally breaks on her face, and she nods her head. "Okay, Killian."

Twenty-Nine
Killian

It's fine.

That's what I tell myself as I wait for her on the hill under the stars.

I'll tell her everything and then it will all be fine.

I can't keep lying to her.

But it just makes things so much easier.

Immediately after the dance with Reign, I left the party without anyone seeing me. I was too anxious and a little bit excited to see Reign tonight, alone, under the stars with me. Plus she is a temptation for me, especially in that dress with those big blue eyes of hers.

I don't know what time it is now, but I have a feeling the party is over since it feels like hours just sitting here waiting for her.

I'd wait an eternity for her.

I hear a car pull up and suddenly my calm heart starts to race.

"I'm surprised you're the one who asked to meet here instead of me," Reign says as she lays a blanket down and puts the extra one next to me.

"You wanted to know more about me so I'm giving you your chance. Consider this your birthday gift."

Reign sits down on the blanket, and I scoot next to her so I can sit on the same blanket. I wrap my arm around her waist and pull her closer to me.

She gives me a look while blushing, making me smirk.

I just love how I can easily affect her.

"Okay," she says, looking up at me.

"Okay." I smirk down at her.

"What's your favorite color?"

"Blue."

"Why?"

"Because that's the color of your eyes."

Reign blushes and shakes her head lightly. "Killian, stop messing around. Seriously, what's your favorite color?"

"Like I said, blue."

Reign rolls her eyes. "Your favorite animal?'

"I'm starting to like lions."

Reign laughs. "You can't keep making them all about me."

"Why not?" I tilt my head to the side, looking down at her lips before meeting her eyes.

"Because this is about you."

"Next question."

"What's one thing you want to accomplish before you die?"

I would say become capo, but plans have changed.

I want something else now, something more than just being a capo.

"I want to be able to live the life I want with no regrets."

"What's one thing you like about Italy?"

"The weather and scenery. It's beautiful there."

"I want to go there one of these days. I've never been."

"I'll take you," I say, making Reign smile.

One of these days I will.

Before the time between us runs out.

"My dad is wrong about you," Reign says, making the guilt invite its way in and make me feel like shit.

Tell her.

Tell her.

Tell her.

"Why do you say that?" I ask, furrowing my eyebrows.

"Because I know you wouldn't do anything to hurt me." I feel my heart clench hearing her say that. *How fucking naive can you be, my sweet beautiful Reign?* Sure, I don't really want to hurt her, but I will. It's inevitable.

I can't fucking control it or how far this thing between us goes. "I like you a lot." She needs to shut up. I don't like how everything I'm not telling her tastes on my tongue. All the unspoken words and lies I'm keeping just makes me feel guilty. "I don't know why my dad doesn't like you. You haven't done anything to prove otherwise. He knows I like you too because I couldn't help but tell him. He knows that I like you even though you're mean, closed off, and dark. He knows how much I trust you and that I've never felt this way about any guy-"

I kiss her to shut her up.

Because she needs to shut the fuck up.

I can't hear her talk about me like I'm some god or praise me like I'm her savior when I'm really her downfall.

Our bodies and souls meld together and the stars above us shine.

This was destined. This night under the stars was meant to happen.

She soon falls on her back and I follow her, getting between her legs. One of her hands goes to my hair to play with it while one of my hands goes to the side of her ass. I pull her closer to me, grinding on top of her.

She is so hard to resist.

I need closer.

I need more.

I sink my teeth into her lip making her moan and if

she'd let me, I'd sink my teeth in her ass making my mark there too.

Reign moans and opens up her legs. Her body is soft and smooth while mine is rigid and hard.

Our tongues dance and we make this kiss our bitch. I feel tingles down my spine when I roll my hips against hers. My hand trails to the back of her dress. I bring the zipper down while Reign pulls me closer to her.

"Killian," she gasps when my finger trails down her bare back.

I'm too far gone to stop this now.

I take off her dress and she lets me. My shirt follows and Reign admires the tattoos while I kiss her neck. I trail the kisses down while Reign watches me with lust in her eyes.

"Tell me to stop, Reign. Because if you don't, I won't be able to," I say, kissing down her stomach. She clenches her thighs together, but she doesn't say anything. "Damn it, Reign," I say before getting below her navel. I look up at her and all I see is trust. This fucking girl. "Tell me to stop."

"No," she says in a breathless tone.

"Reign." My lips nearing her pussy behind the soaked underwear.

"No."

I groan. "You're fucking things up for me."

I take her underwear off and then my nose nudges her

clit. She cries out and moves her thighs, but I keep them pinned down with my arms. I suck her lips in my mouth and lick all the way from her hole to her clit.

"Killian," she moans, gripping my hair, pulling me closer.

I thrust two fingers inside her, making her gasp. "Jesus, fuck. You're so tight. Taking my fingers so well, baby." She clenches around my fingers, and I suck her clit in my mouth. "Come on baby, come for me," I mummer, feeling her clenching around my fingers, slowly falling towards the edge. I curve my fingers, hitting her g-spot, making her moan. I could do this all night if she let me. I swear I've never spent this much time between a woman's legs. She tightens around my fingers and comes apart. "Good girl."

I keep my fingers inside her, softly playing with her as I lean up and press my mouth against hers.

As we kiss, her hand slowly inches down my abs then to the waistband of my pants where my zipper is. "Reign," I groan in the kiss when she slips her hand inside my jeans, her fingers grazing my dick. "Don't go there." I stop kissing her, but she doesn't. She trails her kisses down my neck. Her touch sets my skin on fire, leaving me burning with desire. My dick pulses like it has a heart of it's own and it was saying "Fuck it, let's do it."

I want to cave.

I want to give in to this, to her.

But God, the guilt and the fucking ending begs me not to.

"It's fine. Please."

"Reign-"

"I want to, Killian." She stops kissing me and looks up at me with stars in her eyes as if she trusts me to hold her heart in my hands. "I want it to be you."

But she has no clue that I'll fucking burn her heart until there's nothing left.

"You don't even know me."

"I trust you. It's my decision." Reign moves her hand inside my briefs, and I almost want to just come then and there like a fucking teenager.

"I don't have a condom."

Reign nods. "Just the tip."

I shake my head lightly. "Reign, I've never-"

"It's just the tip. Nothing more."

I bite my lip and Reign moves her hand up and down my shaft making this whole thing even harder to just say no to.

Fucking Reign.

I groan. "Just the tip." She nods happily. My pants and briefs are thrown off and I position myself between her legs. "Just the tip," I say, more so to myself.

The tip of my dick makes contact with her pussy, slipping my way between her folds.

I've never fucked without a condom.

It feels different, better.

We feel closer, it feels more intimate.

Her body curves into mine as she moans. My dick slips past her folds and that's all it took. I trail my eyes up and down her body, the way she holds onto me as if I'm going to let her go.

"Killian-"

"Look at you, Reign." I shake my head lightly, slipping an inch in. "Your fucking eyes, your fucking smile, just you. I never stood a fucking chance," I say before thrusting fully inside her.

Reign tightens her legs around me and moans, scraping her nails down my back. Her walls clenched around me. I roll my eyes from how she feels around. So tight and soft I want to say fuck it all and go hard on her, but the voice inside my head, the one that fucking cares about this girl, tells me to go gentle.

Gentle.

My hand goes down to play with her clit. "Oh my god," she moans.

"How does it feel?" I ask, still playing with her clit. I lean down and press my lips to her neck.

I pull out before thrusting inside her again.

She tightens around me. "Go faster."

She meets each of my thrusts as I pound into her. I suck and bite her neck while my fingers play with her pussy. She moans my name to the stars and for a second everything is quiet.

I look down and see her blood mixed with her wetness on my dick.

My dick twitches inside her. "Please tell me you're close, baby," I say in her ear, and she just clenches around me again. I rub her clit faster making her scream my name and her whole body tightens up. "Come on baby, come for me."

Reign digs her nails in my back, and I pinch her clit.

She falls apart and I follow after her, pounding inside her so hard and fast I feel like I'm hurting her, but she just keeps repeating my name like a prayer.

When she's all spent and calms down, her fingers run down my back, feeling the marks she made.

I stay inside her, kissing her neck softly as I finish inside her.

Fuck.

It's fine, she's probably on birth control and if not there's the pill.

It's fine.

"You're totally fucking things up for me, Reign." I rest my head on her shoulder, relaxing while feeling her heartbeat against my chest.

Thirty
Killia

I can't believe I actually agreed to this.

Showing Reign how I cook my dad's Tagliatelle alla Bolognese, wasn't on my to-do list today.

But Reign asked me what my favorite Italian dish was, and I told her it was Tagliatelle alla Bolognese and then she asked to show it while looking up at me with those big blue eyes of her.

I couldn't say no.

This girl could ask me to go on my knees and I'd do it, no questions asked.

She has no clue what kind of power she has over me and neither do I apparently because I never deny her power and how she makes me do things I'd never thought of doing before.

She's making me question a lot of things about myself.

"Why is this one your favorite?" Reign asks, looking up at me as I cut the pasta.

They obviously don't have any sort of pasta cutter in their house so we're improvising.

"Because it's the one that tastes the best. I also used to make it with my dad and mom whenever they were in the cooking mood."

"Who are you closer with?"

"My mom. Everyone usually assumes that I'm closer with my dad, but we never get along. Mostly because we are too much alike."

Reign is making the sauce right now while the beef is cooking in a separate pan.

Reign told me she doesn't know how to cook a lot of things while I was taught how to cook at a young age, mostly because of my dad.

My dad said it was important for both me and my sister to know how to cook and not solely focus on becoming trained killers, at a young age. My mom would teach us how to cook a lot of easy and basic dishes while my dad taught us how to make true Italian food.

Those were good nights, where my family all got together and just hung out.

As a kid I remember my dad not being so much of a hard ass with me.

But his wife is dying, his empire is falling to my hands, and Thalia got out of control.

It stresses him out even though he won't admit it.

Speaking of my dad, he hasn't called since we landed in Bulgaria from our trip to France.

So, I've been enjoying the peace and quiet, spending time with Reign and being inside her. Ever since we had sex on that hill, I haven't been able to keep my hands off her, which is hard when her dad can't keep his eyes off me.

Reign said he asked what's going on with me and about how I stare at Reign. She just told him not to worry about it. Then Reign told me I need to stop staring at her.

I told her to shut up and then I pulled her to the hallway and kissed her.

Last time we had sex was maybe a couple of days ago when I snuck inside her room.

Still can't get that night out of my head.

I swear that night and the one under the stars just keep replaying in my head.

My hand muffling her moans so she wouldn't wake up the house. How she dragged her nails down my arms, creating marks, the way she would beg for more and how she would try her best to stay silent through an orgasm but fail.

She would also cover my mouth when I groaned which was kind of hot, not gonna lie.

I feel like a fucking teenager whenever I have sex with her.

It's different from all the other girls. I actually enjoy it and don't wish for it to be over.

Instead, I wish I could be inside her all night long, and never leave.

When we had sex in her bedroom I pulled out because she isn't on birth control yet. She did end up taking a Plan B pill the next day because a kid is not in the cards, especially right now.

I know I told my dad there would be an heir but right now, when a war is possibly about to happen with two rivaling families, isn't the time.

"What are you thinking about?" Reign asks and I realize that I've been silent for a little too long just staring at the pasta in my hands.

My body relaxes and I look down at her. "When I was in your room a few days ago." Kind of a lie. I was thinking about that before I started thinking about babies with Reign. Reign blushes and looks away from me. I grab her chin to make her look at me. "Why do you always look away from me? I want to see your eyes on me."

Reign smiles nervously at me. "You're just intimidating."

I furrow my eyebrows. "How?"

"Because you do these eyes. I already explained this to you." Reign laughs.

She tries to take her face out of my hand, but I pull her

closer to me and connect my lips with hers. She smiles into the kiss, and it gets heated as quickly as it started.

I move her around so that I can push her against the counter. She rests her hands on my chest while one of my hands go to her hip and the other trails down to her neck so I can control the kiss better.

I bite her bottom lip making her moan softly which I swear my dick feels. Blood rushes down my body and I rub against her so she can feel what she's doing to me.

Before I can convince her to go to her room, I hear Kyra screaming Reign's name.

"Reign!" Reign pushes me off her and she fixes herself while I lick my bottom lip and stare at her with a smirk. She is flushed red and looks like she just got fucked but in reality it as just a simple kiss. Kyra enters the kitchen and looks between us. A small smile makes its way to her face. "What's going on here?"

Reign clears her throat and smiles. "We're making Italian."

"And Bulgarian?" Kyra raises an eyebrow and looks at me.

I refrain from laughing but Reign's face turns dark red.

"We're making Tagliatelle alla Bolognese," I say, trying to save Reign from the embarrassment from the joke.

That fucking old woman.

"Make sure to clean up after yourselves. Can't have

the Italian and Bulgarian anywhere on the counters if you know what I mean."

Kyra says before leaving, not being discreet about what she knows at all.

Reign cringes and her face stays a dark red shade as she stares at me.

I laugh at her and grab her hand to pull her closer to me. "I can't believe she said that."

"She won't say anything will she?" I ask, raising an eyebrow at Reign.

Reign shakes her head. "No but she also won't pretend she doesn't know anything either. Which makes this mortifying."

I laugh while Reign just buries her head into my chest.

THIRTY-ONE

REIGN

STAR HAS BEEN DISTANT LATELY, BUT I MEAN SO have I.

Ever since I left for France or things between Killian and I started heating up, I forgot about everyone else.

I'm always the one who tries to text first just to make sure he knows I'm still here, but his responses have been short or when he does end up responding I end up getting distracted with Killian.

I am looking over our messages now and am realizing the distance between Star and me.

Hey, how are things going?

Fine. What's going on with you? I haven't heard from you in a while.

The guy I was telling you about, I had sex with him.

You finally lost your virginity? Did you get a cake?

I smile and shake my head lightly.

No but I didn't need one. That night alone was enough.

Is that a good thing or bad thing?

It's a good thing. I like him a lot. It almost feels dangerous liking him.

Why?

Because I shouldn't, especially since Papa doesn't like him. I feel like the more time I spend with him and the more I get to know him, my heart is closer to being in danger.

Does he feel the same way? I remember you saying something about him being afraid of his heart.

He still hasn't talked much about that. I don't want to push him either.

Star reads the message but doesn't reply after a few minutes. I put my phone on my side table and lay on my back, closing my eyes.

I know liking Killian is dangerous but God, the danger feels good.

Spending time with him in the kitchen the other day was nice. It felt good to smile and hangout with him while getting to know him more.

I notice that he smiles more around me and whenever he does, I always take a picture so I can have some sort of proof that Killian De Luca can smile.

In fact, he has one of the most beautiful smiles in the world.

"You know, it's extremely easy to get in your room." I open my eyes and lift my head and see Killian standing in front of my bed. He's wearing a black sweater and gray sweatpants that I always love seeing him in. "Your dad needs to get more security in your room. This is the third time I was able to sneak in." Killian comes onto the bed, hovering over me.

I put my hands on his shoulders while he cages my head between his arms. "Well, I have you stalking me so you wouldn't let anything happen. I don't need guards."

"Stalking, huh?" Killian raises an eyebrow at me.

I smile at him. "Yea, you're always watching me, and you already know almost everything about me without me even telling you."

Killian leans down and kisses me. "It's because I am a good observer. I pay attention to anything that has to do with you." Killian changes his position so that he's lying on his back. He grabs my hand and pulls me over his lap so that I'm sitting on top of him. I rest my hands on his chest and smile down at him. "What were you doing before I came?"

"Texting one of my friends."

"Who?" Killian asks, his expression not changing much.

"Just a friend. Don't be jealous."

Killian shakes his head. "Not jealous. I don't have competition when it comes to you."

Just to tease I say, "I don't know. There's a lot of good-looking guys out there."

"Reign," he warns but I don't care.

I keep going because I like testing him and seeing how far his limits are.

I know Killian has limits that he won't and doesn't show me, but I want him to.

He knows the dark side of things that I like but he never talks about them with me.

But I want to see.

"Maybe I'll finally give Jamie a chance since I lost my virg-"

Killian flips me on my back and puts his knee between my legs, his hand on my throat, and his lips close to mine.

"No one is ever going to fucking touch you. Got it? Good." His lips graze mine. "You're mine, Reign, You'd be smart not to test me on that." Killian rips my shirt off and his lips go for my nipple. I gasp when he nips and sucks. I grind against his leg and bring my hands under his shirt, feeling his abs tighten. "You wanted to test me Reign, you fucking got it." Killian takes off my shorts and his fingers dip between my legs. "Fuck you're already wet baby. This for me? I'm the only one getting you this wet?" he asks, his lips grazing my ear.

I press my head against the mattress, trying not to moan or make any sounds because my parents are literally down the hall.

I spread my legs for him as he moves his long fingers over my wet clit, teasing and playing with it.

Everything throbs, and I swear my pussy feels on edge with how slowly he's moving his fingers.

"Killian-"

"Look at you," Killian whispers in my ear. "Making a mess on my hand with your parents just down the hall. Are you even that innocent anymore?" He nips my ear and I thrust against his hand.

"Please go faster. I need more-"

Killian rips his fingers out of my pussy and holds my legs down to the bed while he takes his sweatshirt and sweatpants off in a hurry.

He puts his hand over my mouth before grabbing my hip and slamming into me in one go. A muffled scream fills the room, and my hands go to his back as he thrusts in and out of me.

"Shh, you're too loud," Killian says with his hand pressing against my mouth. I moan against his palm, my eyes rolling back from the overwhelming pleasure. I feel myself tightening against him as he pushes inside me forcefully. My eyes close but Killian lets go of my mouth and holds my neck tightly. I feel his lips graze mine. "Look at me baby. Look at how I own you, Reign." Killian looks down at me with a dark expression on his face. His hand goes down to my clit, finally rubbing and pinching it fast and hard. "This body is mine." He squeezes my throat. "This cunt is definitely fucking mine," he says, making sure to pound into me harder. "Don't ever question who you belong to."

Killian holds my throat as he fucks me roughly while I scratch his arms and back, screaming into his mouth as he kisses me to shut me up.

I sink my teeth into his bottom lip, moaning while coming around him. I clench around Killian, and he groans in my mouth.

It's not long after I feel his come spurt inside me, filling me until he's completely spent.

Thirty-Two

"Why haven't you been answering? I've called you over 50 times in the last week and I get fucking nothing from you," my dad lectures over the phone and if he doesn't stop, I'll hit that "end" button. "You losing focus or what? Do I need to come down there?"

Jesus, at least mom asks me about my day and what I've been doing. My dad is all business, but he's always been like that.

"No. Everything is being handled." I say in a calm tone even though he, out of all people, probably stresses me the fuck out the most. When Reign isn't off doing dumb shit in warehouses.

I swear that girl and warehouses.

"Then why am I not seeing that momfucker Malcolm

in a goddamn coffin. It doesn't take long to kill that piece of shit. I can do it in my sleep."

"Why are you so hellbent on getting this done right away? You always take your time with shit. Why the rush?"

"Because I want it done, Killian. I'm not asking you to kill him anymore, I'm telling you. Don't make me take matters into my own hands."

A knock on the door brings my attention away from my dad's bitching. "I got to go," I say before ending the call and just turning off my phone.

I'm not answering anymore of his calls until I figure out what the fuck to do.

I open the front door revealing Reign.

Today she has the same smile she always has on her face and a blue summer dress. I don't know how she's wearing that kind of shit when it's cold.

"You're not doing anything today, right?" Reign asks while walking in confidently.

It's been a few days since her bedroom. I sneak up there pretty much every night and then sneak out before the sunrises.

It's become part of my routine every night, just spending it with her.

She'll be reading or texting one of her friends before I barge in and steal her attention, as it should be.

I should be the only one she's thinking of or taking her full attention.

"No, not like I do much anyways."

It's true.

Usually during the day, I have stupid meals with Reign's family, Kyra pulls me into some bullshit she needs Reign and I's help with, training Reign or at least trying to since I can't keep my hands off of her, and just other random bullshit Reign wants to do.

Today won't be any different.

If you were to ask me if I miss the pre-Reign life, I'd say I miss it, but I'd also say it was fucking boring. Being with Reign is like a relief almost and I actually wish the days were longer with her.

I constantly want to be around her, touching her, everything.

"Good, because I want to go to this museum that just opened up a few blocks away. I've been waiting for it to open for ages and haven't had the chance to go because I have no one to go with so now that I have you, I'll finally be able to go and-"

I cut her off by kissing her because she's talking too much and thinking too much about it.

As I kiss Reign she gasps into my mouth and places her hands on my bare chest, her nails grazing my chest.

Something I've noticed about Reign and when she rambles on like that is that she gets nervous when asking me about plans or just talking to me in general. So, she rambles until I kiss the shit out of her to calm her down and shut her mind off for a little bit.

I nip her bottom lip before pulling away with a groan. "I'll go. I just need to change." I kiss her forehead and catch Reign's red, flushed red face before I turn away to go change.

I change into black trousers and a white button up. Reign is sitting on the couch waiting for me when I get down.

We head to my car after Reign explains her plans with me to Kyra and her mom.

During the drive, the music is turned up loud while Reign hangs her arm out the window, softly singing to the music playing. It's pretty empty on the streets today so we get to this museum pretty fast, especially with how I drive.

"How'd you find out about this place?" I ask Reign while parking the car.

"I would sometimes take walks down this road because there's a coffee shop not too far from here. I would always see these people carrying in a bunch of art. I then found out that this place was soon going to open up and showcase renaissance style art," Reign explains.

We get out of the car, and I grab Reign's hand immediately, pulling her closer to me.

"You know how to draw?" I ask her as we walk towards the entrance.

Reign shakes her head. "No. I wish though because artists are so talented. I feel like I just haven't found a passion yet. Yes, I like helping people but there are so many people who are creative and have their whole passion and lives figured out. I feel like I'm meant for more. More than my Papa's business. You know? You have artists creating masterpieces and authors creating different realities with every story," she explains as we walk in.

I pay for both of us to enter before looking down at her. "You're still young. You have enough time to figure it all out."

Reign looks up at me with those gorgeous blue eyes that just keep fucking me over. "What do you think I'm meant for?"

I stop walking and look at her, really look at her. I bring my hand up to hold her jaw in my hand. I stroke my thumb along her cheek and just admire her.

She's made for the fucking universe.

To spoil and cherish.

Reign is like a delicate flower that you should keep protected, like the flower from Beauty and the Beast.

"I think you were meant for me, Reign. In a way you were made perfectly for me."

Reign shakes her head lightly but blushes. She grabs my hand and pulls me towards the art, not saying anything.

But she doesn't need to because I have a feeling, just a

really strong fucking feeling that this girl is going to somehow make my life better.

That's exactly what she was made to do with this life.

While she dances around the museum, looking at the art, I can't take my eyes off her.

There is art all around us, but she is the one I can't keep my eyes off of.

THIRTY-THREE

KILLIAN

AFTER THE MUSEUM YESTERDAY, REIGN AND I spent the rest of the day at the hill, under the stars.

She talked, I listened. When she started rambling a little too much I couldn't help but smile and cut her off by grabbing her throat and kissing her.

When we got back to the house around midnight, I was going to let her go up to her room by herself for the night but Reign gave me those begging eyes that made her kind of look like Puss The Cat for a second and I couldn't say no.

That girl and her goddamn eyes.

It was a struggle leaving her this morning but I had to before her mom or Kyra checked up on her. I told her I would see her for breakfast but she just murmured okay in a sleepy tone since she was kind of half asleep.

Ever since I started sleeping with Reign, I noticed I don't have trouble staying asleep at night. I can sleep a full eight hours without tossing or turning when my body is next to hers. I don't wake up with a heavy beating heart or sweat on my forehead.

It's around 8 in the morning which means breakfast should be ready. I don't change out of the dark gray sweatpants I'm wearing and I just throw on a black hoodie so I don't have my chest out.

When I walk inside the main house I see Reign sitting at the dining table with her grandma who's drinking tea while smiling at Reign as she talks.

Reign has a certain glow on her face that wasn't there before and it's refreshing to see her smile actually mean something.

This morning she's wearing her hair in a loose bun making me able to see all her features perfectly. She has a white tank top on and then a pair of black sweatpants.

She looks absolutely breathtaking.

I sit at the table next to Reign, my hand going on her thigh. I'm pretty sure that Reign blushes but I don't tease her about it.

"Morning, Killian. How'd you sleep last night?" Kyra asks with a smirk on her face.

Too fucking good.

"Fine. And yourself?"

"Wonderful. You two got in late last night. Mind

telling me what you were doing with my granddaughter here so late last night?" Kyra raises an eyebrow at me and Reign.

Reign blushes and tries to cover it with her hands.

"None of your business." I say while gripping Reign's thigh.

"Well then." Kyra says before sipping her cup of tea.

I turn to look at Reign. "How'd you sleep?'

"Good. I had a certain pillow that was comfy to sleep on." Reign says, giving me a teasing look. "I just wish you wouldn't have to leave in the mornings." She says in a hushed whisper but I know that Kyra is probably staring at us, observing every little look and touch.

Because I can't help it, I push a fallen strand of Reign's hair behind her ear.

"Why don't you ever keep your hair up?"

Reign shrugs. "I don't know. I like having my hair down. I feel prettier I guess."

"You look beautiful in any way."

Reign blushes again shyly. I love how easily I affect her.

"Do you have any plans today?"

"Do I ever?" I tease with a small smile, rubbing my thumb softly on her cheek.

"Well I wanted to-"

I hear footsteps making me let go of Reign. "Morning family." Malcom walks in with a bright smile on his face, cutting Reign off.

This should be fucking good.

Malcom this morning looks happy, too fucking happy for my liking.

I all of a sudden have an unsettling feeling in my stomach and my heart feels like it's just suddenly getting tighter and tighter, like something's gripping it but I ignore it.

"Morning, papa." Reign says, smiling at her dad as he sits next to her. "Where's mama?"

"She's coming down now." He says in a calm voice. I expect him to be in a sour mood, especially since Reign and I weren't home all day. Ever since France he hasn't been up my ass like usual which does make me skeptical but I ignore the gut feeling just because then I won't be able to enjoy my time with Reign. "How'd you sleep, Reign?"

"Good, what about you? You seem like you're in a good mood this morning."

"I am Reign." Malcom smiles and then Lia walks inside the dining room with a smile on her face as well. Her eyes dart to me when she sits down and I look at Malcolm who's staring at me. What the fuck. "I want to talk to you after breakfast, Killian." Malcom says, not in a rude way or anything.

He actually has a pleasant fucking tone surprisingly. "Why?"

Reign notices how I tense because I feel her hand slide onto my thigh and grab my hand.

"Well it seems like you aren't leaving anytime soon. I want to get to know you more. Hangout and have some guy time. It's been a while since I only live with girls." This fucking guy. He's got to be kidding. Reign strokes her thumb over my knuckles and I slowly feel tension leaving my body. "Just meet me after breakfast. I have a trail I want to go hiking on so I figured you should come with me."

I don't say anything at that.

Not like I have much of a choice.

Thirty-Four

Killian

After breakfast was over, I went to the guest house to change out of the sweatpants and sweater. When I left, I told Reign I would see her when I get back and we could do something.

I changed into a navy compression shirt and black shorts. I'm hoping this hike with Malcom doesn't take long. He says he wants to go on this hike to get to know each other a little more and have some fucking guy time but I know what his plan his.

He knows he won't be able to get rid of me. He knows I'm here to stay, or at least that's what he thinks.

I'm still trying to figure out myself what the hell I'm even still doing here.

Yea it definitely has to do with the girl who has big

blue eyes and loves playing in flower fields or just talking to the stars.

My dad called me after breakfast, but I ignored it.

Malcom is giving me enough goddamn stress that I shouldn't be dealing with so answering my dad was something that I wasn't going to deal with as well.

Ever since Malcom asked me to hike with him, my stomach has been churning and my mind has been just going into an overthinking drive.

I all of a sudden just feel a wave of anxiety hit because something isn't fucking right.

I usually trust my gut so that's why I bring my matches and gun just in case anything happens.

I walk out the front door and see Malcom stretching. He's wearing a muscle t-shirt and shorts.

I walk up to him, and Malcom turns his head to me. "Killian."

"Malcom," I say in a monotone.

"Let's talk, yea?" Malcom says as he starts to walk towards the exit of his estate. I follow, walking at the same pace as him. "I'm curious, do you know why your dad and I don't get along?" Malcom asks, looking at me with a questioning look.

We end up walking out of his estate and towards the trail he's talking about.

"No. I don't get involved in anyone's business unless it concerns me."

"Well, I'm going to tell you a story. Your dad and I used to be business associates; some would even call us friends."

"What happened?" I ask, indulging.

"Well, a few weeks before the day I met you at the annual ball, your dad killed my brother."

"Why? There must've been a reason. My dad only kills someone who is a threat to him."

"Your dad told me it was because my brother talked badly about your mom." Malcom looks at me for my reaction, but I don't show one.

I just look back at him and say, "Then I have no sympathy for your brother. Anyone who talks bad about my mom to my face will die. I won't even feel sorry for it."

Malcom nods his head. "I understand that. But he was still my family."

"So, this vendetta you have against me is because of my dad for that?" Malcom nods his head. "You shouldn't have any sort of vendetta against me because I'm not the one who killed your brother. I was a kid when that happened and obviously didn't know until now. Plus, I'm not my dad."

"I've realized that now," Malcom agrees. "But you also aren't completely different from him. It's funny, you both have the same weapon of choice while your sister and mom have the same weapon of choice."

"Mom daughter and dad son duo." I shrug. "Do you not like fire?"

"Fire killed my brother," Malcom reveals. I stay quiet, not really knowing what to say. "My daughter likes you," he states, making my heart rate start to speed up. "At first, I didn't like it. I didn't like the fact that my daughter would like a guy like you."

"A guy like me?" I raise an eyebrow at him.

"A villain. You aren't a hero, Killian, and you don't pretend to be. I always imagined my Reign, my sweet, beautiful princess would fall in love with a good guy. Someone like Jamie but then you come in and she made it her mission to make you open up and try new things. Ever since you came into her life, she's been happier."

Why the fuck does he have to tell me all this?

Doesn't he know it makes shit ten times harder?

I can barely even fucking kill you because of that goddamn girl.

"Reign has always been happy."

"She has. But since you came in the picture, she doesn't have her nose stuck in a book or texting someone on the phone. She dedicates her time to you and enjoys spending time with you. Spending time with you makes her happy. Every time she comes home from being with you, she looks like she just finished riding cloud nine. Sure, my daughter smiles and is kind but since you, she changed. She's been glowing recently and Lia notices it."

"I didn't do anything."

"You did. You just didn't realize it. I'm not going to lie and say I didn't hate it at first. But after that trip to Paris, I started to look at things differently."

I don't say anything to him about that.

I don't feel like talking about Reign and I's relationship with Malcom because he doesn't need to know the details.

He doesn't need to know how I'm slowly starting to become afraid of actually losing someone when I've never been afraid before.

I hear a whistle behind me making Malcolm and I stop walking. We turn around and see men in black vests with their guns aimed at us.

And I bet if I turn around...

I turn my head and see three more men behind Malcom wearing the same thing, holding guns.

I look down at their hands, seeing a very familiar rose tattoo on the side of their wrists.

Damn it.

I have the same fucking tattoo on my wrist too. My dad wanted to make the family tattoo a rose because that's my mom's favorite flower.

Everything starts piecing together.

The constant anxiety all day, my dad calling, the feeling of my heart about to explode.

"Not very smart to go on a new hike with no guards," one of the guys says, walking closer to us. "Well done, Killian. Your dad will be proud. Great minds think alike."

Malcom's eyes widen and he turns his head to look at me. "You," he says, glaring at me, his jaw clenching.

I tense but keep my composure calm. "No, I didn't mean for it to go this way."

"Enough with the bullshit, Killian," one of the soldiers says before looking at his men. "Go get him."

All of the guys around us come in closer towards Malcolm but I stand in front of him and help Malcom start to fight off the soldiers.

One soldier from far away raises a gun and shoots, making Malcom fall to the ground. I take my gun out swiftly and put a bullet through his shoulder. I go up to him and hold him against me with the gun pressing against the side of his head.

All the soldiers look at me, shocked that I'm not going along with their plan.

My dad probably set this up to make killing Malcom easier when in reality if I wanted to kill Malcom, I would have done it on the first day I got to Bulgaria.

"I'll shoot him. Leave Malcolm alone or I'll put a bullet through his head," I threaten with a calm tone.

The main guy smiles and laughs. "Killian, be serious right now. You won't shoot family."

"Don't tempt me." I shove the gun against the guy's head harder, making him wince.

"You're really going to disappoint your dad like this?"

Malcom looks at me and I swear I see hurt flash in his eyes. "You've been working for your dad? This whole time?" he says, holding his stomach.

"That was before-"

"Before what?" the main guy says, not keeping his goddamn mouth shut. "Before you fucked his daughter."

I press the trigger, the soldier's body going limp in my hold.

Another soldier puts a bullet through through Malcom's abdomen making him scream. I don't think twice before aiming the gun at the main soldier and shooting him between the eyes.

He falls to the floor with the rest of the soldiers making it just me and Malcolm.

"Fuck!" Malcom screams in pain. I go over to him and kneel next to him. He looks at me with rage and moves away from me. "Get away from me!"

"Let me fucking help you-"

"No! I should have never trusted you. I was wrong to think a girl like my sweet daughter could ever love a man like you. You're dead De Luca. Dead to me. And eventually dead to Reign. Can't believe I was even close to trusting you." Malcom gets up slowly and I try to help him, but he rips my arms off him and backs away from me.

"Malcom-"

Malcom looks at me again, betrayal in his eyes. "I'm not going to tell you again. You're dead to us De Luca!"

THIRTY-FIVE
REIGN

I FURROW MY EYEBROWS WHILE LOOKING AT THE text that Star sent.

It makes me nervous because what on earth can he be sorry for?

I texted him back, asking why but no response.

So, for the past thirty minutes, I've been anxiously waiting for Killian and Papa to arrive home as Baba, and I talk.

Right now, she is explaining to me how everything happens for a reason.

Like how our whole lives are basically planned ahead for us.

Everyone has a destiny and eventually you'll find out

what that is but until then, you're just walking around on the earth just living and breathing.

But all this talk about destiny and fate isn't helping me get my mind off Killian or Star.

Up until Star's message, I've been having a smile on my face, feeling great because Killian's opening up more and everyday feels like a dream, almost too good to be true.

He already knows so much about me while I didn't even know what his favorite movie is.

His favorite movie is Jumanji which is such a classic. That was his favorite movie as a child as well as Marvel movies.

I learned that deep down Killian is such a nerd.

Whether it be about his favorite movies, cars, or just random psychological facts he knows.

I wish I could spend more time with Killian, and he could be welcomed in the house.

I asked Killian if he would want to do anything else but work for his family and he said he can't think of anything that would make him happier.

Talking to him about that made me wonder if Killian would ever go back to his family or if he will eventually leave.

What is his plan for his family?

What's his plan for us?

"What are you thinking so hard about my sweet girl?"

Baba asks and I look up at her, blushing, because I can't help it. "It's that Killian boy, isn't it?" Baba asks, a smirk sneaking up on her face.

I smile and shake my head lightly. "You and your crazy theories, Baba."

"They aren't crazy. A grandmom knows."

No, my Baba isn't crazy. She 100% knows along with everyone else in the house most likely. I know Baba has liked Killian since day one because I would always catch her staring at him or whenever Killian and I were together she would smile at us.

"Yea," I say softly, looking at my hands nervously.

"Killian makes you happy. I missed that smile on your face."

"I always smile," I say, defending myself.

"Not like this."

She's right.

I can't even deny it with the blush on my cheeks.

I can't even deny it when she sees me staring at Killian from across the room.

I can't deny the glow that's on my face when our eyes connect.

He makes me feel like a little school girl with a school crush.

No one has ever made me feel like this.

The front door opens, and I hear grunting.

My stomach feels like it's about to drop especially

when I feel anxiety running through my veins, wondering what happened.

When wheezing follows, Baba and I stand up from the table and run towards the foyer. We immediately see my dad holding his stomach as he tumbles inside the house.

We run over to him before he falls to the floor. Blood covers his hand and drenches his black muscle shirt.

My eyes go to the door, waiting for Killian to appear and explain what the hell is going on.

I'm anticipating him, waiting for him to just show up and make everything better.

"Papa, what happened?" I ask him as Baba, and I carry him to the kitchen where the first-aid kit is. Baba calls an ambulance as I help him.

"Killian," Papa says before his eyes fall shut.

My mind immediately goes back to the text.

The one where Star apologizes.

Thirty-Six

Killian

I never thought I'd ever dread coming back home after a long trip.

Usually I love being home, in my room where no one can bother me.

It's my safe space along with my house in Greata I bought when I turned nineteen.

But instead of feeling happy and relieved, all I feel is guilt and pressure.

So much pressure that I just want to give up already and wish that life would take me.

Reign is back in Bulgaria where her dad could be telling her the worst about me.

But the text I sent her wasn't very vague. Reign is a smart girl, and she knows what her Star meant when he said sorry and then she saw her dad coming back later.

If she didn't figure it out now, she will soon.

While Malcom limped away, I made sure all the other guys were dead and I left them there. Bulgaria's fucking police and Malcom's team can deal with it.

I did all that, killing my own men for Reign's dad.

For fucking Reign Pierce.

This goddamn girl is messing with my head, and I swear I'm going to end up dead faster than I'm thinking with this girl.

I drove fucking fifteen hours, in my clothes that have blood on them in silence.

No music playing in my car because I just can't think straight with music playing.

All that dangerous fucking thinking going on in my head is fucking me up and my heart isn't making things any easier with how fast and rapid it's beating against my chest.

When I open the door to the house it's quiet and empty.

Looks the same since the last time I was here.

I know my mom is probably in her and my dad's room resting. She only ever comes down for meals when she is feeling up for it.

But for some reason, I can't help but have a bad feeling in the pit of my stomach.

I don't go to her like I want to because I know my dad

wants to speak to me after the shitshow in Bulgaria, plus my mom is probably sleeping.

When I push open my dad's office door, I take a look at him, and it looks like I'm staring at a stranger in my dad's chair.

His white button up has the top three buttons unbuttoned, his hair isn't as short as it was last time I saw him, he's grown a light scruff which is strange because he usually always shaves.

He looks torn up.

He is leaning back in his chair, flipping a knife in his hand, there's a glass of what I'm assuming is whiskey in front of him and his eyes meet mine.

"Dad," I state, closing the door behind me and walking towards the chair in front of his desk.

He leans off his chair as I sit in mine, putting his hands on the desk while still gripping onto the knife.

He looks fucked up.

My mom is probably puking her guts out with blood mixed in, she's dying, and my dad can't do anything about it.

For once in my dad's life, he can't fix something.

He has the power to fix everything, but not this.

All the medications and money he's put into her treatments don't do shit, if anything it's making her worse.

She's getting worse every day, my dad knows it, I know

it, Thalia knows it, but none of us are strong enough to say it out loud.

"You fucked up," my dad says, pointing the knife at me. "What were you thinking, Killian? You know how much damage you caused?" He furrows his eyebrows at me. My leg starts bouncing up and down as I try to stay calm. "You let him get away with a bullet wound instead of a bullet to his head. Are you kidding me? I didn't raise you to be so weak. And you're sitting here as if you didn't do shit wrong. As if everything is fucking perfect," he says, getting more frustrated.

"Yea," I say.

That's all I can say.

Because the reality of the situation is something I can't admit.

I just can't admit I've grown weak for the girl with eyes that made me think I was looking at the universe.

My dad furrows his eyes and chuckles lightly, shaking his head. "Yea?" he repeats. "That's all you have to say?" He slams the knife on the desk. "You're fucking done. I thought you'd be ready but after that shit, you're done. No more."

"You're dead De Luca! You're dead to us!"

Malcolm's words flash in my head.

"You created a whole mafia war for mom, right? You seem to be all about the term love but then when your children want something like that or something close to that, you get pissed off. Like with Thalia, you made her marry Alexander when she was dating someone!"

My dad's jaw clenches. "I'm glad I did that because that fucker was a Russian! Besides I knew she and Alexander would end up together. I talked to Thalia about this already, not you because it's none of your business."

I shake my head lightly and laugh. "This is bullshit," I whisper. "You're being unfair. You were unfair to Thalia, even though she was dating a Russian, she still had a relationship with him. Mom was a part of a group you hated! She literally tried to steal from you and kill you the first-time you guys met, didn't she?" I raise an eyebrow at him.

The way my dad is looking at me right now makes me assume he wants to shoot me.

And I wouldn't be surprised if he did because I never disrespect him, ever.

My sister wouldn't think of speaking to him like this. Only person who gets away with calling him out on his shit is my mom but at this point I don't give a fuck anymore.

Everything is falling apart.

What's one more thing like a broken relationship with your dad?

I'll be like every other kid in the world with daddy issues.

My dad and I have always bumped heads because I'm

the type to fight back until I am on my knees bleeding while my dad expects me to act like a dog and follow his demands.

Fuck that.

I'm done.

"You don't know shit, Killian. You think you're perfect? You think you're the king? Think again, son." He shakes his head as if he can't believe me.

"Nobody is. Not even you. But you can't make me hate someone."

I tried and instead it ended up being the complete opposite.

"You want her just for some goddamn pussy! She is just a woman, Killian! You don't love her."

I look at my dad and I already know he can see it on my face.

I haven't admitted it, I'm too afraid to.

And I'm not going to admit it until the very last second because it's just better to ignore it or deny it.

All you do is get hurt.

One way or another.

"Don't talk about her like that," I say, in a serious, low tone.

My dad furrows his eyebrows at me and leans towards me. "Don't tell me you love her, Killian. You barely know her." I don't answer. I get up from the chair and walk towards the door. "Answer me, Killian."

I bite my bottom lip and squeeze my hands into fists, my heart beating hard against my chest.

Reign Pierce happened to pierce her way through my heart, without any restraint or issues. She broken down all the walls with a mere finger touch and those fucking eyes. I was doomed from the moment I met her.

It's a crazy feeling, one I never thought I'd ever feel.

Like you're in heaven, like you've found the one.

I'm honestly willing to lose everything just to see her smile.

Even being away from her now, it feels like a piece of me is missing.

"Does she know?" my dad asks, already knowing the answer.

"No." I say before turning the knob and leaving so he doesn't ask any more questions.

THIRTY-SEVEN

REIGN

THOSE WERE THE LAST MESSAGES I SENT KILLIAN, also known as Star.

My mind has been in circles, and I can't think straight.

All of my secrets and darkest thoughts are known by someone who's just been lying and scheming.

Was I a part of his master plan for this whole thing?

Was I just a pawn in his game?

Everyone's explained how Killian is worse than his dad because he loves nothing and no one, feels nothing for anyone.

But everything we've experienced together seemed different, like I actually mattered to him.

I just need him to tell me it's all a lie.

"Reign," I look up at my dad and see his eyes open. He's lying in the hospital bed in front of me, looking weak and fragile.

Right when he fainted, we had a car get us to our family doctor.

Luckily the surgery went well, and they took the bullet out before it caused serious damage and before he could lose more blood.

I've been with him since he got taken in. I just can't leave him, especially knowing that he could have possibly died. And since we got into the hospital my mind has been in overthinking mode, trying to put all the pieces together and figure out what happened.

I scoot my chair closer to him. "I'm here Papa."

Baba and Mama are at home taking showers since they haven't gone home. Baba went with Mama since she was worried about her.

She's been by Papa's bedside since he got admitted, wouldn't leave his side other than to go to the restroom.

"Water," Papa says in a scratchy voice.

I grab a water cup and hold the straw to his mouth. "Are you okay? How are you feeling?" I ask him as he swallows the water.

He finishes and I take the water cup back and place it on the side table. "I'm okay, Reign. Thank you," he assures me. "It just hurts a little, but I'll survive," he says, sitting up a little.

"Do you want me to grab the doctor for you?"

Papa shakes his head. "No, Reign. I'm okay, thank you sweetheart."

"What happened?" I ask, my eyebrows furrowing at him.

Papa sighs and shakes his head lightly.

I already know what he's going to say is going to be about Killian and it won't be good things.

I can't imagine what happened.

"Killian," Papa says, confirming what I already knew.

"What happened? What'd he do?" I ask, my heart racing inside my chest.

"He's still working for his dad. He betrayed us Reign. He was using us-"

"Killian wouldn't do that, though. We..."

We've done so much and spent so much time together.

It just hurts to think he would do something like that.

Especially since I was so close or pretty much on the verge of falling for him.

"Killian was sent to Bulgaria to kill me. That fire he saved you from was probably a decoy. He used us Reign," Papa says, making me shake my head lightly and my heart clench. *Please don't make it true.* "You may think that he loves you Reign or cares about you, but the harsh reality of this world is that Killian is a made man and made men care only about one thing. I'm surprised I didn't see this coming because he is in line for the role of capo since his sister turned down the role."

But all of the memories and moments spent together seemed perfect.

Almost like it was too good to be true.

I want to argue with my dad but even I know deep down it can't be a lie.

Not when he was Star all along, learning about all my weaknesses and secrets so he could use them against me.

But I can't imagine him doing that.

All of it seemed so real.

"He couldn't-"

"Think Reign, all the facts point towards Killian. Stop being naive, I taught you better than that. His men shot me while Killian walked away, wound-free. We were all just a part of his plan to take the crown from his dad. You aren't allowed anywhere by yourself from now on, he could come back to finish his mission."

I widen my eyes lightly. "What? Why?"

"You are going to have a guard 24/7 from now on."

"That's not-"

"He used you to get to me, Reign!" Papa yells, his eyes turning into glares at me.

"But he acted like-"

"Like he loves you?" Papa raises his eyes at me. "Reign, sweetheart, please tell me you don't actually love this boy! He will only hurt you!"

Tears form in my eyes.

It can't be true.

Killian needs to just explain his side of the story.

He just needs to explain, and it will all be okay.

"You don't know him like I do, Papa," I say, shaking my head.

"I know he is Ace De Luca's son. He will follow in his dad's footsteps."

"Killian isn't anything like Ace." I shake my head again and tears are finally falling. "I know Ace did things that you hate him for, but Killian isn't like that. He's sweet, caring, and protective. He is nothing like Ace, I know it."

My poor naive heart, denying everything Papa says even though the factual evidence that points towards Killian.

"How do you know Reign? Because of a few moments spent together and a few secrets shared? He was lying!" Papa argues. "That's how the De Luca's are, using anyone in their path to get their way. They will take down everyone if they have to. They don't feel an ounce of emotion, Killian especially."

"It can't be true. Papa, I love him."

"Don't have so much hope for Killian. He only cares about himself. He will burn everyone to the ground if he has to."

THIRTY-EIGHT
KILLIAN

My nonna once told me that one day I'd meet someone who's eyes look like embers of the galaxy glowing in their eyes. Like their eyes could look average or like every other person's eye, but her eyes are the only ones that will make my heartbeat.

Being around them is just peaceful and calm.

Like everything is quiet up there.

She died of breast cancer and I'm pretty sure that's why my mom has it because it got passed down. Nonna's death ruined my mom because they were so close.

She was a mess, barely getting out of bed and always crying but my dad was always there to make sure she was okay and strong.

Nonna's death didn't really affect me because I tried my best not to get too close to her because I knew she would eventually die and that would hurt. But seeing my mom so heartbroken hurt a lot.

I made sure she was okay and was taking care of herself but of course my dad was there for my mom. He didn't want anyone to take care of her because he said it was his duty to be there to protect my mom and make sure she is okay.

I now understand why my dad was like that because I thought about if Reign was going through something like that, I would only want her to cling onto me. I want to help her and want her to use my support.

Seeing her happy and smiling makes me feel calm and like my entire world won't fall any second.

After spending so much time with her and slowly falling for her more and more, it made me understand the difference between obsession, lust, and love.

I went back to my room after the argument with my dad to change and take a shower. After I cleaned up a little bit, I went to my parent's room to check on my mom. She was sleeping when I walked in, so I didn't want to wake her, plus she'd probably see the look on my face and know something was up.

She was hooked to an IV which made me pissed off since I didn't know she was getting chemo treatments again.

She got that when she first got diagnosed and it fucked her up. Since I've been away no one has given me any updates, not even Thalia. I didn't know she was back on this shit and I'm not sure why he didn't tell us.

I take another drag of my cigarette, the poison going straight to my heart making me cough. My heart feels like it's on fire with the smoke stuck in my lungs.

It's close to midnight and I'm just walking around the city.

It's nice outside and the stars are shining as if they know Reign is looking up at them, which she probably is.

Watching the same sky as her makes me feel like I'm next to her.

"They say the people with the greatest intentions and best hearts are up there." I hear a raspy voice say in Italian.

I look across the sidewalk and see a bum, sitting against the wall and he is staring straight at me.

There aren't a lot of bums in my city, but you honestly never know who ends up in Lombardy anymore.

But at the same time, I haven't been here for three or so months.

Time has flown by.

I walk across the street and stand in front of him, meeting his eyes.

He has a coat on with a gray shirt underneath and black jeans that have holes in the knees. He has dirt stains all over him and on his face.

He smells fucking horrible but he's a bum so I can't

really expect much. I lean against the wall, standing up next to him.

I look back up at the sky. "Someone I know said something very similar. Do you think it's true?" I reply in Italian.

"That someone sounds like they know what they're talking about. Must be smart."

"She is," I mumble in English.

"You speak English," the bum states in English, making me look down at him.

"Yea, what about it?"

"Well, I don't meet many people who speak English."

"Where are you from?" I ask.

"America. Moved here with my ex-wife but I caught her cheating and now I'm here."

"Oh," I say, not really caring too much.

I don't need to give him sympathy because he doesn't need it.

What he needs is a fucking shower and some cash.

"Do you think it's true?" I raise an eyebrow at him, not understanding what he means. "The tale of the stars?"

I look back up at the stars. "Anything is possible."

"You look lost," the bum comments.

I am.

I don't know what to do.

Everything is falling apart, and I don't have much time.

I can fucking feel it.

I know what I want to do but I also know what I need to do.

I need to make my family proud before time runs out, but fucking Reign Pierce.

The girl who plays with flowers and stares up at the stars as if they have the answer to everything.

"And you're homeless. Are we just stating the obvious right now?"

"Just making conversation. Is it about a girl?"

"Yes."

"Ahh, you love her, and you hate it."

"Unfortunately," I say, grinding my teeth together, getting annoyed.

"Then why are you here instead of being with her?"

"Because I'm scared of the end," I admit.

"The end is inevitable though, isn't it? It's going to happen but right now you shouldn't think about it. You only have the present."

"I just don't want her to get hurt when she realizes I won't be there for her."

"Doesn't mean she won't leave you. Like I said, all you can think about is now. Not tomorrow or next week. If you don't then you won't enjoy the present."

I look away from the stars and back down at the bum.

He has a point.

My heart longs for her, even when we were children, my heart knew.

"Okay then." I lean off the wall and dig through my pockets to find my wallet. I fish out some cash and toss it to the bum. It's a thousand. Won't get him off the streets but it'll help. "Don't be stupid and spend it on drugs. Get yourself off the streets. It's fucking nasty."

The bum throws his head back and laughs. "What's your name?"

"Killian. You?"

"If I tell you, I'm going to have to kill you," the bum jokes.

A smile threatens to appear on my face. I shake my head lightly. "I doubt you'd be able to."

I walk away from him and towards my Bugatti parked down the street.

Time to claim what's mine.

What's always been mine since that night under the stars.

Thirty-Nine
Reign

Reading books always makes my mind clear.

Whenever my mind goes into overdrive I always either go to the cliff near the beach to talk to the stars or I read.

Reading does a good job to take me out of real life for a little bit.

Papa is back home from the hospital.

Ever since things went down, I've been feeling tired from the constant overthinking, and I even threw up in the morning the other day.

Usually, I get like that when I'm stressed out.

Thinking about Killian and how things went down with him and Papa hurts. Everything regarding Killian hurts because deep down I love him, deep down I know that he couldn't have done all this on purpose.

The book I'm reading is "The Truths We Burn" by

Monty Jay. They're a new author I started reading and their books are pretty good.

I think this book will be a new favorite, especially because the main male character is a fire lover, and it reminds me of Killian.

I feel a breeze hit my bare shoulders making me look over my back.

Deja vu hits me as I see a familiar black figure standing at the end of my bed.

Before I can scream, he gets on top of me and covers my mouth.

My eyes connect with his dark ones. "Don't scream," his husky voice says. I put my hands on his chest to push him away, but he doesn't budge. "I'm not going to hurt you. I just want to talk."

He grabs my wrist, soft and tenderly, and slowly threads his fingers through mine.

I let him because no matter how much I fight, I can't.

Killian is just a boy whose heart hasn't been loved.

He removes his hand from my mouth and leans down. "I've missed you so much." He presses his forehead against mine. "I shouldn't be here."

"You shouldn't," I say and Killian leans back. "You're him. You're my Star." His jaw clenches but he doesn't deny it. A tear forms in my eye. "Why? Why didn't you tell me?"

Killian gets off the bed and stands in front of me,

putting distance between us. "Because it would have done nothing. I did it at first because I just wanted to get to know you. I wanted to get to know the girl I met at the ball all those years ago because you were the only person to interest me. I know if I would have revealed who I was it wouldn't have ended well."

"But how do you know that?" I stand up and walk towards him. "You don't know how things would have turned out. But instead of telling me you continue to force yourself in my life-"

"I didn't do that," Killian cuts me off, his dark eyes cutting to mine. "You're the one who was trying to get to know me, making me open up, and bringing down all my walls when I didn't want to. I told you not to make me fall in love with you, Reign. Because me being obsessed with you since we were kids was enough damage. But now you're slowly breaking down all those walls and it's fucking everything up and the ending won't be a good one. I can promise you that."

I furrow my eyebrows at him. "But how do you know? You can't live life constantly on the edge, waiting for a disaster to happen. You should have told me it was you instead of hiding it from me. Things could have ended differently."

Killian furrows his eyes this time and looks like he's about to laugh. "Are you kidding me? Your dad would have shot me if you told him that we started a relationship with a midnight text. Things happened the way they were supposed to."

"But you started off everything as a lie. You didn't tell me about you still working with your dad, you didn't tell me that you were Star, and you already knew everything about me, you lied about you and your dad's relationship. You came here with an intention to kill my dad. You expect me to just welcome you back with open arms?"

"No, I wouldn't expect you to, but I did expect you to understand it from my point of view. I didn't want to tell you about my dad because I fucking liked you Reign. I started to like you more and more as the days went by and then when I did want to tell you it was too late, and my dad found me and your dad. I didn't know your dad was going to get shot or that they were going to ambush us. If I did, I would have never gone on that walk and I would have stayed with you. If I knew it was going to be our last time together, I would have stayed with you and confessed everything."

A tear finally falls. "Killian, you still should have been honest with me, since the beginning." I walk closer to him. "We could have figured it all out and things would have been easier. You know I wouldn't just throw everything away and everything we built because of your dad. I know you probably don't understand love but when people are in love they don't care about the other issues. They still make things work."

Killian shakes his head lightly. "I told you not to," he whispers and looks away from me.

I put my hand on his cheek and force him to look back at me. "It's so easy to fall in love with you Killian. I didn't force it, but I couldn't stop it either. I wish things between us were easier, but I guess the universe has other plans for us. I never felt this way towards anyone, and I know that feeling this way with you is supposed to happen because it happened so easily, and it crept up on me without me even realizing it."

Killian shakes his head again and tears form in his eyes. "You're going to hate me."

"I could never hate you." I furrow my eyebrows at him and bring him closer to me. "Why would I hate you?" Killian's mind and heart are fighting with one another. I can tell he wants to tell me, but something is stopping him. "Tell me," I beg, looking up at him with pleading eyes.

Killian grabs my wrists and kisses my wrists before pulling me closer to him and putting his hands around my jaw, holding my face in his huge hands that make me feel so small.

"Run away with me."

I furrow my eyebrows at him. "What?"

"Run away with me, just for a little while," Killian repeats.

My heart is telling me to go and do it, do it all for love.

Risk it all for love.

But my head, the rational and good girl part of me, is saying to stay home and abide by my dad's rules.

But the heart always gets what it wants.

"Okay."

FORTY
Reign

I can't believe I actually said yes to this.

I can't believe I'm getting on a plane with Killian to run away.

Okay, maybe not run away because I'll probably end up coming back but I can't believe I'm going with Killian.

Papa is going to be pissed.

It didn't take me long to pack all my stuff but once I was all packed, we left through my bedroom window and got into Killian's car.

Killian drove to the plane pretty quick.

We're on the plane now, waiting for take off.

Killian told me to look around the plane while he talks to the pilot. His plane is for sure top tier luxury. His whole plane is basically blacked out. It has some white accents in the interior, but it's mostly blacked out.

I walk towards the bedroom all the way at the end. Killian said the bedroom was nice a big for the both of us as well as a bathroom.

I've been in plenty of jets but this one is by far the most expensive one I've probably been in.

The De Luca's are richer than God and have more money than anyone in the world.

Killian's one of a kind Bugatti Chiron and this jet can vouch for that.

"What do you think?" Killian wraps his arms around my midsection, and I feel his lips touch the side of my neck.

I smile and hold onto his arms around me, blushing.

"It's nice."

Killian turns me around and he gives me a teasing smirk. "Just nice?" He raises an eyebrow. I rest my hands on his shoulders while he rests his on my hips. "I spent a good fifty million on this."

"Why black?" I ask, tilting my head slightly.

"Because it used to be my favorite color. Now I need to make another one."

I furrow my eyebrows. "Why would you spend another fifty million on a private jet when you already have this one?'

"Because I have a new favorite color," Killian says, his eyes almost sparkling or something.

"What is it?"

"Blue. Not light blue though," Killian says while looking in my eyes intensely so that I feel like I'm losing my breath or something. "Like dark blue. Your eye color, maybe?" Killian leans down, his lips nearly touching mine, but he moves back and nods his head. "Yea, your eye color is my new favorite color I think."

I don't reply, I just kiss him.

Killian smiles into the kiss and of course kisses back. He lets me control the kiss for a little bit before he takes over. He puts his hand around my throat and guides the kiss.

Both of our breathing picks up as we chase the euphoric feeling, breathing and swallowing it in.

My entire body is on fire as he squeezes my throat lightly. His tongue traces over my bottom lip and my entire body fills with butterflies.

His kiss is so unexpectedly possessive that it shocks me and sends tingles down my spine to the spot between my legs. I think I might pass out from how much Killian is taking from me.

He is quite literally taking my breath, body, soul, and if I'm not carful, he's going to have my heart.

"Killian," I beg against his mouth.

"You stress me the fuck out Reign. You have no clue how much you're fucking things up for me," he says against the kiss.

I trail my hands down his chest, and they stop at the

waistband of his pants. "Let me help you then," I whisper against his lips.

He groans and bites my bottom lip. "I'll ruin you."

"Then ruin me," I beg against his mouth, my thighs clenching at the reminder of him on top of me.

I've missed him.

I know it's only been a week, but it felt so long.

I unbuckle his belt and put my hand in his trousers. My hand makes contact with his dick and a deep groan spills from his mouth into mine. Killian trails his fingers into my hair and pulls me back. "You better know what you're getting yourself into by doing this."

"I want to," I say, looking up at him through my lashes as I kneel down.

Killian rests his hand in my hair, playing with the strands while looking down at me. His stare makes my entire body heat up.

I've never actually done this before but all I know is that I want to know how to please Killian and make him feel relieved since he's been doing it for me.

I pull his pants down and am faced with his dick. He's long, thick, and has veins running to the tip. He was painfully hard; you can tell by the pre-come leaking out of the tip.

I lean in and lick the tip, tasting him for the first time.

Killian groans and throws his head back from the

simple gesture. I use my hands to hold him at the base and fit whatever I can into my mouth.

"Fuck, Reign," Killian tangles his fingers in my hair, pushing me back and forth on his dick. I get more comfortable and fit more in my mouth, moaning with his dick in my mouth as drool leaks from the side. I feel myself getting wetter as I hear him above me groaning and saying my name. Being on your knees for a man is a sign of submission but I don't feel that at all with Killian. He's giving me complete control and letting me enjoy the feel of his dick along my tongue. "You're doing so good, baby. Just like that," he says, making me feel butterflies between my legs. I squeeze my thighs together and shift, making Killian's dick slide further inside my mouth. I gag but Killian holds my head still. "You're okay, breathe through your nose, baby."

I do as he says and breathe through my nose as he forces himself further down my throat. I moan as he moves inside my mouth, groaning and threading fingers through the strands of my hair, pulling and tugging.

Desire pools between my legs and all I want is for him to bring me back up and just force himself inside me.

I rest my hands on his hard thighs as he thrusts in and out of my mouth. I look up at him and see his face filled with euphoria.

Before I think he's about to come he tugs my hair back and his dick slips from my mouth.

I cough as he throws me on the bed and shreds off my sleeping shirt and shorts, throwing them somewhere behind him.

"Killian-" he cuts me off with a hard thrust inside me. "Oh, my god!" I scream and press my head against the bed.

"Who makes you come, Reign?" he asks, pushing deep inside me to the point where I can feel him in my stomach.

"You," I moan, gripping the sheets in front of me.

He groans and each thrust sends a wave of heat through me. Killian holds the back of my neck and presses my head against the bed as he rocks inside me.

My first orgasm hits me so hard to the point where I scream. I swear I see stars behind my eyes, and I tighten my fists against the sheets, clenching around Killian who's still moving roughly inside me.

"I've been dreaming about that sound, Reign. You have no clue. All night and day that I was away from you." He leans down and trails kisses along the back of my neck while still thrusting inside me.

I feel warmth fill me, him claiming me in a way. He slowly thrusts inside me, making sure I take every drop.

And I swear, I think I just black out.

Forty-One

Killian

A phone buzzing wakes me up.

I turn around and unwrap my arms from Reign to grab my phone.

Ten missed calls on my phone from my dad make me groan.

I turn back to Reign and see her still sleeping.

She's naked underneath the covers so her bare shoulders are on display.

I press a soft kiss on her shoulder. "I'll be back," I whisper, and Reign just groans but I know she probably doesn't hear me.

I get out of the bed and throw on my briefs. I grab my phone and leave the bedroom going to the main seating area of the plane.

I press my dad's contact name and hold the phone to my ear. "Killian," my dad says.

I stay quiet for a few seconds, preparing myself for the fucking headache that's about to come.

"Yea," I mumble.

"I'm going to fucking throw you in the nearest pit of fire I can find and then bring you back to life just so I can do it all over again."

So, before I left, I decided to trash his office.

I burned a hole in his floor.

So now he has a fire stain in the middle of his office.

Think of it as a big fuck you to him for trying to tell me what to do.

"Let's see if you can try and find me. It'll be a fun little game," I deadpan.

"You're not a goddamn child, Killian. Stop running away and come home. You're stressing your mom out and she doesn't need this."

My jaw clenches. "Don't fucking talk about her."

"She's my wife, last time I checked. If you're fucking stressing her out, I'll do everything in my power to make it stop. I can't lose your mom and you know that, so come home."

I already talked to my mom before I left.

I had to see her once because I didn't know how long I'd be gone for.

I told her I was going to be gone for a while, but I'll come back.

She asked me if it was about a girl, specifically the girl I was watching over during the mission.

I didn't answer.

I just left that question hanging in the air because she knows.

She told me, a mom always knows.

She let me leave and told me to stay safe and not to be stupid.

I promised I would call her while I was away.

I know I have to be back home in about a month or so because there is the gala, so I have no choice but to be present for that.

"I'm not coming home. I'll be back before the gala but don't expect me anytime soon."

"Killian, why are you doing this? It's just a girl. Malcolm's daughter out of all people. You could find so many other women. Why waste your time on her? You don't have much time-"

"Because I want to. Insult her again and I'll burn your office to the ground. I'll personally make sure to become boss and I'll fucking burn everything to the ground. Your entire empire, everything. Don't test me and don't ever fucking disrespect her like that again."

"This isn't how you do things."

"What did you do when you fell in love with the enemy?" I ask him.

He stays silent before sighing and saying, "I didn't care."

"Exactly. Ask me if I fucking care," I say before hanging up and throwing the phone on the table. A door opens making my attention shift. Reign comes out of the room with the blanket around her shoulders, covering her all the way up to her chin. My eyes darken, realizing that she's completely bare underneath the blanket. I don't want to risk anyone seeing her like that. Only one allowed to see her like that is me. I stand up making Reign stop in her tracks. "Turn around and go back in the room."

She furrows her eyebrows at me innocently.

Seriously not seeing the problem.

"Why?"

I walk up to her and turn her around, so she faces the bedroom door. I lean down, my lips brush against her ear. "Because I don't want anyone to see what belongs to me."

I move my hand underneath the blanket and grab her bare breast, I pinch her nipple making her whimper and lean against me.

I walk us inside the room and close the door behind me, locking it.

I throw her on the bed and hold myself above her.

I press my lips against her and Reign shivers against

me. She lets go of the blanket and it slowly falls off her chest, making her nipples graze my chest.

My hand trails up her stomach and she inhales and breathes heavily in my mouth. I pinch her nipple again and twist it before massaging her boob.

"You're distracting me because something happened," Reign says against my lips, and I hate how much she knows me already after such little time.

I take my lips off her and trail my kisses down her chest. "It's nothing you need to worry about."

"But I want to worry about it," she says before whimpering when I blow on her nipple. I take her breast in my mouth and Reign gasps.

I nibble on the nipple before licking it and pressing soft kisses around her breast before moving to the next one.

"You don't need to. My dad was just being difficult," I say before taking her entire breast in my mouth and sucking on it. Fuck I love how perfect her breasts are for me. Reign falls towards the edge as I pay good attention to her breasts, struggling to remember what we're even talking about. "I bet I can make you come just from playing with these pretty nipples," I say before biting one of her nipples.

"Stop," Reign says, pushing me off of her. I don't move, instead I lay on top of her and rest my head on her chest. "Tell me what happened," she begs but her eyes are glossy from lust, and I already know she's clenching her thighs together.

I shrug. "My dad's just being difficult. He wants me home but I'm not going. I want to be here with you."

"But won't there be retaliation for you not obeying him?" Reign asks, playing with the strands of my hair.

I nod my head. "Yea but I don't care, as long as I have you."

Reign smiles softly at me before pressing her lips against mine.

For a little while, things will be okay.

But I know eventually the end is near.

It's coming.

I can feel it.

FORTY-TWO

KILLIAN

I took Reign to this property in the Caribbean that I own.

The plane ride wasn't that long, maybe a 10-to-11-hour flight.

We slept most of the flight after fooling around and then we ate some dinner that the attendants provided for us.

I enjoyed the flight because I had Reign in my arms so there wasn't anything to complain about.

"So where exactly are we?" Reign asks as we walk inside the house.

My men on the island are going to bring in her bags eventually because for now I just want to focus on Reign exploring the house and I didn't want her carrying her own bags inside.

"We are in the Caribbean, my island in the British Virgin Islands," I say, closing the door behind her.

"You own this island?" Reign's eyes widen as she looks back at me. I smile and nod my head. "How? Why would you own an entire island?"

"In case I have a moment like this when I want to be alone. No one knows about this property." I shrug and follow Reign as she explores the house.

I bought this piece of land when I was eighteen years old. I bought a lot of properties when I was eighteen so that I could invest in them. I keep all my properties private, so no one knows where to find me in case I want some time alone.

"Who takes care of the island?"

"I hired some people. They live on the island, and I have food and other goods transported so they have everything they need."

Reign walks through the living room. There is nothing special about this house. It's like all of my other properties, they have furniture, some decorations, some small touches but nothing that has to do with me.

All of my personal belongings are at my parents home because that's where I am most of the time.

Reign walks inside the kitchen and she sits herself on the counter.

I stand in front of her, between her legs as she looks around the kitchen.

"I like it. It's a nice house."

"You haven't seen the upstairs yet," I rest my hands on her thighs and press a kiss to the side of her throat.

Reign shivers from just one kiss and me rubbing her thighs up and down.

She's wearing my sweater since I ripped off her shirt. I also gave her some sweatpants so that no one would look at her legs.

Especially in those thin short shorts where you can see the outline of her butt.

But Reign is naive and doesn't understand that people will love to look at every inch of her.

I mean I do.

"You should decorate it more. Put some nice touches on it," Reign whispers, leaning her head to the side so I can access more of her neck.

"Like what? Mm?" I whisper, pressing soft kisses along her neck.

"Um..." she mumbles, closing her eyes and just relaxing in my hold.

She wraps her legs around my waist, pulling me closer. I breathe heavily in her neck, inhaling her.

I'm going to make her start living in my sweater so that she can always fucking smell like this.

She smells fucking good.

She smells like mine.

Reign grabs my shirt, subconsciously pulling me

closer. "Lost your train of thought?" I mumble, moving my hands under her sweater to finish what I was doing on the plane.

She made me talk about what happened with my dad instead of wanting to go for another round with her on the plane. After I talked about my dad with her, she read her book while I was responding to messages and emails from other businesses. I would watch Reign every now and then just because I enjoy watching her read and the reactions she would have when reading certain things.

But now that we're here, away from our families just for a little bit, we can relax and just enjoy each other.

I grab her breasts and play with her nipples. I noticed that she loves whenever I do that or show attention to them.

"You're distracting me," she says, panting softly. "I can't think with you." She tightens her legs around me. I bring the sweater up and over her head, throwing it on the counter. I trail my kisses down her neck towards her chest. Reign leans her head back, enjoying the feel of my lips on her. "Killian," she moans.

"Mmm?" I ask while paying attention to her breasts and taking one nipple in my mouth, nipping at it.

I look up at Reign but she's in her own world. Her eyes are closed, and face is filled with pleasure. I switch to the other nipple, giving her attention because Reign deserves all kinds of attention.

Reign's hand grabs my belt. "We should really stop."

I trail my kisses up and ghost my lips over hers. "But I can't. You are just too fucking good, Reign. Like a goddamn addiction." I press my mouth to hers.

She unbuckles my belt and I take her shorts off.

We're so quick with it, desperate to feel each other as we rip away our clothes. I hiss when I feel Reign grab my dick and put it against her pussy.

The counter is at a perfect height. I could easily slip into her without adjusting her to my level. I hiss against her lips and thrust into her hand.

We keep having sex bare, I know we shouldn't because there's no way in hell, we can have a baby when we might have a war but God, I can't go back to using a condom.

Reign's the first girl I've never used a condom with and after her I can't go back.

And the fact that she swallows up my seed so perfectly, there's no way in hell I'll ever think about going back.

I bite Reign's lip as I push inside her harshly.

Reign gasps.

I groan against her lips.

She's still tight and feels so perfect. It's like she was perfectly carved just for me.

My grip on her hips tightens as I push myself all the way inside. She grips my shoulder and tightens her legs around me, pulling me closer.

"Fuck, baby." I look down at us connected and then

look up at her face filled with intense pleasure and a glint of sweat. "You're perfectly made for me Reign, you feel it right?" Reign nods her head, her eyelids fluttering closed.

I press my thumb against her clit and Reign moans and thrusts against me. "More, Killian. I want more."

"Tell me what you want, baby. I'll give it to you." I kiss down her neck, sucking and biting her skin.

"I want harder. I just need more-" I move us off the counter and slam her against the wall nearby. I grip her ass in my hands and move in and out fast and hard. "Oh my god! Killian! Oh!" she screams, scratching her nails down my back making me feel the burn. Reign clenches around me and digs her nails in my back as she freezes, coming around me. "Killian, Killian, Killian!"

God how could I ever live without this?

How could I ever leave this world without taking Reign with me?

It's like taking coke from a fucking addict and expecting him to be completely okay with it.

"God, I wish I could take you with me," I say against her lips as I come inside her, so deep I'm pretty sure she won't be able to get rid of me.

I'll be fucking everywhere.

Her heart, body, mind, soul.

There won't be any getting rid of me, not if I can't help it.

FORTY-THREE
REIGN

KILLIAN TOLD ME THAT WE'RE GOING ON A DATE tonight.

It's our second day here in the Caribbean.

Yesterday after we were done in the kitchen, we went upstairs and spent the rest of our night there. We only went back downstairs to make some food, but we ended up bringing it up to the bedroom.

The bedroom is so nice and big. He has black accents everywhere, kind of matching his plane.

I can't help but wonder what his bedroom at his actual house looks like.

Killian told me has so many properties around the world like a few around Italy, one in Greece, here, and then an estate in California.

This morning we woke up early to do some training

like usual. Training has become our regular thing. After training we took a shower together and Killian couldn't keep his hands to himself.

He was going to fuck me, but I told him I needed a break because I think in the last three days, he's fucked me a total of five times.

Three times on the plane, once in the kitchen, and once in the bedroom last night.

Plus, he hasn't been using a condom either which I don't mind but at the same time we need to be safe.

But I'm on birth control so I think we're safe.

I still can't help but have this uneasy feeling in my stomach.

Like I should be expecting something.

I went to the bathroom while Killian was eating breakfast and started throwing up. I remember looking in the mirror and feeling that same feeling. I also started to think about how I haven't gotten my period for a while.

All of the thoughts ran through my head as I stared at myself in the mirror this morning.

I was in the bathroom for a good minute until Killian knocked on the door wondering why I was taking too long.

When I get back home, there is no doubt I will be taking a pregnancy test.

But for now, I want to enjoy my time with Killian and just pretend for a little while longer we'll be okay.

But I should be fine I probably haven't had my period because of stress maybe? My stomach looks normal.

I'm just trying to think positive because he can not have a baby under these circomestances.

Tonight, for dinner I'm wearing a dark blue bustier summer dress. It's classy but casual and perfect for tonight's dinner. I have my hair in soft curls and put on light makeup.

Killian told me to meet him downstairs whenever I'm ready.

I walk downstairs and see no sign of Killian anywhere. I look in the kitchen, living room, foyer, and can't find him anywhere.

My phone dings, making me look down.

Come outside.

I do as he says and walk outside, seeing him standing in front of a car.

A dark blue Ferrari.

It's beautiful and matches the color of my dress.

"Good choice with the blue," Killian says, smiling as I walk up to him.

I can't help but blush. "Well, your favorite color is blue."

Killian grabs my hand when I'm close enough, pulls me closer and presses his lips on mine.

I swear ever since he came back, he hasn't let go of me. He is always touching me or wanting to touch me or have me near him.

My heart flutters.

Killian groans in my mouth and forces himself away from me. "God, you taste good."

"What do I taste like?" I ask him with a teasing smile.

"You taste like you belong to me."

I blush.

Again.

I can't help it.

Something about Killian and how smooth his mouth always is makes me feel like a little girl with a school crush.

Killian laughs and he opens the door to the passenger side for me to get in.

When he gets in, he starts the car and drives off.

The drive is quick. We drove for about fifteen minutes until Killian parked the car in front of a hill with stairs leading up.

During the drive I kept looking up at the sky, admiring the stars. It's such a perfect night for a dinner under the stars.

Killian opens my door and holds my hand.

We walk up the stairs and when we reach the top my jaw drops. I look at Killian with wide eyes and a full heart.

I know he knows that I love him, but I never told him directly and I almost want to tell him just from this.

There is a table set up on top of the hill and candles surrounding the table. If you look over the edge you can even, see the beach below.

The whole set up is beautiful and no one has ever done something this sweet for me.

Killian walks us towards the table and pulls out my chair for me to sit down.

"Killian, this is too much," I say as I sit in my chair.

"Nothing will ever be too much for you. You only deserve the best."

Once he sits in his chair, he pours some champagne in my glass.

I don't drink, I just leave it alone on the table.

"Why'd you decide to do this?" I ask.

Killian shrugs. "I don't know, I guess I just wanted to do something nice for you." Killian licks his bottom lip, appearing nervous. "I feel a lot for you, and I just want to show it." Killian reaches over the table to hold my hand in his. "I've never felt this way about anyone. You make me feel crazy, Reign."

"I hope it's the good kind," I joke, laughing softly.

During the whole dinner, Killian holds my hand in his and rubs his thumb along the side of my hand and wrist.

They bring out some Greek garlic style chicken and roasted potatoes.

Killian asks me about Papa and if he's called or messaged me, which he has.

I just haven't mentioned it to Killian because I don't want to focus on our dads right now and what might possibly happen when we return back home.

Papa has been calling non-stop and asking me where I've gone and if it has to do with Killian.

I did text him saying not to worry and that I'm okay. I told him I was going to be gone for a little bit just to figure some things out with Killian and not to try to find me.

That didn't make him happy so I explained the situation to Mama so that she could talk to him and cool him off.

But she told me I was his little princess so of course he was going to worry.

But Mama and even Baba know that they can trust Killian with me.

Killian treats me differently than he does other people.

"Are you not worried about what's going to happen after all of this?" I ask Killian after we finish the food.

Killian looks at our adjoined hands. "As long as I have you, I'll be okay," he says softly before looking back up at me with those intense eyes of his.

And I can't help but believe him.

Forty-Four

Reign

Things with Killian have felt like a dream I never want to wake up from.

It almost feels like we're in a movie and just enjoying each other's company, not worrying about our parents or them calling constantly.

I don't want to go home.

I wish I could stay here forever but I know we'll need to go home eventually.

Something in me knows I need to and that I can't hide away on this island forever.

I get out of the bathroom after freshening up and see Killian isn't in the room where I last saw him. He was waiting for me to get out, on the bed.

I furrow my eyebrows, wondering where he went. I

leave the room to look for him. He isn't downstairs or in the guest room. There is an office down the hall from the kitchen which is the only place I haven't checked.

I open the door and my jaw falls to the floor as I see Killian with no shirt on sitting on the floor, surrounded by fire.

There is a circle of fire around him and I almost think it's a fire that's not controlled but it's in a perfect circle, almost like he created it.

"Killian," I say, making Killian's head lift and look at me.

His eyes are dark and void.

Like there is nothing behind them.

Killian is definitely not a hero and he never pretended to be one either.

Everyone hates villains but they don't know that they love like a hero never could.

I want to go to him but the fire between us stops me.

"Leave," he says only one word that almost breaks my heart, but I don't budge.

"What's wrong? What are you doing?" I say, looking at the fire surrounding him.

"Leave, I don't want you to get hurt," Killian says, and it's like there is a double meaning behind his words. I take a step closer to the fire, but he yells. "What did I fucking say?!" Killian then throws a bucket of liquid on the fire before stepping towards me and grabbing my arms. "Why can't you just fucking leave?! It'd make things so much easier," he says, softly shaking me.

What is going on with him?

I thought that everything was okay.

I furrow my eyebrows and put my hands on his face. "Why are you being like this? What happened?"

"Just go. I'll call a plane, but you need to go and stay away from me," he says, trying to take my hands off his face but I don't let him, and I hold my ground.

"Killian, what's going on? Talk to me, please. We can fix this," I say calmly, because I don't know what he'll do next or how he'll react.

I've never seen something, or someone do something like that before, I don't know if I should be scared or not.

I know I should run away because for some reason Killian is filled with darkness and that darkness will kill me slowly but at the same time, I can't leave him.

Killian makes me feel so much and I can't lose that.

I can't lose him.

"Please, talk to me, what's going on? Is it your dad?" I ask, furrowing my eyebrows, trying to figure out what the hell is going on.

Killian shakes his head slowly and when his eyes meet mine, he almost looks guilty.

Like he's hiding something big.

"You just can't, Reign. You can't be with me."

My heart cracks, I swear I hear it.

A tear forms in my eye. "What are you talking about?"

"You will get hurt. It's not a maybe, it's fucking written in the stars that you'll get destroyed. So please, I'm begging you to run now, no matter what I say."

I shake my head as the tear finally falls. "I don't want to. I love you Killian. I told you, I'm here to stay." Killian licks his lips and shakes his head lightly. I grab his chin and make him stare down at me. "I'm here with you, Killian. I'm not leaving, no matter what."

"You're gonna get burned," Killian whispers, our lips slowly go towards one another.

"Good thing I happen to love fire."

Killian smiles softly and puts his hands on my jaw and brings my face to his.

He immediately thrusts his tongue in my mouth and glides it along mine. While kissing me, he takes my towel off and flings it across the room. He runs his hands down my thighs and groans.

"Fuck, did you shave?" Killian asks, nipping at my bottom lip.

I nod. "I do laser hair removal."

"Perfect," he says, making me confused. He removes his lips from me. "Lay on the floor and spread your legs." I do as he says, eager and confused.

I feel the cold air brush against my bare pussy making

me shiver and want to close my legs, but I know Killian will punish me for it probably.

He walks behind me to his desk. I hear ruffling around, but I don't turn my head. I hear Killian come back and see him cover my eyes with a piece of cloth.

Everything is dark and I feel my other senses heighten. "What are you doing?" I ask.

"I don't know what your limits are, but I want to test them," Killian says, making anxiety rush through my body. Anticipation floods through my veins. "It's going to hurt but it'll feel good. Do you trust me?"

Without a doubt in my mind, I nod my head. "Yes."

"Safe word is 'fire' okay?"

"Okay," I say, a shiver running through my body again.

I hear stuff rustle around in the room before feeling Killian's hands rest on my knees that are bent.

I twitch from the touch and feel his lips on mine. He kisses me softly, as if saying he's here for me and that I can trust him.

Which I don't doubt I can.

I would rip my heart out of my chest and give it to him if I could.

Killian kisses his way down my body until I feel his hot breath hit my pussy.

I moan and my thighs clench as Killian breathes me in before he leans forward and puts his tongue on my clit. Stars explode behind my lids, and I can barely breathe.

Killian brings his fingers to my clit, playing with it before thrusting his tongue inside me.

He isn't wasting time on pleasuring me. My eyes roll behind the cloth and I squirm under his touch. "Killian," I moan, curling my toes and trying to get closer to him.

Pleasure builds up inside me so quickly, like a storm almost.

Killian rubs my clit fast and hard and I can't stop moving from his hold and I try to stay still but as more and more of the pleasure builds, the more I can't hold it.

Killian switches and uses his finger to ram inside me at a rapid pace while his tongue gives my clit one flick before I fall apart on his mouth.

He cleans me up slowly while I relax in his hold while my body starts to slowly build up for another climax.

My head feels fuzzy especially since I can't see anything.

"Remember, it's going to hurt but it'll feel good after. I just need you to trust me, okay?"

"I trust you," I whisper, waiting and wondering what he plans on doing with my body.

I'm his for the taking.

Ready to be burned.

Killian kisses every spot on my body. Paying attention

to every inch and crevice. I moan softly and relax in his arms.

By the time he starts paying attention to my pussy again I'm already on edge and aching for another release.

I flinch when I feel a cold, wet cloth touch my stomach and then suddenly, what feels like fire touches my skin.

I moan and thrash before Killian wipes it with a wet cloth again. "What was that?" I ask in a breathless tone.

My heart pounds against my rib cage and I lift my head as if I can see Killian.

He does it again and I flinch before Killian wipes away the heat with a cold cloth. "Fire." I furrow my eyebrows while feeling an ache between my legs. I feel empty and I need Killian to fill it and make it all better. "What are you thinking?" Killian asks softly.

I shake my head. "I don't know."

Killian moves himself between my legs and I feel his hair graze the inside of my thighs and his breath hits my pussy and I try to scoot closer to him, but he doesn't let me. "Don't move. Under any circomestance. I don't want to hurt you." I hear Killian say before his lips connect with my pussy.

He swipes the cold cloth on my stomach before I feel a hot, burning sensation on my skin.

"Killian!" I yell as I feel his tongue slide inside me.

The burn with Killian's tongue on me feels euphoric. I don't even know how to describe it.

Killian swipes the burn away with a cold cloth and I feel like I'm out of breath and can barely breath. Killian doesn't stop licking me.

Pleasure rages through my body as Killian burns me while licking me.

My release is tipping towards the edge, and I want to let go.

"You're doing so good, baby. Keep holding it," Killian mutters between my legs.

"I can't-I need-I need to come," I yell, trying my best not to squirm.

"I want you to see how you fall apart with my tongue between your legs and my fire on your skin," Killian says before ripping away the cloth. The light burns my eyes first before I am faced with Killian between my legs, his hands holding a lighter and a cloth with his dark eyes staring into mine. "Watch me make this pretty pussy come with the touch of my tongue and the burn of my flame," Killian says before taking a long lick of me.

I throw my head back, but Killian doesn't like that, so he swipes the cold cloth on my stomach making me look back down.

He lights his flame against my stomach, and I see fire playing on my stomach.

I know I should be scared but instead I can't help but feel the pleasure from the burn.

Killian flicks his tongue against my clit and says, "come."

I moan Killian's name as he keeps going, licking me and burning me.

It's all too much.

The pleasure and burn is all too intense.

I can't do anything except scream Killian's name and clench my thighs around him.

FORTY-FIVE

KILLIAN

WE HAVE TO GO BACK SOON.

I've been counting down the days since we got to this island until we have to go back but I don't want to.

But Reign isn't like me.

She doesn't have a broken family where her mom is dying or where her dad is a dick who doesn't care about his kids.

She won't understand running away when she has such a good thing going on at home while I just have a fucked-up ending.

We're sitting on the beach right now.

It's peaceful.

She's wrapped in my arms, leaning her whole body against my chest as she listens to my heart while I feel hers beating against her chest. We're looking up at the stars and just enjoying each other's presence.

We have to leave soon.

We've been here for almost a month, but I know we have to go back because the gala is in a month. We have to do our own separate preparations for the gala, and I have to let Reign get her normal life back.

"What do you think will happen?" Reign asks.

The ending.

No, you or me or us.

"I wish I knew," I say, instead of exposing my truth. Anything is better than the truth, I think to myself while feeling my heart thump against my chest as if it knows. I swear all this fucking stress is making me feel weaker as days go by and it almost feels like fire is constantly surrounding my heart. "It all feels better when I'm with you."

"I think we'll be okay. I have hope." My sweet, innocent girl. My sweet innocent Star who's never been hurt by the world. She has so much hope and holds stars in her eyes that she doesn't even know. I don't say anything. I hold her closer to me and kiss the side of her head before resting my head on her shoulder. Reign looks down at my arms and she trails her finger along my tattoos. "What do your tattoos mean? You have so many."

"Pick one and I'll tell you," I whisper in her ear.

I can't see her face, even though I wish I could, but I

know she's probably smiling. She points to the dagger going through the ace card on my arm.

"That represents my parents' love. I may not like my dad most of the time, but I will always envy him and my mom's love."

Reign turns her head to me and smiles. "I like that one."

I kiss her because I can't help it. She blushes and looks down at my arm after. "And this one?"

She points to a Coldplay album cover tattoo.

"My favorite band. I love their music, so I wanted to tattoo it on my arm."

"I like Coldplay. They have good songs." Reign points to a devil tattoo on my other arm. "What's this big one?"

I lick my lips before saying, "I think of myself as my devil. Everyone says my dad is the devil and everyone says I'm the devil's son. Sometimes they say I'm the devil because I can be worse than my dad."

Reign turns to look at me and holds my face in her hand.

I always love when she does that because then her eyes focus on me, only me, and her eyes are the only place I want to stay in.

"You are not and never will be your dad," she says firmly. "You are Killian De Luca. You can be mean sometimes, but I like it when you're mean."

I smile at her and raise my eyebrow. "Yea?" Reign

smiles back and nods her head. "You love when I'm mean. It gets you all hot."

Reign shakes her head lightly and swats my chest. "Be quiet." She leans back into my arms. "And this one?" she asks, pointing to a patch of stars.

"When we first met, I knew I could never forget you, so I got stars. I knew we'd meet again; I knew you were going to impact my life, so I basically wrote our name in the stars on my skin."

"Really?" she asks as I feel her heartbeat speed up against my palm on her chest.

"Yes. You and I were meant to be. Our fate is written in the stars. I believe that us, here together, was meant to be."

Reign doesn't even know that I plan on getting a lion tattoo for her with the stars designed as the lion's mane.

I don't want to tell her until I actually have it done though.

We have to first survive this.

I tried to make her leave two weeks after we got here but instead, I played with her body.

Since that night in the office, we have just gone on so many adventures and made memories. My dad calls and ruins my mood but Reign always makes it better whether it be lighting a flame on her or just holding me while we sleep.

She loves the fire shit, and I didn't expect her to. She takes the burn like a champ.

She's a goddamn natural when it comes to fire.

And God, it fucking turns me on.

That night in the office, with the fire, I've never done it to anyone, but I've always wanted to do it to someone.

I've done it on myself but that's because I wanted to touch fire without getting burned.

No one told me touching Reign Pierce would quite literally burn me.

And she doesn't even know.

She says she loves me every day.

Before we go to sleep, when we wake up, during dinner, sex, showers, or randomly throughout the day.

Like she knows I need to hear it even though I haven't said those words to her yet.

But staring down at her with those big blue eyes with stars in them.

I can't help it.

"I love you," I whisper in her ear.

Reign turns her head to look at me so quickly I assume that she might have gotten whiplash.

"What?"

I look down at her lips. "I love you, Reign Pierce."

She smiles and presses her lips to mine. "I love you, Killian De Luca."

I'm just hoping our love doesn't go up in flames.

FORTY-SIX

REIGN

IT'S BEEN A WEEK SINCE I GOT BACK FROM THE private island with Killian.

Since then, I've been staying in bed and Baba has been bringing me tea and soup since that seems to be the only thing I can keep down.

I was doing my best to hold down my vomit on the island with Killian and luckily, I only threw up once in front of him. I'm not sure if he heard or knew that I was throwing up a bunch of other times.

I still haven't taken a pregnancy test and I'm not sure I want to because then it will just confirm what I already know.

I don't even look pregnant which is the crazy thing.

My phone dings so I reach over to my side table and grab it.

I miss you.

I smile and my face heats up.

Killian and I text every single day and he always calls me before I end up going to bed. I wish he was here with me, holding me while I fall asleep. It's only been a week, but my body craves his.

I miss you too.

What are you doing?

Just laying down watching a movie.

He messages back but a knock on my door pulls my attention away from him.

I put my phone on the side table as I see Baba walk in.

She has a plate filled with greens, meat, and some baked potatoes on the side. "I brought you something different this time. Hopefully you can keep that down. If not, I'll keep making you soup."

I sit up and lay against my headboard. "Thank you, Baba," I say when she puts the plate on the side table. My stomach instead starts to growl when I smell the meat. It almost feels like it's flipping. I don't want to disappoint her or be rude because she made this, but I really feel like not eating it.

Baba sits down next to me on the bed. "How are you feeling?" she asks, putting strands of my hair to the side.

"Good, I think I got something when I was away."

"How's Killian?" Baba asks.

My stomach churns but I ignore it.

Baba and Mama are the only ones who weren't super pissed at me. Papa though, he was on another level of pissed off.

He pulled me into his office, still bandaged up from the bullet wound, and told me how stupid and reckless I was for leaving with Killian.

But he doesn't understand how I feel about him and how strongly I love him. He has no clue that I would quite literally do anything for him if he asked.

It's stupid to be this weak over a guy, one I have only known for about five months, but I feel like Killian, and I have this strong connection and like we were meant to be together and have our moment.

We were bound to fall in love with one another.

Like Killian said on the island, our fate is written in the stars, and we were meant to fall in love.

Baba understands and so does Mama.

Papa just hates the fact that it's Killian.

"He's good," I say quietly. "He's just busy dealing with his dad and mom."

"Do you know how his mom is feeling?"

I shake my head no.

I would love to meet his mom someday. I don't want to tell him that because obviously things right now between our families are tense, but I know Aria is a sweet woman and she only cares about Killian's happiness. It's his dad that I need to worry about.

"I know she isn't doing well though. He told me that she's back on chemo again."

"Poor Killian, having to deal with all that."

"He's strong," I say, believing it.

"And how are you?" I look up at her and furrow my eyebrows as my stomach churns again. I almost feel like there is something stuck in my throat. "About everything?'

"It's stressful but I believe in Killian and I. That's why I'm not worried. We'll be okay," I say, giving her an encouraging smile but it drops when I feel bile come up my throat.

I fling the blankets off of me and run towards my restroom. I drop down in front of the toilet, and everything comes out.

I can't stop the vomit from coming out. I feel Baba sitting next to me and holding my hair back.

"It's okay, you're okay. You're doing good, keep going. Get everything out," she says softly while rubbing my back.

When I'm done, I spit inside the toilet and rest my head on my arms, closing my eyes.

Damn it.

I need a doctor.

I know I do.

But God, it's not the right time, especially with everything going on and Killian and I just being in the middle of all of it.

"How long has this been happening for? Don't lie."

A few weeks after Killian and I had sex for the first time.

But I don't say that.

"A few weeks," I lie.

If I tell her it's been happening for longer than she'll scold me for not going to the doctor.

She curses in Bulgarian. "Does Killian know?" I look up at Baba and shake my head. She gives me a sad look and shakes her head lightly. "He needs to know."

I shake my head and a tear falls from my eye. "But he can't. Not now, there is too much going on. It will ruin everything."

"Reign, if he loves you, he will continue to fight for you."

"How do you know?" I ask, trying to control my racing heart.

Baba puts a strand of hair behind my ear. "Because men were born to fight for women. And for you and Killian, I have a feeling you both were born to fight for each other."

FORTY-SEVEN

KILLIAN

MY MOM APPEARS WEAKER EVERY DAY.

I come inside her room every day to make sure she is doing okay or to see if she needs anything from me. I never hesitate to get her what she needs or wants.

Ever since I've come back from the Caribbean my dad has been bitching and complaining to me about everything. He's made me do some ridiculous tasks that make no sense and I know he's doing it to frustrate me and push me.

He's stressing me the fuck out and sometimes I just don't leave my room all day because of him. I would ask my mom for help, but she has enough going on to deal with without his and mine's bullshit.

But being with her makes me feel calm and at ease.

Thalia is living her best life with her husband and kid,

so she doesn't give two shits about family drama unless it's serious.

She's supposed to join us for the annual gala which is coming up in less than two weeks.

Time has flown by since Reign and I were last together.

I talk to her every single day. She told me she hasn't been feeling the best and she's usually in her room sleeping or eating whatever her grandmom makes for her.

Her dad rarely talks about me, she said. The only time he does is when he's curious if we've been talking and she always tells him that we do.

There's no point in hiding what we feel for each other because everyone already knows.

I just need to make sure my dad doesn't do stupid shit to Malcom during the gala, and we can settle on an agreement or alliance.

My dad only wants to kill Malcolm because of his brother.

I haven't talked to my dad regarding Malcom or his hatred for him because it's none of my business but if it keeps interfering with my relationship with Reign, then we're gonna have a problem.

"What are you thinking about, my little devil?" I look down at my mom who is smiling at me, weakly.

I have my arm wrapped around her while she lays

against my chest, her ear where my heart is so she can hear it.

Her smile isn't full of life, and she doesn't have her usual glow like she did before.

Cancer kills her every day, slow but deadly.

We never know how long she'll be with us for but we're hoping that the chemo does its fucking job and helps her, somehow, some way.

"I'm fine."

"You know you still never told me about that girl," my mom says in a soft voice. I furrow my eyebrows, wondering how the hell she found out about Reign when I haven't told her shit. Pretty sure my big mouth dad told her. "Don't act stupid, Killian. Your dad was shitting bricks for the past month. I've been waiting for you to come forward, but you never said a thing. Why?"

I shrug. "Because I want to introduce you to her properly. I don't want you to know about her until I am able to bring her over and show her to you."

"Who said you can't?" My mom furrows her eyebrows at me, appearing offended even though I know she isn't.

"Dad is kind of-"

"Your dad doesn't know anything." She rolls her eyes and shakes her head lightly. "Don't listen to him. He can be a dick sometimes. He's just stressed out. He loves you and wants the best for you. My health is just stressing him out because for the first time ever, he can't do anything to help me and it's killing him."

"He's going to be a mess without you. We all are."

My mom shakes her head. "Let's stop talking about it. It's depressing and I want to hear about this special girl instead."

I can't help but smile. "She's amazing, mom," I say truthfully. "She has these eyes, these big blue eyes that make you just want to escape. I love staring into her eyes. They just make me feel calm and like everything won't end up in flames," I explain while my mom stares up at me with a smile on her face. "She instantly makes me have a better mood whenever she's around. If she knows I'm stressed or something's wrong, she'll do everything she can to make me feel at ease," I explain. "I love her."

My mom looks up at me like she's insanely proud of me and that feels good. I've always loved making my mom happy and proud.

"Never thought I'd get to see the day where my youngest falls in love."

"I'm falling more in love with her every day. She makes me want to become a better person. Her love means everything to me."

I still don't know why I would ever risk losing her.

Maybe because I'm scared of the end and how she will end up being alone without me and she'll end up just hating me and I'd never want Reign to hate me.

That's the last thing that I would want.

"Does she know?"

My heart instantly races as if it knows.

"No."

My mom gives me a disapproving look. "She needs to know."

"I know. I'm just- I'm just scared."

"I know, but she needs to know so she can prepare herself."

"I don't want her to have to do that. She shouldn't have to do that mom," I try to explain but my mom just shakes her head.

"She needs to know because then when you go, she'll be even more hurt. Plus, you shouldn't be here wasting time on your dad's bullshit. You should spend your time with the person you're falling in love with. You don't have that much time-"

I tense instantly. "I know, mom. I'm just scared."

"Don't be scared. You'll ruin what you have. Focus on now because if you don't, then you'll never be able to enjoy the present. Enjoy your time with this girl because you never know when your last moment together will be."

She's not wrong.

I know she probably thinks about that since she herself doesn't have much time left.

I know my mom only cries about her time left behind

closed doors with my dad only, never in front of Thalia and me.

She can only be weak with my dad.

FORTY-EIGHT

KILLIAN

THE ANNUAL GALA THIS YEAR IS BEING HELD IN Romania since it's their turn to hold the event. The one who's in charge of the Romanian operations and empire is a guy named Daniel Titan. He recently took the role five years ago, so this is his first gala as boss.

My dad hasn't held a gala in Italy in a long time, mostly because of my mom and because she isn't doing well.

My dad wants to spend most of his time with her instead of working so he tries not to put too much on his plate.

But he does have to attend the gala, even though my mom can't. He didn't want to leave her side before we left for the jet. My mom basically had to force him out of the room.

But she'll be okay. We have cameras all over the house so my dad can do his hourly stalking and we have mom's friends there plus a nurse who is taking care of her if she needs help or anything.

My dad has been talking on the phone with her every other hour and on the phone with Layna and Emma, her best friends, to make sure she is good and still alive and breathing.

I do feel bad that he's forced to come to this event when he wants to stay with mom and make sure she's okay. I can see how stressed he is from being away from her.

Ever since my mom got diagnosed, he's never spent more than a day without her.

"Your last event as an heir." I look in the mirror and see my dad behind me looking at me.

Right now, we are getting ready in the hotel room with Leo, my dad's underboss, Alexander, and his son Landon.

My sister and Jane are getting ready in another hotel room.

Jane's husband, Rowan, was getting ready with us but he finished early and decided to go to her. He never likes being away from her.

momfucker is obsessed to a fault.

So are you.

"I know," I deadpan.

"Do you know what your role is tonight?" he asks.

I run my hand through my hair and take a deep breath.

He's fucking stressing me out again.

Since I've come back from the island with Reign, he's been on my ass, constantly making my life harder.

He gives me constant anxiety whenever I'm around him.

And it's all because I love a girl I'm not supposed to love.

I heard my mom scolding my dad in their room a few nights ago. My mom was yelling at my dad about how he's stressing me out and how it's not good for me. My dad can't help it though, it's his thing.

Especially since his wife is dying so he is trying to control something else.

Ace De Luca only cares about himself and what benefits him.

He's always been like that.

The cold, heartless king everyone knows.

Only person who can tame him is fucking dying.

"Yes," I mutter. My dad expects me to introduce myself as the new capo and the one who'll be running things. "I thought you'd be too pissed to name me capo."

"You are the rightful heir. Thalia won't take it and you still want it, yes?" My dad raises an eyebrow at me and his jaw clenches.

My hands form a fist at my sides. "Yes."

"Then you'll do as I say tonight." My dad looks away from me and instead looks at himself to make sure he looks decent. He shaved the scruff on his jaw and cut his hair making him look younger and not like his world is falling apart. "Have you spoken to that Pierce girl?"

Reign.

Of course, I have.

I call and text her every day and he knows that because he sees me on my phone or sometimes catches me talking to her. He isn't stupid.

This past month has been hell without her in my arms.

"Yes. Why does it matter?"

My dad shakes his head lightly. "Because Killian, that is Malcolm's daughter. He is the enemy and you're in love with the enemy. Don't you see how wrong this is? What kind of issues this will cause?"

I laugh softly and turn around to look at him instead of in the mirror. "Last time I checked, you and mom were both from groups that hated one another. Then somehow you both fell in love, and everything ended up being okay. You aren't being fair."

My dad rolls his eyes. "Life isn't fair, Killian. Get over it. Time to grow the fuck up." He says, slowly getting frustrated.

Good.

"I never expected you to be like this. Mom would praise you, but I feel like she was just talking out of her ass."

My dad's eyes darken and his jaw clenches. His whole-body tenses and he takes a step closer to me. "Don't talk about your mom like that." He glares down at me, and I feel guilt rush through me. He looks physically and mentally hurt. Like he'll do anything to protect her and her name. "I'll be damned if you talk about her like that. Say something like that again, I swear to God Killian, no one will be able to save you from my fire." He licks his bottom lip and sighs, finally calming down from his threat. "I expect you to be great, Killian."

"I will be. But I'm not doing this your way."

He narrows his eyes and looks disappointed. "You're going to fail Killian if you keep becoming weak like this over some girl. She doesn't even know about-"

I get in his face. "You don't know shit," I say in a low, almost deadly tone. "And if you see her, you're going to keep your mouth shut. Don't go up to her, don't talk to her, don't fucking breathe next to her."

My dad laughs and shakes his head, backing up from me. "You're stringing her along, son."

He isn't wrong.

My mom isn't wrong.

I'm only hurting her right now and she doesn't even know.

"You don't care. Stop acting like you do," I say.

"You're so fucked." My dad grins and throws his head back laughing.

"Landon!" I hear Alexander yell from the bathroom at the same time Landon runs out butt-naked, laughing. "Get your fucking ass over here, kid."

I look away from my dad and walk out of the room. I run my hands through my hair as I walk towards my room, trying not to fucking stress out but my heart is racing, as if it knows something I don't. I unlock my door and walk in. It's dark so I turn on the lights and when I do I see Reign sitting on the bed.

She looks up from her hands and smiles when she sees me.

All that stress and anxiety washes away. She stands up and we walk towards one another.

I pull her towards me and press my lips on her.

I haven't seen her in more than a month. My body craves hers.

My heart craves her in general.

I swear it's like my heart is beating so hard, trying to rip itself out of my chest to go to her.

Everything is quiet and my heart stops racing from the stress. "You look so fucking perfect," I say against her lips. "I'm going to try and be a gentleman and not ruin your beauty tonight."

Reign laughs against my lips. "Such a gentleman."

I trail my kisses down her neck as she leans her head to the side. "You won't be saying that when I'm in between your legs and making you scream my name."

She laughs again and swats my chest. "Perv." I give her one last kiss before pulling away. She admires me, her eyes darkening. I love how she doesn't hide her love or attraction with me. She's not afraid to admire me. "You look nice."

"Just nice?" I raise an eyebrow at her, squeezing her waist in my hands. Reign looks breathtaking as usual. She's wearing a long white silk dress. My eyes can't help but go to her breasts that look amazing in the dress, if anything they look bigger than the last time, I saw them. I push a strand of her hair behind her ear. "Be careful out there tonight, okay?"

She nods her head. "I'll be okay."

"I don't trust my dad. I just-" I sigh and lick my lips. "I just can't lose you." I rest my head on hers.

"You won't. We just have to get through this night, and we'll be okay. We'll be together forever."

My heart burns from the comment.

Not forever.

But I can hide the truth and pretend everything is okay for a little while longer.

"I love you." Ignoring the burning sensation in my chest.

"I love you, Killian."

FORTY-NINE

REIGN

"WE NEED TO GO," I WHISPER TO KILLIAN.

His arms around me as we lay in the bed. He just got done fucking me from behind.

He's relentless. Killian and I fucked two times before I told him I couldn't take it and we needed to go.

I kept my dress on because I noticed my stomach looking different in the mirror while changing. Luckily this dress isn't tight enough to show my stomach outline.

I still haven't taken a test, but I don't need to.

I don't feel like throwing up that much anymore which is good.

Now I just need to get the courage to go to the doctor.

"I wish we could stay here," Killian says, while looking at our hands interlocked.

I look up at Killian who looks almost worried.

I wonder how much stress Ace is putting on him.

Killian and I eventually get up from the bed.

"I have to go back to my room to fix my makeup and hair."

"That gentlemanly act didn't last long," Killian says, running his fingers through my hair and fixing some out of place strands. "I did warn you, didn't I?" Killian raises an eyebrow at me.

I smile and swat his chest.

Killian presses a kiss to my lips and stars explode behind my lids like always.

"I'll see you out there," I mumble against his lips.

He grips my waist in his hands and removes his lips from mine before pressing them to my forehead. "I love you."

"I love you."

We let go of each other and I leave Killian's room.

He and I talked about how tonight will go down.

We won't hide our love from our dads or other group members.

Killian said that his dad needs him to marry so he's thinking that Papa and Ace will form an alliance and we could get married.

I have hope.

I'm trying my best to be positive.

Because if I start thinking about the other possibilities, then I'll start stressing out and worrying.

Like for one, I still need to tell Killian my suspicions or that I'm even going to go to a doctor. I've been prolonging the doctor because I don't want it to be true.

Not yet at least.

Not with everything going on and possible war between Killian's family and mine.

Like does Killian even want children?

We never talked much about it, but it's always been a question I wanted to ask him.

But I know it's also a loaded question.

I turn a corner and immediately feel a large hand cover my mouth with a cloth. Panic spreads down my body and I freeze.

"I wish I didn't have to do this. But Killian can't afford this." I hear a harsh whisper in my ear before my eyes close and my body goes limp.

———

My head feels heavy as I slowly regain consciousness. I open my eyes and squint while I look around the room.

A tall figure stands in front of me, his green eyes, so familiar, staring down at me.

I widen my eyes and look closely at the person before I feel a rush of anxiety go through my body.

"Ace De Luca," I whisper as I try to move my hands that are tied behind my back.

Ace walks closer to me. "Reign Pierce. Wish we could have met under different circomestances."

Ace leans down so his face is in front of me. His eyes are the same as Killian's, void and dark. But Ace's don't have any light. It's like there is nothing behind his eyes. Like he cares for nothing. And that's scary to know.

How can Ace do all this and not feel an ounce of guilt or regret?

I can't imagine what Aria would think about all this.

I just wish that I could meet both of them in a different light.

Over dinner with Aria healthy and not dying of cancer.

But Killian and I don't have a normal love story.

We never will.

"Why am I here?" I ask.

"I just want to talk." He stands to his full height.

"Then why am I tied up if you just want to talk?"

Ace shrugs his shoulders. "In case you get any ideas."

"You're a capo while I'm just a mafia princess. I can't do anything to you," I try to explain but Ace doesn't care.

"Do you really love my son?" Ace asks, ignoring my statement.

With all my heart.

Ace doesn't know that I would literally give Killian anything he asks for.

"Yes," I say, no hesitation.

Ace nods his head slowly and licks the inside of cheek. "He was sent to kill your dad and we will get it done. I don't care if I have to be the one to do it."

"I want you and him to talk it out. I don't want a war. I never wanted one," I try to explain but it doesn't seem to matter to Ace.

"This war began long before you and Killian were born, Reign. It's your dad who won't let it go. If he backs down and stops having this vendetta, things would go way smoother."

I furrow my eyebrows at him. "You killed his brother. My Papa isn't a vengeful person. Have you ever even apologized?"

Ace laughs and shakes his head. "Would your dad really accept an apology?"

I shrug my shoulders. "Maybe."

Ace licks his lips, just like Killian does, before shaking his head again. "My son can't be relying on you, Reign. You are simply a temporary matter for him."

"Why do you say that?" I ask, confused.

"Because something isn't right with my son. He-" Ace gets cut off by the sound of a door opening. I look at the person who walked in and it's Papa aiming a gun at Ace. "Malcom," Ace says in a bored tone.

"Ace," Papa sneers while glaring at Ace. "I should kill you right now, with no hesitation," Papa says, making my heart speed up.

"Papa, no," I beg, making Papa look at me. "You can't kill him, please."

"Why? Because you're in love with Killian De Luca?" Papa raises an eyebrow at me. "Reign, no. He can't keep controlling you like this."

"I love him, Papa. Please," I beg, trying to convince him not to shoot Ace.

He can't.

Killian has to have a parent figure.

He's losing his mom.

He can't lose his dad too.

Papa looks conflicted. His hold on the gun loosens but he still aims it at Ace.

Papa is a good, sympathetic man. He isn't vengeful or full of darkness like Ace but that's because both of them were raised differently.

"You shouldn't have hesitated," Ace says before pulling out his gun and aiming it at Papa.

Shit.

Fifty

Killian

"I would like to welcome Killian De Luca to the families officially," Daniel the Romanian leader says, making everyone in the room clap. "I know we'll have good years ahead of us with you taking on the new role. Your dad must be proud."

Everyone in the room agrees which makes me want to roll my eyes.

That asshole could care less what I do.

"One thing, I want you all to know and understand is that my dad and I are not the same. He may be the devil you all are afraid of and talk about but he's nothing compared to me. This is your guys' only warning."

To be completely honest, I want to leave this fucking place and go back to the hotel room with Reign or just go on the dance floor and dance with her. I haven't seen her yet because as soon as I entered the room there had to be a meeting with all the bosses.

Leo is here but not my dad which made me suspicious of him.

"Trust me, Killian, we've heard about you. We know you aren't your dad," Manon says, the French leader.

Manon is the youngest of the leaders. He's twenty-five right now and took the role two years ago due to his dad passing from cancer.

I look forward to working with him since I've heard nothing but good things about him.

He's quiet but deadly, my favorite type of fucked up.

"Good, then we shouldn't have a problem."

We talk about a few more things, what we need to look out for, police force or some secret societies, and other business. In these private meetings we don't talk about alliances or feuds between groups because it causes issues. My dad has brought me to many meetings so I can watch and learn. This is the first meeting I've had as boss and by myself.

During the meeting and the closing statements I notice that Malcom and his underboss isn't here.

The thoughts swarming through my head make my stomach clench, especially since I haven't seen Reign either.

My heart rate picks up as I think of all the possibilities that could be happening.

My dad.

Malcom.

Reign.

Fucking Reign.

Once the meeting is over, we all leave the room, me being the first. I take out my phone and look through my messages but see none from Reign.

I grip the phone in my hand as I look around the ballroom for her, but I don't see those blue eyes anywhere.

I see Kyra and Lia sitting at a table in the back but no Reign or Malcom.

A burn hits my chest making me cough, I try to hold it in as best as I can.

I walk towards Jamie who is talking to some man across the room.

"Jamie, pleasure to see you here," I say, making Jamie turn his head towards me. He raises an eyebrow, basically asking me to leave. I look at the guy he's talking to. "Sorry to interrupt but I have important business to discuss with Jamie, here."

The guy looks annoyed but leaves.

"What can I do for you De Luca?" Jamie says in a bored tone.

"Where's Reign?" I ask, getting straight to the point.

Jamie raises an eyebrow at me. "I thought she was with you. I haven't seen her since she left the hotel room."

My jaw clenches and I feel my heart race.

I don't answer him, instead I turn around and walk towards the exit.

Jamie yells after me but I ignore him.

My dad, Malcom, fucking Reign.

All of them not being here should be a loud enough sign.

I swear if my dad touches a hair on her body, not even Satan himself can save him.

I take the elevators up to the hotel rooms.

My heart racing and my eye twitching from all the thoughts swarming through my head.

I'm overthinking.

I'm being fucking dramatic.

My dad would be stupid to do what I'm thinking.

The elevator dings and as I get out, I hear a gunshot.

My stomach fucking drops.

I take out my gun and run towards the sound of grunting and where the gunshot came from. The grunting and sounds of things falling become more prominent as I get closer and closer to a staff room door.

I push the door open and hold up my gun.

The lighting is dim, but I see my dad and Malcom fighting, punching each other until they are both bloody and bruised.

A gun is on the floor while I notice my dad's gun in his waistband.

Malcolm's underboss and one of my dad's men are fighting each other off.

But what I'm really fucking fuming over is the fact that Reign is watching all this unfold with one of my dad's men straddling her on the floor, begging the guard to let her go.

I run towards her and push the guard to the floor. I press him against the floor and start punching him, banging his head against the floor.

"Don't. You. Ever. Fucking. Touch. Her. Again," I say after each bang of his head.

"Stop! Think about this-"

"Think?" I ask, looking down at him with dark eyes. "You have no fucking clue what I'm thinking about right now."

I take my lighter out, get off of him before setting his jacket on fire.

He screams and yells as the fire spreads to his entire body.

He gets up and tries to get rid of the fire while screaming.

Malcom and my dad pause, looking at the guard on fire while I go to Reign and hold her against me.

He screams, yells, and fucking begs for someone to save him, but my mind goes to Reign.

My pulse slows and my heart feels calm for just a few seconds as I stare into her beautiful blues.

"You, okay?" I ask, holding her face in my hands while looking at every inch of her to make sure she doesn't have a scratches or bruises.

She nods her head and licks her dry lips. She turns her head to look behind me, making me turn my head.

Malcom and my dad stopped fighting as well as their soldiers. They are all bloody and bruised.

They look torn up.

My dad's eyes are void, nothing behind them.

Clouded by revenge.

"I'm so disappointed in you, Killian," my dad says calmly. He's sweating and has blood on his face and suit. I've never seen my dad get down and dirty before. He always taught me never to take revenge with your own hands unless you have to. Let other people do your dirty work. But right now, looking at him, I understand why people are shocked that he, out of all people, fell in love with my mom. It almost makes me wonder how. "I told you-"

"And I told you to fuck off and leave Reign alone! Did I not?!" I yell, still holding Reign to me. "Why can't you two just leave each other alone? What is it with this guy that makes you want to ruin his life?" I ask, mainly looking at my dad.

My dad laughs and looks at Malcolm. "Malcolm here likes being a little baby." Malcom punches him in the face before my dad punches back. Reign flinches making me let go of her and go in between them. I push my dad back as he fights against me. "Killian, move out of the way."

"You're done. Enough is enough. I won't let you kill him," I say, pushing him away from Malcolm.

My dad stops suddenly and just glares at me.

He appears calm so quickly it almost makes me wary.

My dad.

Ace De Luca.

My mom praised him so much and all I see right now is the monster he keeps hidden and tucked away.

It's hard to believe that he actually used to be a decent person and was loving and caring when he met my mom but now, he's finally showing his true colors.

Probably because now, he has no reason to live.

I know the only reason he is being the way he is, is because my mom is dying.

He has no one to impress or love.

His children aren't enough for him.

"Fine. You want to play? You want me to show you the real world and how cruel it can be, Killian?" I look at my dad's hands as he reaches for his waistband. "I'll fucking show you." He pulls out his gun and aims it at Reign.

Everything is in slow motion as I push him to the ground as the gun goes off.

Reign screams at the same time my heart clenches.

And all of a sudden, what feels like fire spreads throughout my body taking me out.

It's happening.

I can feel it.

It's been leading up to this.

I fall to the ground and wince, holding my chest as Reign runs over to me and pushes my hair out of my face.

She is yelling at me, saying something but I can't focus on her.

So, I say my last words to her.

"I love you."

The fire spreads through my entire body and when it gets to my heart, it takes me out.

FIFTY-ONE

AFTER KILLIAN FAINTED, ACE FROZE AND THEN pushed me away so that he could get to Killian.

He held Killian in his arms and kept repeating, "Please, Killian. Don't go yet. Not today."

Now we're in the hospital, waiting to hear from the doctors.

I seem to be the only person who doesn't know what's going on.

Ace is with Leo outside of the hospital because Leo said that Ace needs to take a breather and relax. Papa is back at the hotel. He wanted me to come with him so that I wouldn't be anywhere near Ace, but I wasn't going to leave without knowing what was going on with Killian first.

I'm in Killian's room right now, looking at his sleeping form and holding his hand in mine. He's surrounded by machines and hooked to IVs while so many different thoughts are racing through my head.

Ace wouldn't say a word on the way to the hospital. I wanted to ask him what happened since Ace knew more than me, but I was too scared to ask.

Why did Killian faint?

What didn't he tell me?

"Who are you? Where is Mr. De Luca?" I look up and see a nurse with a clipboard standing in front of me.

"I'm Reign. The girlfriend." I stand up and shake her hand. "Can you tell me what's wrong with him?"

The nurse looks taken back by my question. "I'm sure Ace and Aria or even Killian would have told you what condition he has."

I furrow my eyebrows. "What? No, what condition?"

"He has a coronary heart disease. He had a heart attack and currently is on life support. He's technically in a coma right now. If we were to take him off, his heart could fail so the life support is the only thing keeping him alive right now."

Tears are streaming down my face by the time she's done explaining.

A loud piercing noise rings through my ear as I replay every single moment.

Every single memory between Killian and I.

Nausea rises up my throat and I run to the bathroom inside Killian's room. I kneel in front of the toilet and start throwing everything up while crying.

Once I'm finished, I put water on my face and take deep breaths while looking in the mirror.

It's okay, I have hope.

Everything will be fine.

I walk out of the bathroom and the nurse has a sad and sympathetic expression on her face.

I hold my stomach, as if the child is comforting me. "Is there anything we can do?"

I look at Killian as more tears start to fall slowly.

"There is one thing but with his case, it's hard to find a good pair. He has a very unique case."

"A heart transplant?" I say, following.

The nurse nods her head. "But like I said, his case is unique."

"Is there anyone to donate?"

"Yes, but he's on his deathbed right now. The heart wouldn't make it in time for Killian."

I nod my head, thinking.

My heart beats against my chest, hard and fast. "Can you-" I sniffle. "Can you test me? To see if I might be a match?"

She looks at my hands holding my stomach before

meeting my eyes. "Miss, if you're pregnant, we can't go through with this procedure."

"I'm asking if I can take the test. Not if I can go through with it or not. Plus, you know who my family is, this whole hospital does."

The nurse swallows before nodding her head. "Of course. Follow me."

The nurse walks out and waits by the door.

I go to Killian and press my lips to his forehead. "I'll be back," I whisper.

I walk out of the room and follow the nurse as she takes us to another room. "I'll need you to pee in this cup." She hands me a cup. "And when you come back, we'll take some blood for the test." I nod my head and take the cup from her. Once I finish peeing in the cup, I wash my hands and do my business before giving it back to her. She tells me to sit down on the bed, which I do. "We are going to do an blood test. This will basically tell us what your HLA type is and if you're a match." She preps the area on my arm. "So how do you know Killian?"

My heart thumps against my chest hard and fast. "We met as teenagers and then we ended up falling in love."

The nurse doesn't say or ask anything else. Instead, she starts to take my blood. I look away when she sticks the needle in my arm.

Once she done, she takes the needle out and cleans the

area. "I'll be right back. I'm going to take these to the lap. It should take too long to get the results."

A little while later I hear a knock on the door and look at her as she walks in.

I read her facial expression and notice the stress lines on her face as she looks at me with sympathy. "Well, what a coincidence."

"What is it? What's wrong?"

"You have what he needs."

Everything is silent as my ears ring.

My heart is beating faster to the point where I can't ignore it.

Too much is happening.

Too many thoughts are swarming through my head.

It's all too much.

"Fuck."

"You don't have to-"

"I know, but I love him. I'd rather him live than me. And like you said, he has a rare heart."

"Miss, please don't feel the need to save him."

I shake my head. "You don't understand, I want to. I owe him everything. It just makes sense to do this."

The nurse nods her head, not knowing what to say to change my mind.

I know it's stupid.

I know that I'm just a girl who fell hopelessly in love but it's not a coincidence that my heart was made for him.

The stars wrote our story, and they knew exactly how it would end.

"Your result from the urine test came back. You are pregnant, but you already knew that" she says, making a tear fall from my eye. I knew I was pregnant, but I didn't have confirmation. How long have I been pregnant? "Like I said, you don't-"

"Please stop talking and just let me think," I beg quietly before closing my eyes and resting my head back on the bed. Killian deserves a happy moment. He just deserves this one thing for how much he has gone through. He's losing his mom; he can't lose himself. He's been through so much and he just needs one positive thing in his life. I was that thing, but I'll still be with him. I look back up at the nurse. "Can you take the baby out and is there a possibility of it surviving?"

"We can try. It honestly depends on how many months you are." She looks down at my stomach. "But you don't even look like you've hit the second or third trimester, so I don't want to give you false hope or anything."

I nod my head slowly.

I can't believe I'm doing this.

"Can you check?"

The nurse sighs and she nods her head. "So, the youngest premature baby we've ever had was around 24 weeks," the nurse explains. "With this procedure we would take the baby out first and start on the heart procedure."

I nod my head again for the hundredth time today.

It's all I can do since I can't think straight.

"Okay, do you have a paper and pen? And a phone so I can call my family?"

FIFTY-TWO

KILLIAN

I HEAR THE SOUND OF A MONITOR BEATING AND someone whimpering and crying as I slowly open my eyes.

When I do, it's blurry at first. People are in the room, but the image isn't clear for a few seconds.

I see Malcolm, Lia, Kyra and my sister sitting on my bed in front of me.

Everyone's eyes are red and puffy except for my sister who just looks sad and almost guilty.

What the fuck?

Why am I here?

I'm supposed to be fucking dead?

So, what happened?

Who fucked up?

"Why are you all looking at me like that?" I ask, getting frustrated.

Malcom's face turns around as he glares at me, but he doesn't look just pissed off.

He looks torn apart.

Last thing I remember was tackling my dad and the sound of a gunshot.

Where the fuck is Reign?

"Killian-"

"What the fuck is going on?" I cut Thalia off and look at everyone in the room, no sign of Reign. "Where's Reign?" I look at Malcom, but he comes closer to me instead.

"You don't get to ask where she is. It's your fault! Your fucking fault!" Malcom yells, making me furrow my eyebrows.

"What happened?" I ask, as my heart pounds against my chest hard and fast. It doesn't feel right. There is no burn or clenching around my heart. Something isn't fucking right. I move the hospital gown out of the way and see a bandage right where my fucking heart is located. I look at Malcolm, refusing to believe what this means. "What happened? What the fuck did Reign do Malcom?"

Kyra and Lia start crying and Malcom just lets a tear fall from his eye.

"She saved you. Reign fucking saved you and gave you the most precious thing! To you out of all people!"

And at this point, my heart, Reign's heart in my chest, beats ten times harder.

No, they have to be lying.

This has to be some sick kind of joke.

Because there is no way Reign did what I think she did.

I look at Thalia and see her staring at me, the same guilty and sad expression on her face.

"Why would you let her do that?" I look at Malcolm and sit up. "Why the fuck didn't you stop her?! Where were you when this was happening?"

"I was on my way to the hospital," Malcom says.

I look back at Thalia. "Explain everything."

Thalia sighs and wraps her arms around herself. "You fainted on dad and then he took you to the hospital. After that, they kept you on life support since your heart was about to fail. Next thing I know, Dad gets a phone call that they found a donor for your heart in the hospital."

I shake my head, not believing it. "That's not possible. They told me my heart was rare."

"Reign did," Kyra says, making me look at her.

"They did her procedure and then took you in the surgery room to perform the transplant to give you her heart," Thalia explains.

"Where's Reign?"

"On an ECMO machine in another room. They kept her on that because I know you would want to say good-bye. But after, they're taking her off," she explains.

"I'll never forgive you," Malcom says, making me look

at him. "I will never ever forgive you. The only reason I'm not going to kill you is because my daughter's heart is in your chest, and I'd be breaking Reign's promise. But know this, I'll forever hate you. There is nothing in this world that will make me see you any different."

I can tell how hard Malcom is trying to keep himself together and not let himself break down. I know that once he's behind closed doors he will do it.

I take out my IVs and swing my legs off the bed making me wince. The heart monitor starts beating faster as I place my feet on the floor.

Thalia gets off the bed and holds my arm. "Whoa, what are you doing? You need to stay in bed."

"No, I need to see Reign."

"Killian you can't-"

"Don't tell me what to do right now, Thalia." I look up at her, practically begging her to just make this easy for me. "Where is her room?" I look at Kyra. She sniffs and walks towards me. I put my arm around her waist, and she helps me walk out of the room.

Kyra takes me to Reign's room in silence.

There is nothing much to say.

When we get in front of her door, Kyra stops and turns to look at me.

She grabs my hand and starts crying softly.

"Reign left a letter for you. It's by her bed. When you read it, I need you to have an open mind and not be mad at her for what she tells you. All she wanted to do was save you, Killian. She loves you so much to the point where she would rather you live than her," Kyra explains, and she grips my hands. "I like you Killian, I like you a lot, always have. I know you never wanted to hurt Reign, you were just hurting and wanted to make the pain go away or pretend it wasn't there. Just please, don't hate her."

My hands clench around the door handle.

She lets go of my hand and turns around to leave.

When I push open the door, it's dark inside the room.

The only light in the room is from the moon outside shining through the window.

I walk further in the room and the door closes behind me. The monitors around her beep and I try to ignore it.

Outside the windows, you can see the stars shine bright.

How fucking ironic.

I force myself to look at Reign.

Reign looks so still and pale. She has wires attached to her everywhere and an oxygen mask over her nose and mouth. A tear rolls down my cheek as I kneel by her bedside and hold her limp hand in mine.

"Why, Reign?" I ask her as my thumb runs along her hand. The heart in my chest beats hard and fast as if it wants to go back inside her. I want nothing more than to rip these stitches and put her heart back inside her, where it belongs. "Why did you have to do this shit?" I ask as more tears fall from my eyes. "You were supposed to let me die. I'm sorry I didn't tell you but fuck, Reign! You were supposed to let me die!" I yell at her still form.

She's gone.

My Star is gone.

It hurts so much to the point where I would rather feel any other type of pain than this.

It would hurt way less.

All I want to do is punch something.

More specifically my dad.

He's the one who made me go on this mission. I fell in love with her and then he made me try to kill her.

Who knew I'd fucking fall in love.

He is the reason I lived and turned into this.

"I'm so fucking sorry, Reign. I wish you never met me. I wish I never met you," I cry to her, while still holding her hand. "I told you not to make me fall in love with you. Why?" I ask, as if she'll fucking answer me. "I brought my tragedy into your life and for that I'm sorry. Love keeps can kill you while it keeps you alive to feel it." I hold onto her hand and press my lips to her as my eyes close.

It's quiet in the room with just Reign and I.

I look up at Reign but nothing about her changes. My eyes go to the white envelope next to her.

I pick it up and see my name on the front with stars surrounding my name.

FIFTY-THREE
REIGN

KILLIAN,

I want you to first know that I love you. That's why I did what I did.

You made me genuinely happy and smile like I never have before and for that, I couldn't be more grateful to have been able to learn about you, love you, hold you, and kiss you.

It's been around six or so months since you saved me from the fire.

I remember looking into your eyes and I just knew you were damaged in a way. I knew you were going to destroy everything good and beautiful in my life and I let you.

I have fallen for you so hard that I didn't think of the consequences or maybe I did a little bit, but I didn't care.

I just wanted to be with you and love you and make you happy and I hope I did.

I remember telling you a few times that I wanted to do something great and meaningful before I go. I wanted to be able to make a huge impact on someone's life and I guess I am.

I'm not mad at you, I could never be mad at you for not telling me what you were going through. I understand that you maybe wanted to pretend that things were okay for a while.

I only have a few minutes until I have to go into surgery. I've called my family and they're on their way to try and stop me. The doctors are hopefully going to finish the procedure before they get here but I wanted to write this letter before I go.

It was the only thing I asked of them before I die.

I wanted to be able to tell you how grateful I am for meeting you and for making me fall in love with you.

Because of you, I finally understand why everyone loves love and why everyone is also scared of it.

You never once made me doubt your love for me.

I hope that when I'm gone, you'll still be able to show that love.

I've been kind of prolonging telling you this, but I haven't been feeling well lately and it's not because of food poisoning or me being sick. I knew I was pregnant; I just didn't want it to be true because so much was going on and we couldn't raise a child together while everything was happening.

I don't know if the baby will survive the procedure. They say it's rare for children to survive this early on.

I'm 25 weeks pregnant.

I wasn't showing because the doctor said that sometimes babies are very small to the point where they sometimes won't show until the last few months.

I already have some name ideas for the baby.

For a girl, I want her name to be Luna. It means moon.

For a boy I want his name to be Roman, I know it's your middle name. I found out from your sister.

I've always wanted my children to have names related to the sky or stars. You know how much I love them.

But if you'd like to change it you can. I just thought it'd be nice to give you some ideas.

Also, last thing.

I'm sorry.

I'm sorry for saving you without discussing it with you. I'm sorry for saving you without giving you a proper goodbye. I'm sorry that you're going to live in a world without me while also taking care of our child. That's if it survives but I have hope. I don't want you to be alone. You need someone to love you and care for you and be there for you like I have. You need something to live for and I hope this baby is it.

Don't forget, I'm always here if you need me.

I'm positive that I'm going to be with my grandpa up in the sky.

So, if you ever need to talk, just go outside and look up at the stars, Killian.

I love you with all my heart. Take care of our baby.

- Reign Pierce

FIFTY-FOUR

KILLIAN

I look up at Reign with tears in my eyes.

The letter falls from my hand onto the floor, and I run my fingers through my hair.

Fucking Reign.

I have her heart in my chest and a baby from her waiting for me.

"Why?" I whisper to myself before looking at her. "Why did you have to do this to me?" I stand up and walk towards the wall near the window and start punching it repeatedly. It's the only thing I know how to do. It's the only thing I can do right now to somewhat calm myself down and not start breaking shit. "Fuck, fuck, fuck!" I repeat after every punch. I turn around to look at Reign. "Fucking Reign. I told you not to make me fall in love with you. Why would you do this to me?!" I yell while

Reign just lays still and has no expression on her face whatsoever. I walk up to her. "I didn't want to be here anymore, Reign. I was waiting and I accepted death, but you had to come in and ruin it."

I grab her hand and press my lips to her soft cold skin before making her hold my jaw like she always would. "Please make it stop hurting, baby. Please. I don't want to be here anymore. Just make it stop. Make it all go away," I beg as tears fall from my lids.

Her cold hand against my jaw does nothing to make me feel better.

I feel like the world stopped spinning.

Like my whole world just collapsed and there's nothing left anymore.

I.

Feel.

Like.

I.

Could.

Just

Die.

"Please Reign, don't leave me. Don't leave me here. I don't want to be alone. I can't do this again. I need you here with me, baby. Please, I can't go through this shit without you. I need you."

I lean into her chest, but I hear no heartbeat.

I don't hear anything come out of her.

I cry into her chest and hold her as tight as I can.

And I don't let her go until they come to unhook her from all the machines. I sit in the chair across from her bed and hold her hand as they take the wires and unhook her.

And when they told me I had to let go of her hand, it was one of the hardest things I've ever had to do.

I stay in the room even after they leave.

I stopped crying, there were no more tears to force out.

She's gone.

My Star is gone.

My light.

My Reign.

"Mr. De Luca." I hear, making me look up from my hands and see a doctor walk in holding a clipboard to her chest. "I'm the doctor from the incubator room. I wanted to ask you a few questions and see how you are doing," she says before sitting down next to me. "Do you want to talk about how you're feeling at all?"

"I'm feeling fucking great," I mutter.

She nods her head, probably not knowing what to say. "I understand this is a hard time for you. A child is a lot for a person to handle. But a child is also such an important aspect in a person's life. I know you're going through a lot currently, but I just need to know if you'll be able to handle this baby, especially with all you're going through right now."

A child.

A fucking child.

Reign and I's fucking child.

She didn't fuck anyone but me, so I know it's for a fact mine.

I just can't believe it.

"What is it?" I ask, even though it won't change my mind.

"It's a girl. And she's doing really well, Mr. De Luca. Vitals are normal and she weighs about 1.5 pounds."

God she's fucking tiny.

Probably about as big as my hand.

"I don't want it."

The doctor looks like I just shot her.

"But-"

"I said I don't fucking want it." I glare at her. "See if Reign's parents want the child. I don't. I don't want it. I don't want to see it. Nothing."

The doctor sighs and she nods her head. "Understandable. I know that the grandparents would be happy to take the baby in their care. But I need to ask you since you are the biological dad."

I stand from the chair and my hands clench. "Don't call me that. I'm not the dad and never will be so don't call me that or next time I see you, I'll fucking pour gasoline all over your body before lighting you with my match," I say as my whole-body tenses and that fucking ringing in my ear doesn't go away.

Everything is too loud.

I need to get out of here.

It's too small here.

Everything is too much.

I am about to leave the room before the doctor calls my name again and stops me. I don't turn around, but I don't leave either.

"In my opinion, I think you'd be the best thing for this baby, and this baby for you."

My heart-fuck, Reign's heartbeats uncontrollably hard as I leave out the door.

FIFTY-FIVE

KILLIAN

I SLAM MY CAR DOOR SHUT AND LOOK UP AT THE place I call home.

I would always be so happy and relaxed whenever I was home but all I currently feel is dread.

Dreadfulness that I have to come back to this hell hole and see my fucking dad.

I've been gone for about a week.

Killing off all the doctors that performed surgery on Reign in Romania.

Do I give a fuck that they have families of their own and a reason to live?

Fuck no.

No regrets, at least not yet.

While in Romania, my dad didn't come into my room once to see me.

He probably knew that I would have killed him on the spot because I wasn't thinking straight.

After he heard I survived and that Reign sacrificed herself, he basically caught the first flight back to Italy.

My mom has been blowing up my phone since he got home but I haven't answered her calls.

I haven't answered her calls, Thalia's calls, Rowan's calls, not a single fucking person.

Because I couldn't care less.

I lost the only person I loved and would do anything for in this world and now she's gone.

So no, I didn't want to hear any sorry's or "I'm here for you's."

I don't fucking care.

They don't know what it's like having her heart in my chest.

They don't know how much guilt I felt when killing all those people.

It was a battle between my head and my heart.

I know that the heart in my chest, Reign's heart, is the reason I feel guilty and want to undo what I did.

But then my head cuts in and says they should have never fucking touched her in the first place.

And then let's not forget about my fucking dad. Who's a cunt and doesn't care about anyone but himself.

I hate him.

There is nothing in this world that could make me forgive him or see him any different.

When I walk inside the house, I see the one person I didn't want to see.

Fucking great.

Pretty sure he heard my car.

"Killian, we need-"

I shake my head and walk past him to go upstairs. "Don't."

"Killian-"

I turn around to face him. "Do you know what fucking happened?!" I yell and walk closer to him. "I have the heart of the girl I fucking love inside my goddamn chest." I yell, trying to hold in the tears that are threatening to fall.

"I know-"

"Do you know?" I furrow my eyebrows at him. "Because it seems like you're a selfish prick who doesn't care about anyone but themselves!" I yell. "I have Reign Pierce's heart, the girl I love, inside my fucking chest," I say, grabbing where my heart is located. "Do you understand how badly I want to rip it out of me? It doesn't fucking belong there."

My dad's jaw clenches. "I did everything for you Killian! I have killed for you. I have provided for you and loved you the best I could. I'm sorry things happened the way they did but what more do you want from me?"

"I wanted more time," I say as a tear finally falls from my eye. "I wanted more time to spend with Reign. I wanted more time to have this baby with her."

My dad's face pales, and his eyes widen. "Baby?

I shake my head lightly and nip my bottom lip. "Yea, she was fucking pregnant. She got a C-section before they did the transplant. Con-fucking-grats. You're a grandpa again but not to Landon."

"Is it a boy or a girl?"

"Girl."

My dad looks behind me as if she's there walking.

What a fucking dumbass.

"Where is she?"

"With her family."

My dad furrows his eyebrows as if I'm the fucking problem.

Is he being for real right now?

"You put her up for adoption?"

He looks mad, which he has no fucking right to be.

"No, she's with Reign's family and she's going to stay there."

"Why not you?"

"I don't fucking want her."

"You are her dad Killian." My dad gives me a disappointed look.

This fucking guy.

I want to laugh at him.

"I'm not going to be her dad without Reign," I say as Reign's heart beats against my chest, hard.

My dad looks guilty as he runs his hands through his hair and sighs. "Killian, I'm-"

I shake my head, not wanting to hear it. "No, you're not. This is what you wanted, right?" I raise an eyebrow at him. "You wanted the girl I love dead? You wanted me to not love anyone and be closed off and cold? Guess what, Ace?" I smile and lean towards him. "You got your fucking wish."

My dad's jaw clenches and his expression changes to a sour one. "Don't call me that. You're my son-"

I laugh. "No, if I was your son, the love of my life would still be here in front of me. I would have been raising this child with her!" I yell, getting close to his face.

"I just wanted you to be great Killian. I wanted you to be the best in this world."

I shake my head. "I didn't want any of that. What I wanted was Reign."

"The life you wanted with Reign, wasn't going to last forever and you know that," my dad says, pointing a finger to my chest.

"But it would have been nice to pretend things were normal for just a few years. Reign and I could have done so much with this baby in just a couple of years. And now it's all ruined," I say as another tear falls down my cheek.

I developed a coronary heart disease when I was

sixteen years old. I had heart problems and other complications at a young age, but my parents were never worried about it because I was a healthy kid and the doctors said there wasn't much to worry about.

But one day I got shot and we had to go to the emergency room when I was sixteen and they revealed how damaged my heart really was.

When the doctor revealed how long I had left, maybe 20s to 30s, I knew my time was going to end and so I expected it.

I was supposed to die.

Not Reign.

"I said it would have been fucking nice to pretend."

My dad doesn't say anything to that, so I nod my head and turn around to walk away from him.

He obviously doesn't give a fuck.

He never gave a fuck about anyone but himself.

"You can't pretend, Killian." I stop walking. "Like it or not, you aren't normal. Reign is dead-"

"Stop," I demand, turning around slowly but he keeps going.

"And you're still here, breathing. You need to be more grateful."

"I said stop," I say, my patience wearing thin and Reign's heart racing.

"You won't get her back. Time to start acting like a fucking man and get over it," he finishes.

I lunge towards him and tackle him to the floor.

I straddle his hips and punch him in the face repeatedly.

"It's your fucking fault!" I yell in his face. "You fucking killed her! It's all your fault!"

My dad doesn't punch back, instead he lies there and basically takes it.

"Killian-"

I start laughing like a maniac as I punch the life out of him.

It's funny.

Ace De Luca and Killian De Luca, fighting.

dad and son.

He finally starts to guard himself.

All I can think about while punching him is Reign.

My fucking Reign.

It should have been him instead of her.

"I hate you," I say as tears fall from my eyes.

My dad pushes me off and when I get off him, I take out my gun and aim it at his head.

He kneels on the floor, spitting blood out while I'm standing above him with a gun to his head.

My dad looks up at the gun and I see regret and worry all over his face.

"Enough, Killian." I stay quiet, still holding the gun to his head. I never thought I'd see the day, Ace De Luca kneeling before me with a gun to his head. Reign's heart races as I think about this. If I kill him, mom will never forgive me. Thalia will never forgive me. I'll basically be exiled. "Think about this. You don't want to do this, trust me."

I push the gun against his head harder. "You know all the voices I've been hearing in my fucking head since I left the hospital. Everything is loud and I can't fucking make it stop. The only way to make it stop is literally to kill myself." I lean down to face him, and he looks up at me, his eyes tearing up surprisingly. "I will never forgive you. That dad role you had when I was five is gone. To me you were *fucking* everything. You're dead to me and I will forever hate you." I take the gun away from his head, but he doesn't move or flinch. He looks up at me, his face pale. "Once my mom is dead, I'm kicking you out and you can live in one of your other estates. I'm only going to give one warning. If I see you in this house after my mom dies, I will kill you. I'll burn you alive and make you wish you had a fast, easy death. I'll be the one to say, *'Saluta Satana da parte mia'* to you, Ace."

I don't wait for a response, instead I walk past him and go towards my room.

Who would have thought?

Ace De Luca, kneeling and pleading for me not to kill him.

Fifty-Six

Thalia

Since coming back from Romania, I've been staying with Emma and Leo since my dad and Killian are fighting and going at it.

I've talked to my mom about this whole situation and all she said was, "They're grown men. They can handle it. I can't be here to fix Ace's problems all the time because soon I won't be here to help him. He needs to learn."

Hearing her say that made my heart hurt and I ended up crying to Alexander about it.

She isn't lying and that's what hurts.

"I'll be back, okay?" I say to Landon, who's too busy coloring to even notice me.

"Okay," he says, not looking at me.

Little shit is always mean to Alexander and I.

He has our attitude.

"Dad's going to be with you today, okay? So be good for him."

Landon sighs and rolls his eyes like I just interrupted him. "Fine."

See what I mean by little shit?

I roll my eyes back at him and leave. I go to Alexander who is on the couch, watching something on his phone.

"I'm going to go see what my dad is up to. I haven't heard from them in a while," I say, making Alexander lock his phone and look up at me.

"When are you going to be back?" he asks, standing up and pulling me closer to him.

"Not sure. Probably in a couple hours so I can check on my mom too."

He nods his head and wraps one arm around my waist to pull me against his body. He takes my chin in his fingers before smashing his lips on mine.

"I love you," he says against my lips while I just escape all my problems for a few seconds.

Alexander always makes me feel better and distracts me.

When he was in a coma, I was so lost without him. I couldn't think straight and now that I have him back, I'll never take him for granted.

"I love you too."

I leave Alexander and Landon to head to my parents'.

It's not a far drive since Leo and Emma live in the neighborhood.

Once I get to the house, I park my car and get out. When I walk inside the house it's quiet, but I see my dad sitting on the ground.

"Dad?" I say before rushing over to him. He spits out blood as I wrap my arm around him so I can help him up. "What happened? Where is Killian?"

My dad lifts his head, and he almost looks unrecognizable.

There is no way Killian did this.

"He came back home. But he made sure to make it clear how much he hates me."

I help him to the couch and sit him down.

He looks bad.

His eyes are swollen and has a busted lip.

Blood is covering his face and he looks like he's going to pass out.

I go to the kitchen and get a first aid kit to clean him up. "Has mom seen you?"

I hope not because if she did, she'd probably start freaking out and crying and she doesn't need that.

But if she isn't sleeping, I'm sure she heard what went down.

"No. She's still upstairs. Killian left not too long ago."

"I don't blame him," I mutter as I clean dad up.

"He told me once Aria dies, I have to leave and never

show my face and if I do, he'll kill me." I keep my tears back because the only person I'll ever cry to now that I'm older is Alexander and my mom. I remember crying around my dad when I was a child, but things have changed. "How mad do you think your mom will be?"

"She'll be devastated. That's why you have to clean yourself and get your shit together before seeing her. She can't see you like this. It will break her, and she doesn't need this."

"You think she'll forgive me?" he asks, worry filling his eyes.

I know the only person my dad truly cares for is our mom. Me and Killian will always come second.

"Of course, she will. You're the love of her life. She'll always love you no matter what. But she also loves Killian. You shouldn't expect her to be happy with the whole situation. This is too stressful for her, and she shouldn't have to worry about two grown men fighting."

He leans his head back and closes his eyes. "I don't know what to do, Thalia."

I feel bad for my dad, I do.

The love of his life is dying and he's taking it out on Killian.

He put himself in this position.

"You fucked up, dad."

He laughs and shakes his head lightly. "At least one of my kids calls me dad."

I furrow my eyebrows at him.

What the fuck?

I know it's a defense mechanism, him laughing and joking about this because I know he loves and cares about Killian. He feels bad because how could he not?

He ruined his son.

He is what everyone says he is.

The cold, ruthless devil that no one would dare cross.

He made Killian into the devil, maybe even more than him.

"You're so stupid. Do you know what you did?" I ask, making him look up at me. "You made Killian go on a mission to kill Reign's dad. After he fell in love with her, you didn't care, you went and tried to kill him yourself and when that didn't work, you tried killing her before sending Killian to the hospital for a heart attack. And now you're joking about it? Are you serious?" I furrow my eyebrows at him and stop cleaning his face up.

He looks down at his hand and licks blood off his lip. "I know."

"You can't control everyone. You certainly can't control Killian, no one can. You tried and look at what happened. You lost a son, and he lost a dad and the love of his life in less than two weeks. You were supposed to be there for him, be a dad to him and accept him and all his decisions. You failed him."

"I know, Thalia." He sighs.

"Then why aren't you doing anything to fix it?" I ask, getting a little frustrated.

If he knows then he should go and fix it!

"Because I don't know what to do." My dad looks at me and looks defeated and like he's just given up. Who knew, the king everyone was afraid of, would finally lose and fall. "Your mom's dying, and I can't do a thing about it. I can't fucking control her health. No amount of money or fucking doctors will fucking save her, Thalia." He sighs and runs his hand through his hair. "Killian is a dad."

I swear my face pales and I widen my eyes at him. "What?"

"Reign was pregnant."

That's not possible.

No one said anything.

I lick my bottom lip slowly and sigh too. "I wouldn't be surprised if Killian did kill you. After everything that he's been through in the last week, he actually let you go." I look at my dad. "The thing about Killian is that he never had anyone to truly love him. He never got to experience the kind of love that Reign gave him. And you tried to kill her. All of this is your fault. Reign killing herself and saving the baby and Killian. She left the world and left a baby for Killian. Her love, the love that was meant for Killian and that child is gone forever. And it's your fault." My dad nods his head and I notice a small tear fall from his eye. "Your punishment is to see how you made Killian so heartless and unlovable. You're going to see Killian the way you wanted to. But instead of being happy, you'll feel guilty for the rest of your life."

"And the love of my life will die along the way. I know, I'm fucked Thalia, you don't have to spell it out for me."

FIFTY-SEVEN

ARIA

THREE YEARS LATER

THE TIME HAS FINALLY COME.

I'm coming close to my last few days.

I honestly don't know how to feel about it all. I'm super tired and just feel weak. I can't stomach anything without throwing up with some blood.

The doctor said I should say my goodbyes soon since it's coming.

I can feel it coming.

I wonder if this is how Killian felt when he felt like he was near the end.

Layna was telling me how much she'll miss me and everything she wants to say before I go.

She's been my best friend since we were in diapers. I

know she will never judge me, and I can be myself around her.

While she was talking to me and saying how much she'll miss me, I started to cry because that made this whole thing even more real.

Like it's finally happening.

I'm dying.

I will never be able to hold or love my family ever again.

And that's such a scary thing to think about.

But I can't break down.

Not yet.

When Thalia came to see me all I did was hold her while she cried.

My girl, she is strong.

One of the strongest people I know.

She raised a child while Alexander was in a coma so I know she will be able to get through this. She apologized for every spark of attitude she's ever given and also told me how much she doesn't want me to leave and how scared she is.

It breaks my heart.

Not just hearing her say that but hearing everyone say that because they aren't wrong.

I'm leaving them and I can't control it.

"Mom," Killian says from above me. I asked him to cuddle with me because as much as I love Ace's cuddles, I love Killian's hugs. Killian rarely shows affection but when he does, it always means so much. "I don't want to let you go," he whispers in my ear.

I'm lying my head against his chest, hearing Reign's heartbeat.

He doesn't call it his heart; he says it's Reign's because it makes him feel closer to her.

It's been three years since she passed, and my Killian still has that cold heart he developed. There is only one thing that can mend it and it's his baby girl.

I just have to encourage him to be strong enough to get her back.

He's had so much heartbreak in his life, and I feel horrible for leaving him in this world.

But I know he can do it, he's strong.

My boy has been through so much from going through so many health issues as a child, losing his friend in high school, and then losing the love of his life and daughter now.

I look up at Killian, trying not to tear up. "I love you so much, Killian." He looks down at me with sadness in his eyes. "I shouldn't say this, but I love you more than your sister, more than your dad. More than anything in this world." I put my hands on his face. "You have to know that no matter what happens, I'll always love you just a little more, because you deserve a little more. I wish that you could have your happy ending and be with whoever you want to be with. If I could, I would have sacrificed myself instead of Reign," I say, making a tear finally fall from his eye. "I believe that I was put on this earth to have you and love you. Everything has been leading to you, Killian. I just need you to know you mean so much to me. You're going to do such great thing-"

Killian shakes his head. "No. Not without you. It's just hard mom. I can't lose you too," he says as a tear falls from his eyes. "I've just lost so much and I'm at the end of the fucking bridge mom. If I lose you, I don't know what else to do. I won't have anything to live for anymore."

"But you do, Killian." I smile up at him. "You have your daughter."

Killian shakes his head. "I can't. That's too much, mom. That's too hard."

I smile softly at him. "You can do anything, Killian. You can get your daughter back and be a good dad and man that I taught you to be for her. Just promise you'll do this for me Killian. I need you to have someone."

Killian licks his bottom lip and lets out a shaky breath before nodding his head.

We don't talk for the rest of our time together. He lets me hold him as he sleeps on my chest. I feel his heart with my hand and hold him extra tight, never wanting to let him go.

My poor boy, who's been through so much, deserves a better life.

Killian eventually ends up leaving and I tell him to bring his dad in.

Ace and him are still not on talking terms and Killian is still not living in the house.

Ace tries to make up for it, but Killian is a firecracker and if you get on his bad side, it takes a while to get back in his graces. Ace fucked up with Killian and I scolded Ace for it because Killian didn't deserve any of that. I would have stopped Ace if I knew what was happening but unfortunately, I don't have that power anymore.

Ace walks in and I can't help but start tearing up.

Ace's eyes are puffy, and he looks like he's been crying.

Ace De Luca.

My husband, the dad of my kids, my enemy, tormentor, my savior, and my forever always.

"Come here," I say, making Ace strip to his briefs before sliding into bed with me and wrapping his arms around me. When I rest my head on his chest that's when I start crying. "It's so hard, Ace."

"I know, *amore*," Ace whispers as he kisses my forehead. "Love is poison."

I nod my head and can't help but cry into his chest. "It's a menace." I lick my lips and look up at Ace. "I'm so scared. I don't want to die."

"I know," Ace says as a tear falls from his eye. "Trust me, I know."

"You need to make up with Killian. However, you

can, I need you to do it because if you don't, I can't leave knowing that he is going to do something stupid. He won't tell you or anyone, but he needs you, Ace. He needs his dad. No matter how much he pushes you away, please never stop being there for him. I can't have him lose you."

Ace doesn't hesitate. He nods his head and says, "Of course. I'm trying the best I can. I'll do everything I can, *amore*." Ace kisses me on the lips, and even after so many years, I still feel the spark between us. I'm still so in love with him, all of him no matter what. "Close your eyes, *amore*. I'm not letting you go."

"I love you, Ace."

"I love you more. Till death do us part," he whispers in my ear.

FIFTY-EIGHT

KILLIAN

I PLACE THE WHITE DAISIES ON THE GRASS IN front of her grave.

Reign Pierce
Daughter, friend, lover, mom.
A wonderful soul who had the biggest heart in the world.

It's officially been more than three years since Reign died and this is the first time, I've visited her grave.

They buried Reign here in Bulgaria because it's her home country. I haven't been back here since I dropped Reign off after we returned from the island.

Since that day she gave me her heart, I haven't been able to look at the stars or sky the same.

Everything hurts too much, and I hate thinking about all the moments but at the same time, it's all I think about.

Looking in the mirror hurts the most because I see that stupid fucking scar from the decision Reign made.

"Hi, baby," I say softly and kneel at her grave. "I finally had the courage to come after so many years. I'm sorry I didn't come sooner. I just needed time. But I felt like I needed to come today," I explain. "My mom died last year, and she told me to see you and ask for another chance. Plus, I met this guy named Hayden Night. He's a boxer who's in love with a girl named Jaclyn. You would like them a lot. They are very good people, especially Jaclyn. She's been through a lot but she's strong." I sigh and try to hold back my tears. "I wish you were here to meet them and know their story. They've both been through a lot and Hayden is probably my best friend. He's special to me but I'll never say that to him."

Hayden is my second in command for the Mafia. He used to just be one of my underground fighters that made me money but long story short, he ended up getting promoted. I met him through Rowan because I guess Hayden is his little brother. So, we just got closer over time from hanging out. Him and Jaclyn are in love and have a little boy and soon another baby as well.

Seeing their love makes me jealous, because why can't I have that?

"Things without you are hell, Reign. I miss you so much and looking in the mirror where your heart is breaks me everyday. I don't know how I'm still here. It hurts, you know. Having your heart inside me hurts. It doesn't feel right. I'm not mad at you, I could never be mad at you because you were just trying to help. God, I wish you didn't. I wish you would have just left me to die," I say after a tear finally falls. For the first time in three years, I break down at Reign's grave. "I love you as much as I did three years ago, and I always will. You'd probably hate who I've become because I'm nothing like the guy you fell in love with. I blame my dad for everything. We haven't talked in so long and it's my fault because I keep pushing him away. I just can't look at him the same. After you died and my mom died, I went on a killing spree. I know you probably don't want to hear it but it's the only thing that made everything stop. I just felt so insane," I say truthfully. "I haven't spoken to your family since you passed but now that I'm here, I was hoping today I could see them."

"You didn't text me you were here."

I turn my head and see Malcom with flowers in his hand.

He looks like he's aged pretty well which I'm not surprised about because Malcom takes care of his body.

I stand from her grave and face him. "Malcom."

"Welcome back, Killian," he says, walking towards her grave and placing the flowers down next to mine.

"Wish it was under different circomestances."

Malcom looks at her grave with sadness in his eyes and touches the stone. "Don't we all?" he says, more so to himself. He kisses her grave before standing up and facing me. "Can I ask for a favor?"

"Only if I can ask for something in return."

Malcom shakes his head lightly. "Still an asshole."

"You didn't expect any less, did you?" I furrow my eyebrows at him.

"No, I expected you to be worse."

"Sorry to disappoint." I shrug.

Malcom sighs before looking at my chest and back to me. "Can I hear her heart?" I don't hesitate to nod my head. Malcom comes closer and he wraps his arms around me and puts his ear against my chest. I don't hug him back, I let him do his thing and hear Reign's heart. I swear I can feel her heart pound hard against my chest. "I hate that you have her heart." Malcom says, letting go of me.

He wipes a tear and controls his emotions. "I hate it too. I was waiting for death, but she had other plans for me."

"What are you doing here?"

I place my hands in my pocket and take a deep breath, licking my lips.

My whole body feels like it's shaking from the anxiety and tension.

There's only one reason I'm here and I know that Malcom suspects why.

"I want her."

Malcom immediately knows what I mean, and his eyes turn into slits and his body tense. "No."

"It wasn't a question."

"She isn't a fucking object that you can give and take back, Killian. She is a kid with organs and feelings. How do you expect her to react when she sees her dad after more than three years of not being in her life?"

I nod my head. "You're right. She isn't an object. I know I fucked up but that's why I'm here trying to do better for her and for Reign."

"Luna deserves someone who has been there and loved her since the beginning. You weren't there for the sleepless nights or the constant crying and tantrums, Killian."

Luna.

My daughter's name is Luna, just like Reign wanted.

"Luna, that's her name?" Malcom nods his head. "I know, you're right. I should have been there from the beginning. It's not your responsibility to take care of her because she's mine. You and Lia won't be around for long, so she needs a dad, not grandparents. I mean that with full respect, I'm just stating the truth."

"A child is a big responsibility, Killian. They need your attention and love not just for a couple hours or days but forever no matter what. Can you give it to Luna? Can you be both of the parents that she needs? You can not ever just give her back, that's not how this works."

"I know. I wasn't ready then but I'm ready now. I want to meet her, get to know her, love her, everything."

I'm not fucking perfect.

I know taking care of a child is hard and to be honest I never wanted a child but with Reign, my mind changed.

I would kill for another child with Reign.

"I'll give her the world if she asks for it."

Malcom gives me a sad smile. "She doesn't need the world, Killian. She needs a dad. She needs you. Can you give her that?"

She's half of Reign and me.

Of course, I will.

"Yes."

FIFTY-NINE
KILLIAN

MALCOM AND I ARE IN HIS CAR DRIVING TO MY daughter.

Luna.

I didn't bring my car here, instead I had a driver take me to the graveyard because I didn't think I'd stay long.

But I also didn't think Malcom would so easily let me see my daughter. I would have understood if he didn't let me see her at all.

I'm scared shitless to meet her.

I've never seen her before.

I don't know how I'll react when I see her.

"Tell me about her," I say to Malcolm, hoping that will just distract me.

Malcom smiles while driving. "She is the sweetest little girl ever. She has the purest soul and is always smiling. She has the best laugh and will end up making you laugh with her. You can never stay mad at her. She's my mini-Reign. Sometimes I think that Reign was put inside her when she passed."

"How were the three years with her?"

Malcom chuckles softly. "They were an experience, that's for sure. She reminds me of Reign a lot. You'll be able to see a glimpse of Reign in her as a child. It was hard to act as a mom and dad to her because like you said, we were just grandparents. We aren't going to be here forever, and we can't keep up with her because she's super active and a little all over the place."

"What kind of stuff does she like to do? Tell me more. I want to know everything about her."

Malcom smiles at me. "She likes to sing. She is always singing when she is coloring or eating, all day long. She is also energetic and will keep you on your feet, so you have to have your full attention on her," he explains, reminding me of Reign. "She has Reign's beautiful blue eyes, thank God. She is a mini version of Reign. If you were to put baby Reign next to Luna, you wouldn't be able to tell the difference. She has a huge smile on her face all the time. And her hugs are the best. They always make you feel better. She loves saying 'I love you' which I can't help but smile over." Malcom's smile drops. "Sometimes it's hard because of how similar she looks to Reign. Of course, there are days where it's hard and Lia and me cry when looking at her. But we love her. We always will."

Reign's heart beats against my chest hard as if she just knows how much I'll end up loving her. "She sounds amazing."

"She is Killian."

The rest of the drive is spent with Malcom telling me more things about Luna while I listen with a smile on my face.

When we are in front of the front door, my hands start sweating and I swear I feel like I'm going to have a panic attack.

"What's her full name?"

"Luna Reign De Luca." Malcom says as he unlocks the front door.

Luna Reign De Luca.

God, she sounds perfect.

I'm surprised that Malcom kept my name but I'm so happy he did because she has some part of me.

Malcom and I walk inside the house and as I look around, I notice nothing much has changed.

It feels weird but also kind of good being back here since this house just holds some sort of positivity.

"Luna!" Malcom yells before closing the door.

Reign's heart beats faster.

Thump Thump

Thump Thump

Thump Thump

"Papa!" I hear a little girl yell and I swear my hands start shaking as the laughter comes closer.

"Luna, not so fast!" I hear a familiar voice yell.

A little girl comes out from the corner and her smile widens when she sees Malcolm.

She has long dark brown hair, just like Reign, the biggest blue eyes I've ever seen and then her smile.

Her goddamn smile, she is Reign's twin.

No doubt.

She literally looks like a mini-Reign.

Luna is wearing a pink dress with her hair down and a big wide smile on her face. As I look at her, Reign's heart goes crazy inside my chest, like she fucking knows.

Luna Reign De Luca.

"Papa," she cheers when she knocks into Malcolm's leg and hugs him.

"You're here." I turn my head and see Kyra, looking like she's about to cry.

"Kyra," I state and smile at her softly.

"You came back," she says with a sad smile.

I nod my head. "I did." I look down at Luna who is now looking at me with those big blue fucking eyes.

"Luna, this is Killian De Luca," Malcom says, kneeling to her level.

"Hi," she says with a smile. "I'm Luna. Wait! You have the same name as me."

I kneel down to her level and look at Malcolm. He nods his head and gives me an encouraging smile. "That's because I'm your dad."

Fuck.

I said it.

She furrows her eyes, confused and then tilts her head. She looks up at Malcom for confirmation.

I'm not going to just grab Luna and take her with me now that I met her. I'm going to be staying in the guest house while getting to know Luna and getting closer to her. I don't want to take her away from her home or grandparents and what she's used to.

But eventually I will be taking her with me back to Italy. I have a bedroom set-up for her when she's ready.

Over the past year I've changed a lot.

I've kicked my dad out and now he lives in one of his other estates. When I kicked him out, I redesigned and renovated everything.

It's not the same as it was before.

"This is your dad, Luna. He's going to be staying with us for a little while so he can get to know how amazing you are," Malcom explains to Luna.

Luna looks at Malcom before looking at me.

Her eyes gloss over before she smiles softly at me. She walks closer before wrapping her tiny arms around me.

I tense up and look at Malcom who just smiles and nods his head at me softly.

I slowly wrap my arms around her and start crying quietly.

"Don't cry, I'm here now," Luna whispers in my ear but that just makes me want to cry more. "I'm not going to leave you. I promise." Her hand touches Reign's heart beating hard against my chest.

Like she fucking knows how close her mom is to her.

"I'll take care of you, Luna. I promise. I'll make your mom proud."

SIXTY

ACE

FIVE YEARS LATER

I NEVER THOUGHT I'D SEE THE DAY I'D COME back here.

I haven't been here since Killian kicked me out after Aria passed. I have another house near this estate, but Aria told me to just give Killian this house.

I take a deep breath before walking towards the door and pressing the bell.

I'm sure Killian's security already notified him that someone was here.

The door opens and when I look straight, I don't see anything.

"Hi." I look down and see a girl with big blue eyes and

long dark brown hair. "I'm Luna, what's your name?" she asks, a smile on her face.

I furrow my eyes at her.

Luna is wearing black shorts and a white shirt. Her long hair is in a messy ponytail.

She looks like she is maybe 10 the most. As I study her, I see all the similarities she has with my son and Reign.

Killian got her back.

"Daddy!" Luna yells and looks behind her.

I hear heavy footsteps before seeing him.

Killian looks the same but a little bigger. He's put on more muscle and has a light scruff on his face.

He looks shocked that I'm here at first before his eyes start shooting glares at me. "What the fuck are you doing here?" he says, moving around Luna and putting her behind him. She peaks around him to watch what's happening. "I remember telling you to never show your face."

"I want to talk."

I realized then I made a wrong move, demanding to talk.

Because Killian is a mini me and mini-Aria but ten times worse.

"Talk to my foot, Ace."

My hands clench in fists. "Killian, what will it take for me to have a conversation with you? I just want to talk."

Killian licks the inside of his cheek before looking down at Luna. "Go to your room, Lu. I'll be up in a bit, yea?" Luna nods her head and Killian kisses her on the forehead before she runs upstairs. Killian walks towards the kitchen and I look around the house and see everything that's changed. He replaced a lot. There are toys in the living room, and it reminds of how Thalia and Killian would leave their shit everywhere. "What do you want, why are you here, and how can I get rid of you?" he says, bringing out a clear glass from the cupboard.

"I want my son back. I'm here to make things right. The only way you can get rid of me permanently is to kill me."

"Want anything to drink?" Killian asks, opening another cabinet and pulling out my favorite whiskey.

Of course, he has the same taste as me.

"I want to fix what I broke before I start drinking." Killian gives me a glass of water and pours himself some whiskey. "It's no excuse how I acted. I was a dick to say the least and I never should have treated you like I did. You were in love, and it was unfair."

"Damn straight," Killian says, taking a sip of his drink.

"I want to be your dad again. Not Ace. I know after everything that happened between us you hate me, and you have every right to. When it came to you, I never knew how to be a dad. I always treated you differently than Thalia because I saw myself in you. I'm scared of you

Killian, I shouldn't be but after what happened in my childhood, I was just cautious with you."

Killian's jaw clenches but he listens.

"When I saw you, I was fucking terrified Killian. I knew I was going to fail as a dad. It's not an excuse, it's just an explanation. I knew that when it came to you, I was going to be a shitty dad just like mine because I saw myself in you. When I saw you, I saw my past. I hated how you made me think of that," I say as tears start to form in my eyes, but I don't let them fall. "As you got older, things got harder and then the love of my life was dying. I had no way to control it so instead I tried to control you which I regret every day. Like I said, I have no excuse, I just wanted to explain to you."

"Why didn't you come sooner?" Killian asks, his cold stare still present.

"Because I wasn't ready. I wanted to give you time," I explain. "What do I have to do to be your dad again, Killian?"

Killian downs the whiskey before slamming it on the counter.

He then looks me dead in the eye, in all seriousness. "I want you to bring back Reign."

A pang of hurt hits my stomach. "You know I can't do that."

Killian leans forward. "Trust me, I know." He takes off his shirt and my eyes go to the huge scar on his chest where Reign's heart is. "Every morning when Luna and I work out together I take off my shirt because I don't like working out with a shirt. And every day whenever I'm not wearing a shirt Luna always looks at this scar and asks me something."

"What does she ask you?"

"Why did mommy give you, her heart?" Killian says and I swear hurt fills up his eyes. He looks pained. "Every fucking time I hear that question, this heart, Reign's heart, breaks. I feel like breaking apart. I don't know the answer. I can't answer that question and every time she asks that question, I hate it. So instead of answering I always tell her to ask me another day. And she keeps asking me and I never know what to say," Killian explains. "So, the only way I'll forgive you, other than the impossible, is if you answer that question for my daughter."

At this point I'll do anything I can for him.

I lost the love of my life and I only have my children left.

I realized I lost everything when Aria passed.

And Killian means the world to Aria.

I always knew Aria felt closer and protective over Killian because he's always had a hard time.

"I will."

Killian nods his head before leaving the kitchen. "Follow me." I follow Killian all the way up to Luna's room. He knocks before opening the door. She's on her bed coloring and looks up at us when we walk inside her room. "Luna, baby, come here." Luna gets off her bed and walks towards Killian. She looks at me with a confused expression on her face before looking at Killian. "Remember that question you ask me every day about the scar on my chest."

Luna nods her head. "Yea."

"I want you to ask him." Killian nods his head towards me.

Luna looks at me with a skeptical look on her face. "Who is he?"

"Your grandpa."

"Like dyado back in Bulgaria?" Luna's eyes sparkle when she asks that.

I can tell she loves her grandparents, especially since they helped raise her.

Killian looks at me. "Yea but he's, my dad. Ask him the question, Luna."

Luna turns her attention back to me with those big blue eyes. "Why did my mommy give my daddy her heart?"

She looks genuinely so confused why Reign's heart is in Killian's chest. It's so clear to everyone but her because she wasn't born yet and she's still a kid.

The world hasn't destroyed her yet with the power of love or heartbreak.

I crouch down to her level. "Well, your mom and dad

fell in love. She couldn't see your dad pass, so she gave him her heart to let him live. Reign, your mom, was a very generous and selfless person like your grandparents from Bulgaria. She saved my son, your dad, so he could live and raise you. Your mom loved your dad and love like that isn't easy to find."

Luna looks at Killian sadly, almost like she knows. She wraps her arms around Killian and hugs him tightly, pressing her hand against his chest.

Like she fucking knows.

Killian tears up but he doesn't let a tear fall. He looks up at me and smiles softly.

A weight lifts off my shoulder and I take a deep breath before looking out the window.

It's almost like Aria is watching over me and taking care of me from above.

I can't wait to join you, *amore*.

THE END

THANK YOU

If you enjoyed this book please feel free to leave a review as it would mean a lot to me.

I always enjoy reading good reviews and I always love reading reviews that have criticism in them. Criticism makes me a better author and I always love knowing what I can work on as a writer.

A simple, "Great Book" would be amazing.

Appreciate your love and support so so much!

Acknowledgment

And that's the end of the De Luca series.

I don't even know what to say or how to feel knowing this is the last book in the De Luca series. I'm been writing this world since I first started on Wattpad back in 2018-2019. And it finally ends here with Killian's book. The Blinded By Series and the De Luca Series will always be such a huge part of my writing journey and I'll never not be grateful for this series and the opportunities it has brought me. I would have never started writing if it wasn't for Wattpad. No matter what reputation Wattpad has or how other readers see it, I will always be grateful for Wattpad and the support I've gotten from that platform. For my readers who have been with me since the first chapter of Ace De Luca was written, you guy mean the world to me and it's just crazy seeing how far we've come. Thank you for watching me grow.

Killian De Luca has always been a special character to me because I always saw him as my golden child who I would want to protect from the world. I took my time writing Killian De Luca because I genuinely loved this story line and everything about this story and I didn't want it to end. This book along with Blinded By Love and Broken Beauty is my favorite, taking the top three places. I love how this story closes off this world so perfectly. It might have been sad and could have had a better ending but I never saw Killian having a happy ending. It sucks to say but it's the truth.

So with that being said, with Killian De Luca published, there will be no more books from the De Luca and Blinded By Series world I'll be publishing or writing other than Hayden's friends book, Kayden. But that won't be for a while since I want to focus on other projects and new stories with new characters. But like I said, that doesn't mean I won't ever come back to this world. I still would love to maybe write a Novella for the Blinded By Series and then Kayden's book.

Now I have to say thank you to Antonia, my editor. She has been with me since day 1 when I decided to start my publishing journey. She is such a wonderful human being and I will forever be grateful for her and her work. I don't even know if I would be publishing books if I didn't find her. It's crazy that I've been working with her since 2021, so almost or about three years. Thank you, Antonia! I am forever in debt to you.

My readers, who have supported me since Ace De Luca and my Wattpad days, thank you so much. Like I have said before and in all my other books, I would never be writing or publishing without any of you. Thank you for making my dreams come true.

About the Author

Jaclin Marie is a Self Published Author who lives in Southern California. When she isn't writing a compelling story or reading, she either spends her time at the gym or watching Disney Animation movies.

Jaclin started writing at the age of sixteen but she has always been a book lover. She started writing on this writing platform called Wattpad before she decided to publish her debut, Ace De Luca. Although that was her first published book, it wasn't the only book she has written. Since she started writing, she couldn't seem to stop and just like she found her passion.

Darkness evades Jaclin's mind and it demands to be heard. Writing darkness down on paper is something she loves doing. She makes her readers not only think about her plots but completely sob over them.

Her current works published are just a taste of what goes on inside her head.